OPERATION RENEGADE

Операция Ренегат

The untold Cold War story

JEREMY AKERMAN

Operation Renegade
© 2025 Jeremy Akerman

Cover design: Rebekah Wetmore
Editor: Andrew Wetmore

ISBN: 978-1-997827-09-2
First edition November, 2025

Moose House Publications
2475 Perotte Road
Annapolis County, NS B0S 1A0
moosehousepress.com
info@moosehousepress.com

Moose House Publications recognizes the support of the Province of Nova Scotia. We are pleased to work in partnership with the Department of Communities, Culture and Heritage to develop and promote our cultural resources for all Nova Scotians.

We live and work in Mi'kma'ki, the ancestral and unceded territory of the Mi'kmaw people. This territory is covered by the "Treaties of Peace and Friendship" which Mi'kmaw and Wolastoqiyik (Maliseet) people first signed with the British Crown in 1725. The treaties did not deal with surrender of lands and resources but in fact recognized Mi'kmaq and Wolastoqiyik (Maliseet) title and established the rules for what was to be an ongoing relationship between nations. We are all Treaty people.

Also by Jeremy Akerman

and available from Moose House Publications

Memoir
Outsider

Politics
What Have You Done for Me Lately? - revised edition

The Marc LeBlanc Mysteries
Holy Grail, Sacred Gold
Unspeakable Evil
The Plot to Kill the Premier
Best Served Cold
My Brother's Keeper

Fiction
Black Around the Eyes – revised edition
The Affair at Lime Hill
The Premier's Daughter
In Search of Dr. Dee
Explosion
Decline and Fall
The Man who Came from Away: a Cape Breton Odyssey

This book is dedicated to the memory of Carl Abbott
physician, author, painter, friend and gentleman.

For Nell

This is a work of fiction. The author has created the characters, conversations, interactions, and events; and any resemblance of any character to any real person, with the exception of historical characters, is coincidental.

Operation Renegade

1	11
2	12
3	16
4	24
5	27
6	31
7	33
8	37
9	40
10	45
11	50
12	53
13	56
14	58
15	61
16	66
17	69
18	73
19	75
20	79
21	81
22	85
23	88
24	89
25	90
26	94
27	99
28	101
29	105
30	107
31	111
32	115
33	118
34	123
35	125

36..128
37..131
38..135
39..139
40..144
41..147
42..148
43..150
44..157
45..160
46..161
47..163
48..165
49..169
50..174
51..178
52..180
53..186
54..191
55..195
56..198
57..204
58..210
59..215
60..220
61..227
62..233
63..238
64..244
65..249
66..251
67..255
68..259
69..266
70..272
71..275
72..277
73..281
About the author..283

Operation Renegade

Jeremy Akerman

1

This is not my story, except insofar as I have collated the evidence and narratives provided by many people, living and dead, and presented them as best as I am able in this book.

This is Harry Posen's story, which his death earlier this year from Primary Progressive Aphasia has finally permitted me to tell.

The book comprises verbatim recordings of Harry and interviews with eyewitnesses, some of whom can be named, some not, and of passages where I have reconstructed events according to the information given me by those who would not allow me to record them.

The book tells the story of secret intelligence officers—American, Russian, British, German and others—most of whom must remain unidentified, who, in 1985, saved the world from what might have been a disaster of unthinkable proportions.

2

One morning in 2018, I received a visit from an RCMP officer, who asked me to accompany him to H Division headquarters in Dartmouth, Nova Scotia. I was seriously rattled and, since he would not tell me the purpose of the visit, I searched my mind for any crime I might have unwittingly committed.

While I realized that I could probably refuse to accompany him in the absence of any warrant, I thought it wiser not to offer any resistance, so I climbed into the back of the cruiser and off we went.

Crossing the Halifax Harbour Bridge, I again combed my memory for any reason the RCMP might want to question me, but could think of nothing. Maybe they had been falsely told I was involved in some criminal activity, or even that someone had suggested I had been a witness to some criminal act.

When we arrived, I was taken straight to the top floor, to the office of the Chief Superintendent, where I was politely ushered in.

The Chief Super introduced himself, shook my hand and asked me to sit, not in one of the arm chairs in front of his desk, but at the desk itself. "I guess you're probably wondering what this is all about."

"Indeed I am," I said, not a little put out.

"I wish I could tell you, Mr. Akerman, but I can't."

"Then who the hell can?" I was getting tired of this game.

"All I can tell you is that at ten o'clock our time, two o'clock London time, you will be getting a call on that phone," he said, pointing to a brown phone. "Or it could come through on that one." He indicated a white phone alongside it.

"London time? Oh my God," I said.

"What?"

"Has my brother died?" My younger brother by ten years was living in Bristol in the United Kingdom. That could be what the expected call was about, but it would not explain the extraordinary lengths to which they had gone to communicate the news to me.

"I can't say," said the Chief Super, "but I don't think so."

"I don't wear a watch. How long do we have to wait?"

"Three minutes, so I'll leave you now."

"You won't be here for the call?"

"No, I must leave. The call is coming from MI6"

"*What?*"

"I'll see you before you go," he said, and left the office.

Those few minutes felt like an hour. I had never in my life had any dealing with MI6 or any other intelligence service.

At length, the brown phone rang and I picked it up.

"Hello."

"Hello, Mr. Akerman?"

"Yes."

"I am calling on behalf of Sir Alexander Younger."

"Who's he?"

"He's the head of the British Secret Intelligence Service."

"Jesus! And who are you?"

"You can call me Mrs. Peverell, but that is not my name. The Chairman's is the only name in our service which is ever made public."

"Look, what is this all about?"

"I believe you were for years a close friend of Mr. Michael Foot, former leader of the Labour Party."

"Yes, but that was before he became leader. We were friends for about a decade and a half, ending in the early eighties."

"I see. Is the name Ben MacIntyre familiar to you?"

"Yes, of course. He's a writer."

"Like yourself."

"Yes."

"The Chairman wanted Mr. Foot's friends to be aware that Mr. MacIntyre is shortly to release a new book entitled *The Spy and the Traitor.*"

"So?"

"In it Mr. MacIntyre intends to say that Mr. Foot was a KGB agent—"

"Not this foolishness again. This is about Oleg Gordievsky, the defector?" I was livid.

"Yes, that's right."

"*The Sunday Times* carried this lie some years ago. Michael sued them and won in court!"

"Yes, that was because the accusation did not appear in any of Mr. Gordievsky's five books and he refused to elaborate at the time."

"That's right."

"But now Mr. MacIntyre will say that Gordievsky indeed confirmed that Mr. Foot was an agent. Not a high-level one, but one who took money from the KGB and had regular meetings with them."

"I find that very hard to believe."

"Indeed. But we are satisfied that the information is accurate. Sir Alex wanted his friends to be prepared rather than read it in a book."

"I see. That was most considerate of him. Thank you."

"That is the *official* part of my business with you," said 'Mrs. Peverell'.

"Official? There's *un*official business?"

"There could be. If you're interested. Call it a consolation prize."

"Go on. I'm listening."

"There's a story which needs telling, but no writer so far has picked up on it. And, naturally, we can't tell it ourselves."

"Naturally. MI6 is not in the business of writing books."

"Indeed not. Incidentally we haven't been called MI6 since World War II."

"Sorry."

"I can only say so much."

"I understand."

"But I can point you in the right direction."

"Please do."

"It was called *Operation Renegade.*"

"An MI6 operation."

"Oh dear, no, it was much more than that! It involved the CIA, KGB, and other intelligence services, too."

"How could it?"

"My dear, it was a *joint* operation."

"You mean, the Russian, Americans and Brits working together?"

"You're getting the idea. But I can say no more."

"Well, that's not enough! I must have more to go on than that."

"In Northern Virginia there is a little village called Zulla—"

"Zulla?"

"Yes, Zulla. There is a retired employee of the CIA named Harry Posen. He'd be about 75 now, and he is in poor health."

"Is that all you can tell me? Hello? Mrs. Peverell? Hello?"

But she had hung up, presumably to return to the considerate ministrations of Sir Alexander Younger.

3

On a quiet, sunny day in early September, Harry Posen finally agreed to see me. This occurred after I had tracked down his whereabouts in Zulla, Virginia, unsuccessfully writing to him, then unsuccessfully trying to discover his phone number, and finally turning up on his doorstep.

I expected to be shooed away by a large, aggressive dog or by a housekeeper of equally impressive dimensions, but he answered his own door.

"I knew you wouldn't give up," he said gruffly after I had introduced myself. "It's too good a story to miss. I don't know who put you on to it—no, please don't tell me. I don't want to know—but there must be a dozen or so of us still alive who were involved."

He led me through the house and out into his back garden, an enchanting place overflowing with flowers and exotic shrubs. I expressed delight at the surroundings.

"I deserve no credit," he said, "I have a gardener come in every day. Poor feller lives in an apartment with only a window box, so he gets his kicks here."

"He does a marvellous job."

"Yeah, I guess he does."

We moved across a carefully-manicured lawn to some chairs arranged around a wrought-iron table. I sat down and, while I continued to appreciate the wonderful plants, he disappeared into the house.

After a few minutes he reappeared, carrying a tray bearing glasses, a jug of lemonade, bottles of Coke, club soda and Aberlour single malt. He put the tray on the table and indicated that I should help myself to whatever I preferred. He sat down heavily with a long wheezing sigh.

"Cephalinol."

"I beg your pardon?"

"Cephalinol. That's what it is all about."

He raised himself, pulled a thin file from under his buttocks, and pushed it across the table.

"Of course, that's a translation from Russian. The original report was to the Soviet Committee on State Security."

"What was it?"

"I'm no chemist. In fact, not a scientist of any kind." He took a sip of scotch. "But, in a nutshell, it was a self-replicating bio toxin which could produce hideous effects in humans."

"So the Russians had it and we wanted to get it?"

"No, both sides could get it but both decided to sit on it—indefinitely."

"Rather like the nuclear bomb."

"Exactly. We knew that if either side employed it, the result could be devastating for both."

"So, what was Operation Renegade all about then?"

"A third party had got hold of Cephalinol."

"A third party? You mean another country?"

"No, not another country. Our own people. And theirs."

"I don't understand."

"Work it out."

I thought for a few seconds, looking hard at Harry's face. He seemed to be testing me, or playing with me.

"Are you trying to tell me that persons on both the American and Russian sides ganged up and procured this substance?"

"That's exactly what I'm trying to tell you."

"Who were they? Who had the capacity, the skills to pull off something like that?"

"The CIA and the KGB."

"I'm sorry. What are you driving at?"

"Before we go any further, you need to know the setup as it existed in both services at the time. Rather than rattle it off for you, I have put two organization charts in that file."

"Yes, I saw that. What do they show?"

"In a very simplified form –they omit much more than they show, but the rest is irrelevant for our purposes—they set out the basic chain of commands in each of the CIA and KGB.

"I have to go to take my meds. You take a look while I'm gone. You'll also find the report on Cephalinol in there, although I don't think you'll be able to make much of it if you're not a biochemist."

I opened the file and started to read.

   UNITED STATES OF AMERICA
   CENTRAL INTELLIGENCE AGENCY.

   President: Ronald Reagan
   Secretary of State: George Schultz
   Director CIA: William Casey
   Deputy Director: John MacMahon
   Head Department X ("Dirty Tricks"): Edgar Sollows
   Deputy Head: Harry Posen

   UNION OF SOVIET SOCIALIST REPUBLICS
   КГБ (KGB)
   General Secretary of Communist Party and President of the Soviet Union: Mikhail Gorbachev
   Minister of Foreign Affairs: Eduard Shevardnadze
   Chairman, Committee for State Security (KGB): Viktor Chebrikov
   Section Head, Action Services: Colonel Valentin Repnin
   Deputy Head: Major Zina Varenko

That seemed easy enough to comprehend, but Harry was right about the other report. Most of it was gobbledygook to me, but I struggled through it as best I could.

COMPOUND		LF	FUSARIUM SUB-SPECIES
deoxynivalenol (vomitoxin)		70	F.roseum
cephalinol	See appended report for this agent		
DHN		15	F.nivale
			F.scirpi

Pathology: vomiting

hemorrhaging

loss of muscle co-ordination

fever

visual disturbances

death, often occuring from secondary

  causes -- dehydration

Delivery: aerial spray (100Kg cannisters)

fine powder mist (42Kg cylinders)

Evaluation of efficiency:

With the exception of cephalinol (see appendix) most trichothecenes have little strategic or tactical value except for psychological value as a "shock" weapon against third world populations. The main factors are:

    - large amounts must be absorbed to insure

      lethality

Vomitoxin	500MT British Forces, Northern Ireland
T-2	760MT Soviet Fourth Army, Vladivostok

APPENDIX: CEPHALINOL

Within the past eighteen months reports about the development of a hardier and more reliable trichothecene have surfaced in Rome and the middle east. Upon investigation by agents of the Committee on State Security it has been learned that the Italian chemical firm of Calermi has produced this agent on contract for the Government of Iran.

Characteristics:

Produced:	c.albidium
	c.oxysporum
Lethality:	.0001
Range:	As Cephalinol is believed to be a self replicating biotoxin, estimates on deployment parameters cannot be provided with assurance.
Delivery:	aerial spray (25Kg cannisters)
	talc-based powder (10Kg bombs)
	Possibly other methods

<pre>
Vomitoxin   500MT   British   Forces,   Northern
            Ireland
T-2   760MT Soviet Fourth Army, Vladivostok
</pre>

<u>APPENDIX: CEPHALINOL</u>

Within the past eighteen months reports about the development of a hardier and more reliable trichothecene have
surfaced in Rome and the middle east. Upon investigation
by agents of the Committee on State Security it has
been learned that the Italian chemical firm of Calermi
has produced this agent on contract for the Government
of Iran.

<u>Characteristics:</u>

Produced: c.albidium
               c.oxysporum
Lethality: .0001
Range: As Cephalinol is believed to be a self
               replicating biotoxin, estimates on deploy-
               ment parameters cannot be provided with
               assurance.
Delivery: aerial spray (25Kg cannisters)
               talc-based powder (10Kg bombs)
               Possibly other methods

Pathology: Severe muscle dysfunction

Extreme nausea

Hemorrhaging

Hallucinatory episodes

Death from respiratory arrest

Constraints: Dry air

Initial evidence would indicate a fairly narrow range of effectiveness somewhere between 14° and 31°

Estimated military effectiveness:

Excellent strategic and tactical choice in situations where rapid results are required, although uncertainty of control could pose problems should deployment be close to native borders. This is an extremely potent and long lived agent which requires utmost care in handling and deployment. The use of this agent in advance of further experimental research would be exceptionally unwise.

Sources: Due to Italian environmental laws, Cephalinol is neither stored nor tested at the Calermi laboratories at Palermo.

All known quantities are currently in
Iran:

100-200G Calermi, Teheran

4-10Kg test cylinders with Iran first
Army Group.

<u>Note:</u> Depending upon the success of the forthcoming
field trials Iran is expected to place a 2000Kg order
(8.4 million rubles) with Calermi in the fall of 1988.

The only thing which was apparent to me was that this substance was downright evil and, in the wrong hands, could wreak untold havoc.

4

"Did you actually meet any of the Russians on this chart?" I asked when Harry returned to the garden.

"Yes."

"Which ones?"

"Varenko."

"Only her?"

"Yes."

"So you never met this Repnin, who would have been the equivalent of your boss in the KGB."

"Not really. I understood that he and Varenko had some kind of intimate relationship. Apparently they had a lot in common. They were both lovers of opera."

"Would that relationship have been forbidden in the KGB?"

"I have no idea, but I imagine it would have been discouraged."

"How long did that last?"

"What?"

"That relationship."

 "I guess right up until he went off the rails."

"What does that mean, 'off the rails'?"

"We'll come to that."

"Okay. I guess Varenko would have been your own opposite number?"

"More or less, yes."

"What was she like?"

"She was the love of my life," Harry said, taking me completely by surprise.

I did not know what to say. Given that the tensions of the Cold War had not yet softened, such a liaison seemed highly improbable.

"Did she…I mean, were your feelings reciprocated?"

"Yes."

"I imagine it must have been against the rules."

"You're not kidding. When they eventually found out, they could have interrogated me and kicked me out of the Agency. If the operation hadn't been a success they probably would have."

"Both of you must have had to make a special effort not to reveal your countries' secrets to each other."

"It never arose," he said, refilling his glass and holding up the bottle of Aberlour. "This is awful good stuff. You want some?"

"No thanks. I'll stick to lemonade."

"Suit yourself."

"You were saying…?"

"Oh, yes. We were far too busy pursuing the objectives of the operation. And being in love."

He sighed deeply. "You need to put this in the context of the times, Jeremy. Gordievsky's defection had told us that the Soviets really believed that the West was about to launch a nuclear strike on them—"

"They really believed that?"

"Oh yeah. Andropov was not only neurotic; he was utterly paranoid. Chernenko was not much of an improvement, so until we got Gordievsky's info, you could say the state of the world was hanging in the balance."

"What was the West's response when they heard what Gordievsky had to say?"

"Well, for one, Reagan pulled back on his 'Evil Empire' talk and Mrs. Thatcher toned down her hawkish comments. We were also instructed to start opening up dialogue between the two services."

"The CIA and the KGB?"

"Yeah. Also MI6 and the Ruskies. In his second inauguration, President Reagan said he was ready to consider easing relations and that a number of initiatives would follow. Then came the meeting which kicked it off."

"What meeting?"

"In Paris, between Schultz and Shevardnadze. Of course, I wasn't there. Schultz took ******* with him, among others, on that occasion. I'm still in touch with him. I can give you his number. I think he might tell you what happened. Of course, you can't reveal his identity because he is still a serving officer."

"He must have been extremely young at the time if he's still serving."

"Naturally, he's not full-time any more, but shall we say he's still on the books."

"Are you 'still on the books'?"

"No. I am very much off the books."

"I understand. Does that mean I can reveal your name?"

"No. I'm sick. Something called aphasia. It's in its early stages. They tell me it'll get a whole lot worse. I don't know how long I've got left, but I don't want to spend my last few years in prison."

"I see. Well, thank you very much, Mr. Posen. I'll see what your 'on the books' guy has to say. If he'll talk to me."

"Oh, he'll talk, provided you swear to keep his identity secret."

5

Interview with Harry Posen's contact.
Informant A. Washington D.C.

At the time of the Paris meeting, George Schultz was 72, said my informant, and had the distinction of having held four different cabinet positions in Republican administrations. He was no slouch, having a distinguished military record, holding a PhD in Industrial Economics, had taught at MIT and was Dean of Chicago's School of Business. As Nixon's Labor Secretary, he was the first to make use of racial quotas in the federal government. He accepted President Reagan's offer to become Secretary of State three years earlier, in 1982. Short, bald and stocky, he was considered "a tough cookie" as a negotiator, but a patient one who acted as if he had all the time in the world.

On the Russian side, Eduard Shevardnadze was 57, burly and full-faced, and was used to getting his own way. He had been kingpin of the Communist Party in his native Georgia for over a decade, but his rise to power had been punctuated by turmoil, including demotion and Stalin's purges, during one of which his father-in-law had been executed. He was a close ally of Gorbachev and was believed to be a strong supporter of *Glasnost* and *Perestroika*.

My informant A said there were conflicting opinions about Shevardnadze in the State Department, some of the Ivy League diplomats considering him a peasant, but astute observers recognizing his talent as a wily bargainer. Unlike many of the Russian communist members of the *nomenklatura*, he was thought to be a gentleman.

The French had chosen a medium-sized, extremely elegant, extremely expensive hotel for the meeting place. In the centre of a large, ornate room overlooking the Champs Élysées through enormous windows with heavy brocade curtains, stood a huge, oval, gleaming walnut table surrounded by high-backed armchairs with padded red velvet seats. The table was situated underneath two oversized, multi-tiered chandeliers, the myriad twinkling pendants of which were mirrored in the wall-length, elaborately-framed mirrors.

My informant told me there were approximately twenty people at the table, more on the American side than on the Russian. Although Schultz and Shevardnadze had already shaken hands outside the huge oak doors, they did so again across the table, but could only do so by stretching.

"I remember thinking how stupid it looked, their reaching across the table like that," A said. "Just for appearances."

Even more ridiculous, said A, was that when the two main protagonists were anxious to get down to business, the French Foreign Minister, Roland Dumas, insisted on interrupting with an interminable speech about the historic nature of the meeting, how France had a noble history of bringing warring parties together ("which was news to me", said A), and how President Mitterrand dearly wished he could be present to welcome such honoured guests but that great affairs of state had detained him elsewhere.

When Dumas had finally completed his address and fussily withdrawn from the room, Shevardnadze opened by saying that, their underlings having agreed on broad parameters, they could now deal with specific matters.

"Yes," said Schultz, "You will have received and studied the list of possible areas of easing tensions?"

"I have," said Shevardnadze, "and you will have studied ours?"

Schultz inclined his head to indicate that he had. "We find that proposals for scientific co-operation in the Bering Sea to be quite acceptable."

"And General Secretary Gorbachev has instructed me to proceed to a mutually verifiable arms reduction program. The question of neutral observers needs some clarification. I doubt we would entirely agree on which nations would be 'neutral'."

"Okay." Schultz grinned broadly. "It's time we did this. The game has been going on far too long."

He glanced down at his documents. "You know I can't go along with you on Central America?"

The interpreter seemed to be having some difficulty with the expression "go along", but when she had sorted it out, Shevardnadze nodded impatiently. 'We'll set that aside. Possibly for another meeting."

"Rome wasn't built in a day," said Schultz.

"What?" Shevardnadze did not understand the interpreter's rendition of the phrase and, A said, there was an hysterical few minutes during which the Foreign Minister and the interpreter seemed to be arguing.

"These gatherings are usually so stuffy, boring and full of bullshit," A told me, "that any amusing relief takes the form of high comedy."

It was at this juncture that a sour, heavy-set man, believed to be Anatoly Kovalev[1], pushed a slim file along the table to his chief.

Shevardnadze frowned then glanced down at the file. He seemed irritated. "What do you say about this Cephalinol business? I expect you have managed to get hold of our toxicological report?"

"Why yes," George Schultz replied with a smile, "I happen to have it in front of me. At least a translation of it.[2] Our own research confirms your findings. We have no objection to cooperation on this matter—in fact, we would encourage it. If this is a matter of priority for the Soviet Union, as it is for us, I should like to know how you propose to deal with it."

"Let us be frank with each other," said the Georgian, leaning forward. "We both know the Iranians are religious lunatics. The whole world knows it. I see you nodding your head, so you agree.

"What the whole world does not know is what religious lunatics will do with deadly material which none of us properly understands. At the moment our intelligence tells us they are sitting on the only deployable quantities of this unstable, highly-unpredictable and devastatingly-virulent toxin."

"What do you suggest?"

"The stuff is being manufactured in Palermo. The United States should deal with the Italians and get them to stop production immediately. And see to it that all your allies keep their research only at present levels. We will do the same within the Warsaw Pact and wherever else our influence extends."

---

1 Not the KGB agent of the same name charged with election interference in the 2016 US elections.

2 This was the report Harry had given me in Zulla.

"Agreed," said Schultz, "but what about Iran?"

"We must go and take it."

"Take it?"

"Precisely. We will send a joint KGB-CIA team to find this stuff and destroy it."

Informant A told me that Schultz looked as if "he had been sloshed by a wet haddock." He said the Secretary of State sat back in his chair and gazed up at the twinkling chandeliers. Then, he inhaled deeply.

"Our experience of sending agents into Iran has not been"—he coughed—"wholly successful in the past. I'm not sure I could sell President Reagan on your suggestion."

"You haven't been successful because—how shall I put it?—we have not exactly been helpful behind the scenes. But this time we would be working together."

"How large a team?"

"Two. It must be kept very small, very manageable. One of yours, one of ours. The best men we have."

"I shall have to call the President. Can you give me, say, thirty minutes?"

"Take an hour," said Shevardnadze. "It is time for lunch."

He rose and left the room, the other Russians following.

When they had gone, the American delegation huddled around Schultz as he made the call. My informant said, "We couldn't hear what Reagan said, but when Schultz put the phone down, he said to one of my colleagues: 'Bill, go after Eduard and tell him we've got a deal.'"

6

A few days after my conversation with Informant A, I got an unexpected call from Harry Posen. It was surprising because Harry sounded considerably more eager for my project to succeed than he had seemed when I met him in person.

"I forgot to tell you," he said, speaking more slowly than on the previous occasion. "There's a crucial part of the story you must know if you're going to make sense of how it all ended."

"Okay. I'm listening."

"Pete Roussel."

"The name seems vaguely familiar. Should I know it?"

"He wrote a book. I think it was called *Ruffled Flourishes*. It was about White House reporters."

"I may have heard of it. I haven't read it."

"It doesn't matter. The point is he was Special Assistant and Deputy Press Secretary to Reagan from 1981 to 1987."

"Is he still alive?"

"And kicking, so I hear."

"What could he tell me?"

"What I just said. Making sense of it all."

"Would he see me?"

"If I call him. I became sort of friends with him around that time."

"Where would I find him?"

"Houston. Last I heard he was teaching at the state University. But he may have retired from that. Could you get down there?"

"My finances are a bit strained," I said, very truthfully because I was almost broke. "But I'll do my best."

"Got a pen? Write down the address and phone number."

I did as Harry instructed and thanked him.

"You can call me from time to time if you need any more leads or other info," he said. "But if you've got questions, the sooner you get them to me the better. I'm finding it hard to organize my thoughts when I'm speaking. It's gonna get worse. The doc says that's why they call the disease 'progressive'."

When I had finished my call with Harry I did a little research on Peter Roussel. Apparently his years in government began in 1969, when he was only 28, as press secretary to George Bush Sr., staying with Bush until 1974. Then Roussel went on to serve two tours of duty in the White House, as Staff Assistant to Gerald Ford. He became Assistant to Presidential Press Secretary James Brady and subsequently to Larry Speakes.

I was intrigued at the prospect of learning a new (to me) aspect of the story, so I waited a day to allow time for Harry to call him, and then placed my own call.

"You a newspaperman?" he asked after I had introduced myself. He had what one might call a cultured Texas drawl.

"I was for a while."

"I can smell 'em. In my blood. My mom, dad and me, we're all newspaper people."

"I confess, I haven't read your novel."

"Hell, I don't care about that. It weren't no best seller!" He laughed. "So, how d'you wanna do this?"

"Harry explained what I want?"

"Yeah."

"Can you tell me what he thought was relevant?"

"Yeah. But not on the phone."

"I understand. I'll have to wait a bit until I have the funds to fly down."

"Huh. Well, let me know when you can make it. Give me a coupla days' notice in case I have to leave town for any reason."

Unfortunately, it was not until after Christmas in early 2019 I was able to afford the air fare. I earnestly hoped that the information Pete Roussel could give me was worth the time and expense involved.

7

Interview with Peter Roussel
Houston, Texas, January 18, 2019

It was a lousy winter, but then I find nearly every winter awful. I am a man of the sun and summer is definitely my season. I was particularly disappointed to find that the weather in this part of Texas was not a huge improvement on Nova Scotia, it being only 10°C the night we met.

At his request I met Pete Roussel for dinner in a large restaurant in downtown Houston. I imagined he had chosen this venue because of its noise level and consequent lower susceptibility to listening devices.

He was a very pleasant-looking, likeable man in his late seventies who cracked a number of good jokes using professional timing. I guessed he would have been fun to work with, but something in his eyes also told me he was someone to take very seriously.

The food was good and we got along extremely well, but as the evening progressed the sounds of other diners became almost deaf-ening. I found it difficult to hear everything he said, and I had to con-stantly ask him to repeat himself.

As we finished dessert, he pulled his chair up to the table and in-dicated that I should do the same.

"Right. Strictly speaking there is nothing classified in what I am about to tell you, but everything said by and to the president in the oval office is privileged. What's that?" He nodded toward my little recorder. "You taping this?"

"Yes, but I do not intend to identify any sources in their lifetimes. That is a solemn undertaking."

"Good. You see that you stick to that." He wiped his mouth with his napkin. "Now, what I'm going to describe may strike you as a not particularly important or significant regular meeting of staff. And it wouldn't be if not for its subsequent importance."

"Okay."

"So, one morning the president sent for us—"

"Excuse me. Who is 'us'?"

"Oh, me; my boss, Larry Speakes; Don Regan, the Chief of Staff; his deputy, Mike Deaver; and, of course, the president's secretary, Kathleen Osborne."

"Is that all? Anyone else?"

"Let me see. I think Cap Weinberger may have been in for part of the meeting. Yes, he was."

"He was Secretary of Defence?"

"Yeah. Oh, and Faith was there, too."

"Faith?"

"Faith Whitllesey. She was the Director of Public Liaison. She was quite a gal. She'd been a Member of the Pennsylvania House before working for the boss."

He drained the bottle of Cambria Pinot Noir and called a waiter to bring us a bottle of Diamond Creek Cabernet Sauvignon. I got a glimpse of the label and noticed that the vintage was 2000, so I guess the cost must have been considerable.

"Now I come to think of it," he said, frowning, "it may have been Faith who came up with the idea."

"The idea?"

"Here's how it went. The president was in a great mood, joking and ragging everybody in turn like he usually did. Then he turned to Don Regan and said..."

"Now that I've had to back away from the Evil Empire stuff because of what we learned from Gordievsky, I need to have another kind of message. A kindly message. Something uplifting. Something the press would lap up and the people would love."

"Free beer for a month," Larry said.

"Larry, I'm sure you'd like that, but that's not quite what I had in mind," said the President. "Maybe a national festival of some kind."

"We need to be careful," said Deaver. "If something is just done for show it may appear gimmicky. I don't think we need you to be associated with gimmicks, sir."

"No indeed, Mike. God forbid an actor should be accused of gimmickry."

"Excuse me, Mr. President," said Weinberger, "but I'm hearing a lot about these Americans for Peace. Frankly, I don't take them very seriously, but they're loud and they're growing. Could you—how shall I put it—harness their energy and put it to constructive use?"

"You mean exploit them."

"No sir," Cap said with a smile, "I didn't mean that exactly."

"May I speak frankly, sir?" Larry asked.

"Well," Reagan gave that famous drawl, "Larry, you usually are frank, so why should today be any different?"

"It's just that when the President himself is…well…venerable—"

"Venerable!" The President hooted with laughter and slapped the desk.

"What I mean is that it's always good for you to be seen, photographed, et cetera, with young people. And these Americans for Peace sure photograph well."

"Before we go any further, someone tell me these kids are not Communists."

"No, Mr. President. They are not," I said. "They're mainstream, naïve kids who want peace."

"That's what we all want, Pete. So tell me, how would this work? It's got to be more than a photo shoot. Can anyone put the flesh on the bones of this thing?"

"Here's how we do it," Don said, "We tie this in with your recent approaches to Gorbachev. To show that the whole nation —including its youth—extends good wishes to the Soviet Union, we make it a national movement, a national demonstration—"

"Now this, I like!"

"Yes, sir. We could hold lunches here at the White house, inviting Americans from all walks of life and all parts of the country to talk about peace."

"Yeah," interrupted Faith, "but all this is bringing the mountain to Mohamed. Sure, bring people here, but you, Mr. President, must go to them—almost like another election campaign. A huge Fourth-of-July-like celebration in all major centres, at each of which you tell Americans that we want peace."

"I can see you saying to the crowd, 'Come join your voice with mine, my friends, as I say 'Mr Gorbachev we want peace,'" Deaver said.

"That's a very good impersonation of me, Mike, but I hope you always do it with respect and not in mockery."

"Mr. President! Mock you? Perish the thought!"

As the laughter subsided, Faith said, "Why don't we do it by balloon?"

"Balloon?" The President frowned. "Sounds like baloney to me. Larry, what do you think?"

"Maybe it's not as silly as it sounds. One of those Air Force contraptions we used in 1940. But all spruced up and decorated with huge stars and stripes and doves of peace on the sides."

"I don't want to go up in flames like the Hindenburg," the President said with a grin.

"Oh, the humanity, and all the passengers screaming around here!" Kathleen Osborne chipped in from the corner.

"Okay, okay," the President said. "I can see the possibilities, but I'm not there yet. Faith, you work with Mike and Larry. Cap, check out the security angles. If you people can work it out, come back to me and tell me. Make sure I can't go up in flames or look like a jackass."

"And did he go for it?" I asked Pete.

"After some refinements, yes."

"That's quite a story. Funny, too."

"That was Reagan. He was always full of fun."

He dusted himself off, drained his glass and stood up. "Anything else?"

"Yes. I don't see how this fits in with the stuff Harry Posen told me."

"You will," said Roussel, and left me without another word.

8

When I returned from Houston, I quickly realized that it would be impractical for me to keep calling Harry Posen to fill in the details, even if he would talk to me about such matters on the phone. This was especially true in light of what then seemed to be a rapid deterioration in his condition. I did not know then that he would hang on for four more painful years, and even if I had known, his powers of communication would still have been severely diminished.

I came to the conclusion that I would have to go back to Zulla, get as much of the complete story as I could and then insert into Harry's narrative contributions from others in chronological order. To accomplish that I would have to obtain Harry's consent to record our sessions, and even if he agreed, due to financial considerations I would again have to wait until I could afford to fly to Virginia and stay for possibly as long as a week.

I phoned him, ostensibly to report on my meeting with Roussel, intending then to lead into my true purpose.

"Harry, I got along very well with Pete Roussel."

"Thought you would. So?"

"I've been thinking. The only way I can see of doing this thing is if I can get your side of the story first and then fill in the details from the people you point me towards."

"Yeah. I figured that, too. After you went home. We should've thought of it when you were here."

"It means I would have to record you."

There was a very long silence. Just when I was certain he was going to tell me to forget the whole venture, he agreed. I thanked him profusely and explained my financial situation. There was another long silence.

"How many days do you think it would take?" he asked.

"You would be able to judge that better than me."

"I would only be good for, say, three hours a day, max. I get tired more quickly than I used to."

"So how many days would that be?"

"I'm guessing two or maybe three."

"Is there a cheap motel in Zulla?"

"Jesus, no. There's nothing here. There are places in Middleburg, Plains, Paris and Haymarket, but the cheapest would be around $300 a night."

"US dollars?"

"Of course. We don't take Monopoly money here."

"Ouch."

I did not know what else to say. I knew there was no way I could afford those prices, especially as I would have to hire a car again and keep it for several days. Together with airfare I was looking at something like $2,500 Canadian. I knew it was impossible.

"Unless something turns up, I guess that's it," I said.

"Like Mr. Micawber."

"Sorry?"

"Not a Dickens fan?"

"No."

"Never mind. Well old son, you call me in a month and we'll see where things stand."

I called again in early April and told him that my finances had improved, but not enough to permit me to make the trip.

"Tell you what. If you can swing the rest, you can bunk up here," he said. "You can get a bus from Dulles to Haymarket and I'll get my gardener to pick you up there."

"That would be great. Thank you, Harry."

"When will you be here?"

"It'll take three weeks to get my ducks in a row."

"Okay."

~

Thus, for one reason or another, it was not until late May of 2019 that I found myself in Zulla for the second time. The foliage on the trees was rich and green, and rural Virginia looked like a rustic paradise.

Harry's gardener, whose name was Hernandez, told me that the daytime temperatures were around 24C, a full ten degrees warmer than it had been back in Halifax.

When Harry welcomed me at the door, I could see that his long, hopeless journey was well under way. He walked with more difficulty and his speech was sometimes painfully slow.

He showed me to a very nice bedroom and told me he would likely not see me at dinner, which the gardener's wife would serve at seven.

"I may feel up to it, but if not I'll see you tomorrow around eleven for our first session."

"Second."

"What?"

"This will be our second session."

"Oh, yeah."

I did not see him at dinner, which was a lovely meal of pork tenderloin with tiny asparagus and early cabbage from Harry's garden.

After listening to the booming of a nighthawk, and later a whippoorwill, I slept extremely well.

9

"Okay," said Harry. "I'm going to ramble on. Interrupt me if you need to, but only if absolutely necessary."

"I'll try."

"Happy birthday, by the way. I did some research on you. You've had a strange and varied career."

"That's one way of putting it. But thanks for the birthday wishes."

"You're welcome. Alright."

First taped session with Harry Posen
Zulla, Virginia, May 28th, 2019

POSEN: I was 42 at the time. Not particularly good looking—you could have guessed that from what you see today—and overweight. I was always working on that—you know, eating nectarines for breakfast with bran and skim milk. Ugh. Don't know why I put myself through that. The nectarines were tasteless before June—leathery. I guess I figured that if I tortured myself at breakfast and didn't have lunch, it was okay for me to have a nice meal with good wine in the evenings—which I did frequently, either at home or at La Grande Boucherie, Le Diplomate or Lupo Verde. I had a morning exercise routine before breakfast of 15 minutes on a stationary bike, then 20 minutes of stomach exercises, including 50 sit-ups, but it was always a losing battle against a growing waistline.

I had a nice little house—a bungalow, really—in the Palisades district of DC and drove to work in Langley each day over the Chain Bridge and along the George Washington Parkway. On a good day I could be there in twenty minutes, even less early in the morning or late at night.

I had never married, though I came close several times. At that time my current entanglement was Marjorie, the eldest daughter of a United States Senator. She dragged me, kicking and screaming, around a series of boring cocktail parties or dinners where they always seemed to serve up fried chicken, corn bread, candied yams, pecan pie and piles of mashed potatoes.

Every one of these horrendous affairs started with a fight about my shoes. As you can see, Jeremy, I like to be comfortable and always wear battered hush puppies –remember them?—and these holey sneakers —these must be at least ten years old. Marje wanted me to wear shiny, stiff shoes and was livid when I didn't.

Anyway, enough of that. You want to know about work. Well, I guess you could say I was a spy. With the CIA. I'd been with them for about 15 years and at the time this all kicked off. I was second in command of X Division, which was known in the shop as the "Dirty Tricks" Section. This covered almost anything clandestine you can think, of ranging from a lightning kidnapping on a street in Guatemala City, through running guns, to arranging the disappearance of troublesome individuals."

AKERMAN: At home and abroad?

P: Just abroad. As far as I knew. Anyway, I rose through the ranks in what you might call a steady but not spectacular way. I started as a field agent in Vietnam for the FBI and was transferred because of my work on the Winstanley Affair—

A: What was—?

P: If you don't know, I'm not going to tell you. It's not relevant anyhow. I always had more of a police mentality than the outlook of a spy, and I kept my nose clean and never bucked the bosses. I worked very closely with the Brits in Buenos Aires during the Falklands War and, apparently, it was this that convinced the gang upstairs that I was management material, so that's when I was moved to Section X.

Before you ask, the answer is 'yes.' You try not to think of the ethical implications of your work in a department like X, you have to assume that the bosses have got it right and that what you do is in the best interests of the USA. If you didn't, you would go mad or become a drug addict or a drunk—which many did.

A: Excuse me, Harry. How would that impact things like national laws, regulations, and international agreements, not to mention moral codes?

P: If we stopped to consider any of those, we couldn't have done our work. I often thought about it, but figured I had to get on with my job.

That brings me to Edgar Sollows. He was one of the three Assistant Directors of the Agency, in charge of Section X, reporting to Bill Casey. I'll tell you about the other ADs later. Sollows was my boss. He was an extraordinary man in so many ways, more like a professor or a great artist. He was immensely cultured, went in for opera, ballet, theatre and all that stuff. And he was an expert on wine and food. I guess people would have said he was urbane. He was the one who got me involved in wine. I never became as knowledgeable or as fanatical as him, but eventually I had quite a good cellar.

I don't want to bore you with unnecessary details, but since Sollows played the leading role in Operation Renegade, I need to give you an idea of the kind of man he was. I think I can best do that by describing one night I went to his place for dinner and a wine tasting.

Excuse me, I need to take a drink.[3]

Like I was saying, he invited me over and I got there at about eight. He lived in Georgetown, which, as I expect you know, is a very swanky neighbourhood, and Edgar's place was swankier than a good many. You might say it was discreetly set back from the street behind several trees and a lush shrubbery. The house and the surroundings whispered— well, a little louder than whispered—'money'. I believe Edgar's family were Boston Brahmans from way back.

Anyhoo, I got there on time and was greeted by his sister, Barbara, who appeared as a theatrical apparition, shimmering on a wave of exotic fragrance. Ed wasn't married and the sister lived with him. She led me—yes, by the hand—to what they called the den, but what most of us might call the 'Imperial Suite', it was so opulent.

Oh, I forgot to tell you what Edgar looked like. That's important. He

---

3 He poured himself half a glass of Aberlour and threw in some ice and a dash of soda. I hoped he would drink it slowly, because if he did not he would soon be too sloshed to talk.

was about fifty-something, but looked younger—not a line or wrinkle anywhere on his face—and tall, with long, elegant fingers. He played—not the piano, but the clavichord! I didn't even know what one looked like until I saw it at his house. I'd only heard them on records. You alright there? Do you want a slug of Scotch?

A: Thank you, Harry. I think I might have a little drop.

P: Little drop, my ass.[4], Soda?

A: Yes, please.

P: Here, help yourself.

I was describing what he looked like, and here's the strangest thing about him: he was—what do they call it?—Alopecic. He didn't have a hair on his body—nowhere, he told me. I don't know whether he was born that way or got some infection or something when he was a kid, but it meant his face and head were shiny—almost gleaming. And tanned, too. He spent his free time somewhere in the Caribbean—I don't know where, on some island or other. He had a slightly fleshy nose, a wide mouth with full lips, very deep brown eyes, and when he spoke he gestured as if he was conducting an orchestra.

Anyway, we all sat around a big, beautiful table—Harry said it was rosewood, but I wouldn't know the difference—and had five glasses of wine in front of us. Oh, I should mention—not that it matters—that the other guests were a guy called Hancock who was commodore of Edgar's yacht club and Walter Winterton, the wine columnist for the *Washington Post*, a tubby feller with fat fingers, pink ears and a polka-dot bow tie. Just the five of us—Barbara joined in, too.

To cut a long story short, we all smelled and sipped and swirled and spat and made copious notes. Then Edgar called on us to say what we thought the wines were. Winterton led off and gave his guesses, followed by the rest of us. Then, in a very prissy way, Ed told us what they were and gave us a lecture on each one. His triumph was catching all of us out by following a Château Palmer 1966 with a '67, which we all thought was the '61.

After that was over, we were led into an even swankier dining room

---

4 Harry filled my glass half full.

where we had lashings of foie gras and lobster salad. With that he gave us a sweet wine. I think it was Château D'Yquem 1967. I didn't think that was appropriate and kept my mouth shut, but Winterton and Hancock whined like banshees. Edgar glowered at them and declared in an imperious tone that Sauternes was the perfect accompaniment to all food except dessert. That was the kind of guy he was.

I'm getting a bit tired now, Jeremy. Do you mind if we leave it there for this morning?

A: No, of course not.

P: We'll have another go at it after lunch.

10

Interview with Informant B.
Former member of the Federal Security Service (FSB)
of the Russian Federation and of
the Committee on State Security (KGB)
of the Union of Soviet Socialist Republics

It took me a long time to track this man down. Harry gave me his name as a possible source and I finally found him in one of Canada's Maritime provinces—of all places—almost at my own back door!

He was very old and was terrified at the prospect of talking to me. He said, "Until Putin goes, nobody is safe."

Only after I gave him assurances of absolute anonymity would he agree to see me.

"I knew Zina Varenko very well," he told me. "I cannot reveal precisely the nature of our relationship—but I assure you it was entirely professional. In any event, her affections were for our superior, Colonel Repnin.

"If she is still alive she would be about 75 today. She was a very attractive woman, a little on the *zoftig* side maybe, and always immaculately dressed. That was difficult to do in the Soviet Union in those days. The quality of clothes she liked were not always available and were extremely expensive. She loved fine food and wine and adored opera, something else she shared with Repnin."

"Tell me about him."

"I will. in good time. One thing at a time. You must let me tell it in my own way."

"I'm sorry. I apologize."

"No matter. She had been posted to Vienna at one stage and clearly fell in love with the place. She despised Moscow although she knew it —how do you say?—like the back of her hand. At the time of Operatsiya Renegat she had twice been decorated for outstanding work.

"Of course, we both worked at the Lubyanka in Dzerzhinsky Square and she often spoke lovingly of the beautiful, polished oak doors and 19th-century elevator with its grillwork cage. But she could not stand the smell of boiled cabbage and fried sausage in the canteen. It was strictly segregated according to rank, captains and above had a slightly better dining room, but it was invariably full of smoke and Zina said it made her sick. So she always brought something from home and ate at her desk—usually a brioche with butter and apricot jam.

"Just as the eating arrangements were separated by rank, so also were the floors on which we worked. As you went up the flooring, the furniture all became more luxurious until, at the corner at the very top, Comrade Chebrikov had a massive, sumptuous office. Under normal circumstances only colonels would be allowed up there. Occasionally majors—like Zina—might be summoned for a specific purpose. The only others who were..."

He paused here and seemed nervously uncertain. He rubbed his leathery face with a gnarled hand.

"Is there something wrong?" I asked.

"Er...I find myself in some difficulty." He fidgeted in his chair. "I am trying not to say anything from which the FSB could identify me from your book."

"For a variety of reasons my book can't come out for at least another two years—maybe more."

"Ha-ha, and you think I would be dead by then, eh?"

"No, I didn't mean that, but Putin could be gone by then."

"Don't you believe it! That one will rule Russia until someone assassinates him. I'll deal with his role in this later."

"You mean Putin was involved in Operation Renegade?"

"Oh yes. At the time he was working with the *Stasi* in Dresden. I don't know what else he did there, but it must have been diabolical because they promoted him to Lieutenant Colonel."

"Tell me more!"

"You are trying to rush me again. We have others to deal with long before we get to him. Back to Zina. She had spent some time in Bulgaria, where she received the Medal of Friendship from the Bulgars, although she said the stink of roses of attar in that benighted country was almost intolerable.

"Then she returned to Moscow, where she eventually became assistant to Colonel Repnin, head of Special Services. It was in 1985 she was given the task of investigating Cephalinol and preparing a report for the bosses."

"I have seen that report," I interrupted. "At least, a translation of it."

"Have you indeed? I won't inquire where you got it. Now what was I talking about?

"Ah, yes, Repnin. Now there was a man! What a brain! In light of what he did he must have been a genius—of sorts. He was a Cossack from Stanista Nagutskaya, now Stavropol Krai, which was the same place Andropov came from. I guess you know that Andropov went to great lengths to hide his origins—who the hell knows why—and the gossip was that somehow Repnin, through his family connections, knew what they had been. They said—and again this is sheer gossip—that Andropov had a meeting with Repnin at which he had decided to have him eliminated, but was so charmed by the young fellow that he inserted him directly into the KGB.

"Repnin not only had great charm and an enormous intellect, but he was extremely handsome. 'Dark and dashing' was the way my dear, late wife used to describe him. He too liked the good life. Opera was his great passion, just like Varenko. So much so that even though his rank and position gave him the influence to obtain the very best seats at the Bolshoi, he always preferred the cheap *fauteuils* down at the front on the left where he could see the conductor. Anyway, to the day."

"The day?"

"The day Repin and Varenko were summoned to the Chairman's office, which, as I have said, was sumptuous, with thick carpets and comfortable chairs of leather and velvet. It seems strange in retrospect, but in those days it was thought important for certain meetings that there be a secretarial employee taking notes and a supervisory person sitting with them to make sure the essential points were recorded."

"And you were—?"

"One of those people. I will not say which one."

"Understood."

"Before I go on I should say something about Viktor Chebrikov—'old squint eyes,' he was called in the Lubyanka building because his sight was very bad and he peered through very thick glasses.

"He was a sour, humourless man who would then have been in his early 60s. He was from Yekaterinoslav, now called Dnipro, in Ukraine. He attended military school and, by all accounts, fought bravely in World War II. Because of his poor eyesight he had quit the military, so he went in for engineering and the Communist Party. Nobody really knows how or why, but in 1967 he was summoned to Moscow as personnel manager for the Central Committee of the Party, then the next year they made him Deputy Chairman of the KGB under Andropov. Imagine those two sour apples in the same barrel!

"It was Chebrikov who managed the American spy Aldrich Ames, whose work led to the deaths of countless CIA and MI6 agents around the world. He was also 'the Butcher of Uzbekistan', when he cleaned out the party there and eliminated Sharof Rashidov and many others.

"So, there they were around a big table, with Chebrikov blinking away at the head. There were several KGB colonels there, including Bauer and Roston, who envied Repnin's 'in' with the boss, and Vladimir Kryuchov of the First Directorate, who later succeeded as the Chairman. There were five of them under Chebrikov, the other was a man called Ivanov, but I don't think he was there on that occasion.

"Oh, I should have asked you. Would you like some tea, Mr. Akerman?"

"No, thank you."

"Some vodka, maybe?"

"Oh, no."

"Right. Repnin was not the most senior of the colonels in terms of age or length of service, but because Action Services was considered most prestigious, he was treated as if he was junior only to the head of the First Directorate and the Chairman.

"Repnin, with gallantry and a flourish, asked Varenko to hand her report to the Chairman. Chebrikov attempted to go through the report, but soon gave up and threw it over to Kryuchov, saying:

> "I can't be bothered to read all this. It's packed with technical jargon, Vlad, you go through it. What is the *itogovyy rezul'tat*? Repnin?"
>
> "It speaks of a highly toxic material which nobody understands which is currently being produced in Palermo."
>
> "So?"
>
> "Excuse me, Comrade Chairman," interjected Kryuchov, "but

this is the matter Comrade Shevardnadze was handed by George Schultz just the other day."

"Ah, yes. That must be what Shevardnadze was calling me about yesterday. I was at the Kremlin. So this is that?"

"Yes."

"Is there a problem with the Italians?"

"No, the Iranians."

"*Sumasshedshiye!* Those bastards are a fucking hemorrhoid. What's the proposal?"

"A two person team—one of ours, one of theirs—to draw up and execute a plan to steal it from the Iranians."

"Fine. Repnin I appoint you as our representative on this task force. Who will Casey choose?"

"Probably Sollows."

"You know him?"

"We've never met, Comrade Chairman."

"Well, you soon will. And, Repnin..."

"Sir?"

"This is not an opportunity for you to wallow in capitalistic pursuits. It sounds as if it could get you both killed."

Informant B. shifted in his seat. "I noticed that the Chairman did not give this an Operational Title, which meant it wasn't set up formally. That turned out to be a serious mistake. It was the first I heard of Celphalinol. But it was not the last."

11

Second taped session with Harry Posen
Zulla, Virginia, May 28th, 2019

I didn't see much of Bill Casey. There was nothing unusual in that. I mean, I was three ranks below him. I did see John MacMahon, the Deputy Director, from time to time, although not often. Most of the time we observed the chain of command and, for the most part, my link with John and Casey was through Edgar, my boss.

John was a super guy, a New Englander, and a lot of us were sorry when he quit over assistance to the Afghanistani and Nicaraguan so-called freedom fighters. He was highly suspicious of all-out support for those crazies and I think time has proven him right. That happened the year after Operation Renegade.

Now, Casey was an Irish, Catholic, New Yorker who liked to get his own way and didn't suffer fools gladly. No sir! He got the Directorship because he had been in the OSS under Bill Donovan during World War II, and—more importantly—he was Reagan's campaign manager in the 1980 election. Apparently, he was the man who brought Reagan and Bush Senior together, which, as you know, led to Bush becoming Vice President.

At Sollow's level there were three Section Heads. An old fart called Clayborne Morse—who had been some kind of naval hero—as head of Administration, Phil Lacusta in charge of recruitment and personnel, and Sollows in Special Services.

Phil was in command of the agents and residents around the world. He had been with the agency for decades and was a 'hands-on' man. At one time or another every CIA operative had passed through Phil's hands and been subjected to his scrutiny. He was a great guy who looked much younger than his age—I guess he would have been around 62 at the time—and although he was Italian, he looked like an

Irish leprechaun, with a big red nose and cheeks and curly hair, and a big, grinning, mouth missing a tooth. To Sollows' wealthy, cultured mentality, Phil was considered as the black sheep of the family, and he absolutely hated Phil's habit of chewing on cheap cigars.

Anyway, now we come to the day we learned about what was to be done about the Cephalinol business. I'm not really sure why I was at the meeting, but Edgar dragged me along. I think it made him feel good to have someone there he could tell to get coffee or water. So, there was Casey at his desk, John MacMahon on his right, Lacusta on his left and Edgar and Morse in the middle. I sat behind Edgar. Oh, yes, and Casey's secretary was there, too.

Casey thumbed the thin red file with what appeared to be disgust. I guessed he was mulling over in his mind how he could handle it so he would be in the clear if anything went 'tits up', as he would put it.

"It's a presidential order." He sniffed. "The Russians have pushed it and Schultz took it to the president and got the okay. Ours is not to reason why, ours is just to do or die. I assume you've perused the material."

"Director, there are no special problems," said Morse, "except money."

"Why, Clayborne? Are we short of the readies?"

"Not really, sir, provided you are willing to tap the contingency fund."

"How much is in there?"

"$23.7 million."

"Alright, as long as you don't blow the whole frigging lot, allow a reasonable amount."

"How much is reasonable?"

"You make that determination and don't tell me what it was until later."

"Understood, Chief."

"Phil?"

"It'll be weird working with the bastards instead of against them. I don't see this as a job for regular operatives because of the security clearance level, so it won't actually be my show. I think it's up to Ed."

Sollows frowned because he hated being called "Ed".

Impatiently, the Director pushed the file aside. "I'm assuming that's why we have Harry here. Can you handle this task okay?"

"Certainly, sir," I said.

But before I could continue, Edgar cut in. "Ah, that could be a problem. Of course, Harry is more than equal to the task, but he doesn't speak Farsi and not a lot of Arabic. And he would need to be fluent in Russian if he is going to work with their man on a day-to-day basis."

"How is your Russian, Harry?" the Director asked.

"Good" I said, but I didn't want to upset my boss, so I added, "but maybe not good enough for this."

"Then what the fuck are we going to do?" Casey was angry. It was getting late in the day and he probably had a dinner date.

"I can do it myself," Edgar said.

"You?"

"They're likely to send Repnin or Verenko. I can deal with either."

"You know them?"

"Not personally."

"Well, unless Phil objects, I won't stand in your way, Ed."

"Not really, boss," Phil said, "but Ed, you've been at a desk for a long time and you're not as young as you used to be."

"You are most solicitous of my welfare, Phillip, for which I am deeply grateful, but I think there might be a vestige of life in the old dog."

"Fine," Casey said, getting up. "Do it."

I always prided myself on my instinct, Jeremy. My nose and my antennae were very sensitive and the best in the place.[5]

But I have to confess—to my eternal shame—that I did not smell a rat when Edgar butted in to get the mission for himself. And—and this is even more shameful—I didn't smell a rat when, purely by chance, I came across some documents which showed that many of Edgar's previous overseas postings happened to coincide with Repnin's.

If only I had smelled a rat then, we all could have been saved a great deal of trouble.

---

5 Harry hitched himself up, looked at his watch, and poured himself a glass of Scotch.

12

Reconstruction

There is no direct, first-hand knowledge of these events. I have reconstructed them based upon suppositions offered by Harry Posen, Informant B and others.

We know that a rare telephone call occurred between Viktor Chebrikov and William Casey sometime following the meeting in Casey's office. We cannot know with any degree of precision what was said—via an interpreter—but it is not unreasonable to suppose that the following might approximate the conversation:

"Mr. Chebrikov. good morning."

"Mr. Casey. This is a pleasure I do not expect to see repeated many times. Of course, I know you from your file and know of your bravery in the Великая Отечественная война—"

"I beg your pardon?"

"The Great Patriotic War. What you call World War Two."

"Ah yes. I see that you, too, acquitted yourself with honor in our fight against the Nazis."

"Yes. But to business. I got your file on Edgar Sollows. Do I have your personal assurance that it is accurate, that it has not been falsified, and that significant information has not been redacted?"

"You have my word. I have your file on Valentin Repnin. Do you make the same assurances with reference to that document?"

"I do." Chebrikov chuckled. "Although you understand I could not let you have all the supporting files?"

"Likewise," said Casey with a hearty laugh. "So, we hand it over to these men to carry out the mission as they see fit?"

"We do, Let us hope for success. Between ourselves, these Iranians are a bunch of Чертовы идиоты."

"What?"

"Excuse me," said the interpreter, "the Chairman said 'fucking assholes.'"

"I see. Well Mr. Chebrikov it was an honor to speak with you, I doubt it will happen again any time soon."

"No. *Do Svidaniya,* Mr. Casey."

~

With a yawn he stubbed out an evilly-pungent, half-finished *Belomorkanal* cigarette and reached down to pick up his assorted belongings. There was a light-blue German raincoat, a small canvass bag, and a large, bulky camera case. Reaching into the breast pocket of his nondescript grey suit he withdrew his boarding pass and the cheap, paperback novel he had picked up the day before, and entered a long tunnel leading to the tarmac.

When he emerged from an equally long and boring tunnel almost twelve hours later, he felt filthy and out of sorts. It was very hot and humid. The vodkas he had on the plane were of a cheap variety and left a metallic taste in his mouth.

He stopped at a small tobacconist's stall and bought some *Kilyubatra Subar* cigarettes, which he considered insufficiently strong, but better than nothing under the circumstances.

The perspiration was pouring down his neck as he waited for a taxi to appear. On all sides it seemed as if people were accosting him, in Arabic, French and English, offering to shine his shoes, or show him a "good time".

He cursed them, and there was something cruel, ruthless in his eyes which made them back away.

At length, a taxi pulled up and the driver, stinking of *raki*, threw his bag into the back on the ancient, decaying Citroën.

"*Tu veux un hôtel américain?*"

"*Non.* Hilton."

He sank into the dilapidated back seat and drew deeply on his cigarette, contemplating a long shower and, if he could find one, a decent meal.

~

At that moment, Flight TWA 662 from New York via Rome skidded on the tarmac. The flight had been a long and uneventful one for the man who sat, virtually alone, in the First Class cabin, sipping glass after glass of Dom Perignon Champagne. He marked a passage in *Decanter* with an elegant, embossed, silver pencil and replaced the magazine in his black, leather attaché case,

He retrieved his Louis Vuitton luggage from the carousel, and at once a porter appeared at his side, placed his bags on a tin *kuli* and respectfully folded and draped the navy Burberry over the top.

"You want taxi?" asked the porter, displaying an expanse of yellow teeth.

"No, the Menah House's Daimler."

The smile disappeared from the porter's face. People who stayed at the Menah House knew the country and seldom tipped generously.

The Daimler was summoned and, for his troubles, the porter received a few *piastres* dropped into his shirt pocket.

The Menah House was where his parents had stayed in days gone by. He had preferred Shepheard's and had transferred to the Menah only when rioters had destroyed the former in 1952.

By the discreet light in the *tonneau* he scanned a leather-bound notebook containing the telephone numbers he had learned in Rome. Then he flicked off the light and gazed at the passing illuminations artificially focused on the pyramids. Ah, he thought with some disgust, how the tourists love the *sons et lumières,*

Repnin and Sollows had arrived in Cairo.

13

Much to my surprise, Harry said he would eat dinner with me that evening, and we sat down to a lovely meal cooked and served by Mrs. Hernandez. We had tenderloin steaks with mushrooms, tiny Brussels sprouts and fried potatoes. With the meal, Harry served a bottle of Mayacamas Mount Vedeer Cabernet Sauvignon 2002, which was utterly delicious and showed little signs of its age.

I could not help but notice that Harry was slow in eating, found it difficult to eat and carry on a conversation, and occasionally was unable to name simple items like salt and pepper. Under the circumstances I expected him to leave me right after dinner, but he insisted on getting the tape recorder and conducting the third interview of the day.

Third taped session with Harry Posen
Zulla, Virginia, May 28, 2019

The agreement was that at precisely 11:32 EST the radio operator on the priority channel at the Langley annex would receive a short burst of signals in a pre-arranged pattern. Her instructions were merely to report this fact to her supervisor, who then would tell Phil LaCusta.

Neither the operator nor the supervisor had any idea what this meant, nor could they have discovered it because the signal itself was unintelligible, uncoded and of no literal value. In other words, it was just a noise. This noise, which was to be repeated every night at the same time, only had significance for Phil and me, to whom it meant different things on different days.

Only if the signal changed would it convey a message which would indicate that something had gone wrong, and then it would be decoded. Since we were working with the Russians on this, these security measures were in place, mainly to avoid Iran intercepting our traffic.

The way it worked was that the operator walked along a bank of electronic equipment—don't ask me what it all did, because I couldn't tell you—and tapped at the window of the office-sized glass booth at the end of the hall. The supervisor—a nice Nebraskan called Herbie—would wave his thanks and then call Phil.

I was with Phil when Herbie called. Having established every-thing was okay, Phil called the Director on the scrambler, and said, "He's in Cairo."

The next night, the performance was repeated, and this time Phil called Casey and said, "Sir, contact with Repnin has been established."

On the third night when Herbie brought his news, Phil told the boss, "Planning complete. Everything is on schedule."

The following night, Phil had difficulty raising the Director. His wife, Sophia, said he had the flu and was too ill to come to the phone. So Phil asked her if she would just tell him that they were going in tonight and there would be no further message for three more nights.

You know, Jeremy, I have to say that it crossed my suspicious mind that having the flu might be a good excuse for not getting the mes-sage.

14

*Statements taken from Mahmoud Ali and
Mostafa Hassan, August 2019[6]*

Statement by Ali:

My master, Alsayid Dimitriou Giannopoulos, own a shop in the
Sherif Gardens. On front door was card which say: "Hasni Karim
Jeweller." There is no Karim. He does not exist. In the window
we display high-priced carpets. Too high for most peoples except maybe tourists.

I am not long working for Alsayid Giannopoulis—cleaning,
and minding the shop when he is out—that I am aware that he
does not depend upon sales to pay his way, and that he don't
care if or not he sell stuff. I have opinion that he was some kind
spy, but not know for who he is working. In case he work for
State Security Investigations Service I keep my mouth shut.
Hāfiẓ 'alā naẓāfatuk.

I see strange people come and go and they not buy anything.
No jewels, no carpets. And always they meet in back room
where Alsayid think I cannot hear but is hole in wall—how you
say?...level of knees—where I hear most what they say.

One day this man come in shop and ask for Alsayid. He is bald
with no beard or moustaches. He look like *altabaqat aleulya:*
nice clothes and shine shoes. He ask for Alsayid Giannopoulis
and I say—as I am instructed to do-- that is me, I am Giano-
polis, but man get angry and say he want to see the real Giannopoulis.

Then Alsayid come out and greet man by name of "Da-vid."

---

6 While taken at a much later date, than those statements which precede it, they
   appear here to present the narrative in chronological order

They disappear in back room and I crouch down to hear what they say. Alsayid offer him Ouzo but the man David say no, so he get him mint tea.

I only understand little of what they say, but is plain that David is pressuring Alsayid and threatening him to do something. I think David say "discontinue contract" and say something about the accounts not in order. David ask him if he want transfer to Bombay. Alasyid say no, no, no.

Someone come into shop and I have to leave my hole for maybe five minutes. When I return to hole, Alsayid is saying that he have no choice and 'iin sha' allah, he must do what David say.

I not see this man David again in shop and soon Alsayid close place and kick me on street. Later I hear he has open new place on Al-Muiz. I not see him again.

Statement by Hassan:

I am bartender at Commodore Hotel. I do not drink alcohol, but I have to make a living. One of my regular customers is man who call himself Serge—I never hear his last name. He always drink vodka and sit in velvet booth close to bar, but away from other tables.

I not know what this man do for business or work, but he always has plenty money and meet many mens and womens in the bar. I do not think any of this meetings was for social reasons. He take notes and then dismiss peoples like they was servants. I tell myself he is collector of information, but why I do not know.

One evening, a dark handsome man come into bar. He is Russian. I can smell Russians. Not mean his expensive Turkish cigarette, but him. The way he move. The way he look this way and that way. This man walk straight to Serge's booth and he disappear behind the drape. I move from my end of the bar to that end.

The man's name is Valya and it is clear that Serge is terrified of this man who is saying that Serge will be sent home to Russia. Serge say he will do anything to stay in Cairo and Valya say that is good because he wants that...Suddenly this Valya jump up and look around. He see me and give me the evil eye so I move down the bar. That is all I know.

15

Although Mrs. Hendandez had laid places for two, Harry did not appear at the table for breakfast. I waited for about twenty minutes then continued without him. I attempted to engage Mrs. H. in conversation but was unsuccessful, so I ate in silence.

When I had finished eating I wandered out into the garden, which was splendidly in full bloom. The morning was exceedingly fine, and I saw from the thermometer on the garden wall that the temperature was already 24°C.

As the morning wore on, I began to fear that Harry had experienced a bad night, and worried that he would be unable to see me at all that day. To kill time, I counted the varieties of flowers and shrubs in the garden. When I reached 58 varieties (one more than Heinz, I reflected), I was loudly hailed from the patio.

It was Harry, looking quite well, and speaking clearly and loudly, if rather slower than usual. "Sorry I'm late. Had a good night. Mrs. H has instructions to let me sleep. Are you ready to start again?"

"'Morning Harry. Sure, I'm ready." I joined him on the patio.

"I see in your file that—"

"I have a *file*?"

"In a manner of speaking, yes. I see that this is your father's birthday. How old was he when he died?"

"Ninety-nine."

"Wow. You've got good genes, then. I know I won't live that long. Maybe two more years if I'm lucky."

"Oh, I hope not."

"Where did your old man hang out?"

"You mean, where did he live?"

"Yeah."

"In England. On the south coast."

"Too much rain for me."

"Shall we start?"

"Ah. Okay, let's get to it."

Fourth taped session with Harry Posen
Zulla, Virginia, May 29th, 2019

Now we come to the day. In the afternoon, Phil called me in and asked me if I would go to the Annex that night and 'keep an eye on things'. I asked him what exactly he meant by that, and he said he wanted me to be one who brought the nightly message to him. I told him that, although I didn't relish the task, I would do it. Herbie was entertaining to a point, but after he had trotted out his five or six well-worn jokes he became a bore.

Phil was fidgeting in his chair and chewing on his cigar.

"Are you nervous, Phil?" I asked.

"Yes. I can't tell you why. It's something in my water, if you know what I mean."

"Yeah, I do. Will you be here or at home?"

"I'll be here."

"Okay. I'll see you later."

Some hours later I glanced at the clock and saw that the appointed hour was approaching, so I sauntered along to the operators' quarters and idly chatted with Herbie.

After a while, I saw our operator putting aside the sweater she had been knitting and turning a few knobs on the control bank. She carefully placed a notepad and pencil on the ledge in front, switched on the recording apparatus and put on her headphones.

The designated time approached, then passed. She waited another five minutes, then looked at me, shaking her head. I told her I would see Herbie and take it from there, so she put her headphones down and picked up the knitting.

"Everything alright?" Herbie asked.

"No. Zip. Nada. Zilch."

"Really?"

"Yeah, really. I'm going to head on over to see Phil."

"Okay. See you."

When I crossed into our building, Phil was halfway down the corridor, coming towards me.

"What the hell happened?"

"Nothing."

"What do you mean, nothing?"

"No message. Nothing at all."

"Fuck. Come with me. We'd better call the boss."

Casey was sniffling and coughing when we called, so maybe he really did have the flu. And he did not take our news well. He said he was running a temperature of 101 and needed to sleep.

"What did you think it means, Phil?"

"Don't know, Chief. I have to say I thought Ed's three days was optimistic. My guess is that it doesn't look half as easy on the ground as it did on paper."

"Harry, any ideas?"

"I think we should give it a few more days, sir."

"How many?"

"Two. If we haven't heard by then I think we have to assume that the ragheads have caught them. In that case we must expect a show trial, or at least a press conference where they announce they have been executed."

"Mother of God! I'm off to bed, and I'd advise you to do the same."

"If this has gone tits up, it won't be my fault," Phil said after he had hung up. "Harry, you should have grabbed the job when the Director offered it."

"Jesus! Don't blame me. It was clear Edgar wanted to take it. I couldn't argue with my own boss in front of the Director!"

I was good and mad, I can tell you. Here we were only a few days behind schedule and already Phil was running for cover.

"Alright, alright. Calm down." He spat the end of the cigar into a wastebasket. "I don't know why Schultz or Chebrikov wanted this to be a two-man job. Could you do it without extra muscle?"

"No, of course not. I just assumed Edgar would recruit help. Maybe that's what has delayed him."

"Yeah, that could be it. Say, why don't I contact the head of Cairo Station? Maybe Ed checked with her."

"Her?"

"Yeah, Marg Benson. She took over from Fussy Freddie Fry only last month."

"I didn't know that."

"There's lots you don't know. Why don't you toddle along to your own office while I make the call?"

It was the middle of the night, and a good two hours had gone by before I heard Phil's heavy footfall outside my office. I could tell by his face that he wasn't a happy man.

"No luck?"

"No fucking luck is right!"

"Did you talk to Marg?"

"'Course I did, and I told her to check with her stringers to see if Ed made contact with any of them."

"And..?"

"The answer was 'no', but she said two of them had vanished."

"Vanished?"

"Yeah. She said all traces of them had disappeared."

"Who were they?"

"You wouldn't know them. Low-level chaff."

"Could be a coincidence."

"Maybe. But Marg had an idea. It may be a bit early to press the panic button, but she suggested we check the contingency file."

The contingency file was a document any field agent, of whatever rank, was required to draw up before leaving indicating his or her extrication plans in the event of an emergency. That would have been left in Edgar's office, in a very secure safe.

"You think that will tell us something?"

"I dunno, but if it's anything like his usual stuff, it'll be a Bible of info down to the last detail. I'd put my money on the answer being in there."

"Okay. Let's do it."

I called Larry Cathcart, head of internal security, and he told me he would get out of bed and come in. While we waited, Phil started on a new Macanudo cigar, this time actually lighting it, and blowing out clouds of stinking smoke. As discreetly as I could, I moved away from the desk to the door and looked down the corridor, gratefully breathing the only slightly better air.

After what seemed like an eternity, Larry arrived, wearing his overcoat over his pyjamas. He nodded to us, grunted, and presented us with a form for each of us to sign, listing the time, date and purpose of the "intrusion".

We walked to Edgar's office, which was notably different from the others in that it boasted a rosewood desk, Chinese porcelain vases, a thick Axminster carpet and pre-Raphaelite paintings.

Larry pulled aside a Frederick Sandys painting of a languishing girl with long red hair—Ed loved that painting, but I thought it was sickly and mawkish—and punched a code into the wall safe. Then I entered the section code.

"Please look away, Phil," I joked.

"Fuck you, Harry. I can get into every one of four million files come 8:30 this morning so quit farting around!"

Larry cautiously slid the door open. "Huh," he said.

"What is it?" Phil demanded.

"Take a look."

The safe was empty.

16

I met Informant B, the former KGB officer, only once. I tried to see him a second time, but he refused, whether out of fear or for some other reason I never discovered.

By sheer chance I happened to be in Southern New Brunswick, for reasons unconnected with this book, when a strange headline in the Saint John *Telegraph Journal* caught my eye:

Mystery Man Dies in Strange Circumstances

A Grove Hill man known to the local community as Fred Mac-Donald has died under circumstances which authorities have not fully explained. Locals say MacDonald, believed to be about 85, came from somewhere in Eastern Europe, and settled in Grove Hill about thirty years ago.

Police said the death was suspicious, and an inquest, held last Wednesday, ruled that it was "death by misadventure". A confidential source in the pathologist's office told *The Journal* that traces of Novichok A242, a deadly nerve agent, were found at the scene.

This gives rise to speculation that MacDonald was somehow connected with Vil Mirzayanov, the Russian chemist known for revealing to the West the existence and scope of secret chemical weapon experimentation in the Russia.

Mr. MacDonald is not known to have any living relatives. The Prothonotary said it was likely that his house and land at Grove Hill would revert to the Crown.

Had Putin finally caught up with him? I wondered. It was probable he had made a number of enemies in his time in the USSR, but few would have access to that kind of poison. I set the question aside, because I knew it could never be answered. Instead I thanked my lucky stars that I had most of what I wanted from B on tape.

The following extract was, therefore, recorded at the same time as the previous interview on page 49, but I did not then understand its significance. That is why I insert it at this point.

Extract from taped interview
with Informant B

One day the Comrade Chairman Chebrikov held a meeting—I forget what it was about—and I dutifully attended, together with the stenographer. There was a large number of people in the room, so we were relegated to a far corner.

When they had ploughed their way through three quarters of the agenda, there was hammering on the window not far from where we were perched. It was Varenko, red in the face, trying to attract the attention of Vladimir Kryuchov of the First Directorate.

Her knocking was of no avail, so she opened the door and shouted, "Excuse me, Comrade Chairman, but I have news for Comrade Kryuchov. It is very, very urgent. Extremely urgent!"

"Well, spit it out, woman," said the Chairman, obviously annoyed by the interruption.

"Sir, I cannot." She looked around the room at the faces. "It is Security clearance A."

"Bauer, Roston: you stay," bawled Chebrikov. "The rest of you get out!"

The room cleared much more quickly than the stenographer and I could gather up our papers and equipment, and Varenko started talking while we were still there. We froze, not knowing what to do.

"There was no signal again last night. Repnin has disappeared."

"Disappeared?" I thought the Chairman was going to have apoplexy.

"It has been nearly a week. If he'd been caught by the IRGC's Quds, they would have been done with torturing him, and by now would have had a public event denouncing the Soviet Union for spying."

"Vlad?"

"I'm afraid she's right, Chief," Kryuchov said. "I think we have to assume that he's missing because he's dead in some ditch, killed by the *Türk mafyası* somewhere between Ankara and Gurbulak, after a misunderstanding."

"*Svyatoye der'mo!* What the hell are we going to do?" Chebrikov shouted and got up from his desk.

He stretched, wiped his glasses on the end of his tie, and then started pacing. After about six paces, he stopped dead and stared at our corner of the room in total disbelief.

"What the fuck are you doing here?" he shouted at us. "Are you recording this?"

"No, no, Comrade Chairman," the stenographer stammered. "We just didn't want to interrupt."

"Interrupt? Fuck off out of here before I have you both taken down to the basement!"

Needless to say we scurried out of that room as fast as our legs would carry us.

"*Udachlivyy Pobeg!*" The stenographer muttered as we scuttled down the corridor. I agreed. It was a lucky escape, and I wondered if Comrade Repnin would be as fortunate.

17

After we had broken for a light lunch, I was anxious to record more of Harry's memories about Operation Renegade, but he said he could not organize his thoughts sufficiently well. I noticed that before our meal of omelettes and salad, Harry had invited me to take a "table", obviously meaning "chair" and, during the meal, strangely asked me if I wanted "vinegar", by which I suspect he meant "wine".

After lunch, of which he partook very little, Harry said he wanted to go for a walk because, he said, it was one of the few things he could still do.

We left the house and set out up a narrow country road on either side of which were fields of wheat. In another field at some distance was a herd of handsome-looking cows. It was a splendid day and we walked in silence for about half a mile.

Unprompted by me, Harry suddenly started to tell me about his illness. "The first thing I noticed was that I was hesitating unnecessarily, pausing all the time and searching to find the right word. You've probably noticed that. The tapes must be a bitch to transcribe, since there must be an awful lot of silences."

"They're remarkably good," I said, "When I transcribe, I don't show the silences, and so far, I haven't noticed too many slips or substitutions. But there were some at lunch."

"Oh yeah? That's to be expected. The doctors tell me that soon I'll be speaking in foreshortened, or stupid, sentences. Struggling to articulate. As you say, I'm already using the wrong words or words in the wrong order. Then, they say, I'll have difficulty understanding what some words mean, or I won't be able to follow a conversation. I won't be able to spell properly, read, or even make sense of a page."

"Harry, I'm so very sorry."

"Thanks, but there is no sense in bellyaching about it. Later on, they say, I won't be able to walk or even move."

"Jesus, that's terrible."

"It's a good thing I'm not married. I think it must be worse for a spouse, knowing there is nothing they can do. Every day must be a heartbreak. I can see that the Hernandezes take pity on me, but I'm not much more than an employer to them. When I go, so do their jobs. I think we'll go back now, Jeremy. I feel I could do another session. Probably only a short one."

"If you're sure you're up to it."

"We must try to do it while I still can. How long can you stay?"

"As long as necessary, I guess."

"Good. Let's take a shortcut across the fields."

Fifth taped session with Harry Posen
Zulla, Virginia, May 29th, 2019

It would be boring to describe all the things I did the next day, but basically they consisted of my trying to retrace, as best I could, Sollows' steps from Langley to Cairo and beyond. I was stuck in the office round the clock, having only been able to get home to grab a change of clothes and toiletries, and then come back to work.

It was unbelievable drudgery, but I tracked him as far as the Turkish/Iranian border. This involved using all of Phil's agents as well as our own section's "trick or treat" characters from Beirut, Ankara and Port Said.

There was a sighting from Soltaniyeh—about 150 miles west of Tehran-- which might or might not have been Repnin and Sollows. The observer didn't know what the former looked like, and said the second man was wearing a hat, so that was pretty inconclusive.

Around lunch time I wandered along to Phil's office and gave him a rundown of what I had found. Or, rather, what I hadn't found. I shared a tuna fish sandwich with Phil, then we went to the Director's office, bumping into John MacMahon on our way.

Morse was already there when we arrived. He was sitting close to the boss's desk talking to him in undertones, but abruptly stopped when we entered. I glanced at Phil, who gave me his "search me" look.

I told the director my bad news, ending by saying that Sollows had vanished from the face of the earth.

Casey didn't like that one bit. "Alright Posen," he snapped, "spare us the dramatics. We have established that Edgar got to Cairo?"

"Yes, we've known that for nine days," I said. "He hadn't checked out of his hotel room and left luggage there as if expecting to return. We are fairly sure, but not positive, that he reached the Iranian border."

"What about the 'chain'?" Casey asked, clearly irritated.

"Director, there were four people in the 'chain', including the Cairo resident. She can't tell us anything. The guy we think helped Edgar to cross the Turkish border has disappeared. It's as if he never existed. The men who transported them are both dead, apparently as a result of a fire in a doss house."

"Mother of God!"

"Giannopoulis, who we believe was at the start of the chain—"

"Do we know him, Phil?"

"Yes, sir. He'd be the first one Ed would see in Cairo. He's been on the books for some years. A bit of a fly one, but he's done some useful work for us."

"And?"

"Giannopoulis says he hasn't laid eyes on Edgar."

"Is he telling the truth?" the Director asked.

"Who knows?" I said, "But I can't think of a reason for him to lie about this."

"That's it?" Casey asked bleakly.

"Just about," said Phil.

"What about Kimberly?" Claiborne Morse piped up. When we turned to him in astonishment, he added, "Yes, I know about Kimberly."

"Well, you shouldn't know!" barked Casey.

"Some additional funding was needed for Kimberly some time ago and the info slipped out. It wasn't my fault."

I should explain here, Jeremy, that Kimberly was one of our top secret—probably our *most* secret—prize sources for Iron Curtain and third-world material. He was very highly placed and had come over about five years before, and in that time had provided us with pure gold. It was all top level info on Warsaw Pact military commands, KGB, East German Stasi and the Czech Státní bezpečnost.

Over and over again, we had found that when we struck out with our other sources, Kimberly came through with the goods. The man who found Kimberly and subsequently ran him as an agent had persuaded the Director—and, as we found out, also Morse—to free up large amounts of dough, and a large part of the fourth floor to analyze and evaluate his product. Until now it had all proved to be excellent value for money.

While only six people knew about Kimberly, only his handler knew who he was and how to contact him. This was not unusual, because the existence and identity of someone of that stature had to be kept secret at all costs.

It was because that asshole Angleton knew of Gordievsky's existence and started digging to find out who he was that that even bigger asshole, the traitor Ames, figured it out and Gordievsky, the poor bastard, had to be lifted out through Finland in the trunk of a fucking car.

So, the fewer people who knew the identity of Kimberly, the safer he would be. So, on that day in Casey's office there was nobody at the CIA who knew where or who Kimberly was. That was because his handler was Edgar Sollows.

"Clayborne, all you need to know is that we have nothing from Kimberly," the Director said curtly.

"Okay," Morse said, standing up and stalking around the room, "I see that, but do you know what I think? I think the fucking Russkies have double-crossed us. This whole charade was staged so they could get their paws on an Agency Section Head and sweat the hell out of him, and then ransom him off in exchange for some fucking KGB hoodlum!"

"Oh, boss," John MacMahon hastily interjected, "I don't think—"

"I think you could be right, Clay," the Director said. "I'll have to call the President."

"But first, I beg you, call Chebrikov," John urged.

"Humph!" was the Director's only comment.

18

Reconstruction of events following the meeting of senior CIA staff in Director Casey's office[7]

Reluctant though he might have been to follow John MacMahon's advice, when his senior staff had left this office, William Casey did arrange for a call to be placed to Viktor Chebrikov in Moscow. And he did so prior to calling President Reagan.

The conversation cannot have been an easy one, and the call must have taken considerable time, as both sides would have verbally fenced, trying to discover what information the other possessed without revealing too much of his own material.

When Casey finally informed his opposite number that Edgar Sollows was missing and that the Agency had no idea where he was, there must have been a pregnant silence before Chebrikov told Casey that Sollows was not the only one on the missing list. Valentin Repnin had also disappeared.

It was almost a matter of form in such exchanges that each side had to accuse the other of breach of trust and foul play, but it would not have taken either man long to deduce that if both operatives had vanished it had to be a third party which was responsible.

Casey likely asked Chebrikov if China (a) would have the ability to pull off such a kidnap and (b) what would be their motivation. Chebrikov immediately countered with the suggestion that Israel had "gone rogue", but Casey would have said they would have too much to lose: If they double-crossed the United States in such a way, they stood to lose an immense amount in money and matériel.

Together they would have gone through the list of possible suspects, almost immediately ruling them out as soon as each was put forward.

---

7   In the absence of any eye-witness evidence for this sequence of occurrences this seems a logical inference from subsequent events.

Chebrikov would scoff at the idea that North Korea would have the necessary organization in the world at large, while Casey would have said that Britain as the culprit was a ridiculous notion.

For some time, the two men would have seriously considered Mitterand of France. "A sly fox," Chebrikov could have said and Casey might have added, "A real trouble maker. Almost as bad as De Gaulle."

It seems clear that, finally, they agreed that the most obvious conclusion was the correct one. Iran had caught Sollows and Repnin and had either executed them or were torturing them in some hideous dungeon. The silence from Tehran was puzzling, it was true, but there had to be a sinister motive for the mullahs holding off on their public delight in the superpowers' humiliation.

Pending approval from President Reagan and General Secretary Gorbachev, they tentatively agreed to further co-operate to find, and if possible, recover their assets.

19

Harry disappeared after our walk in the country, I assumed to rest, and I was not sure whether he would be joining me for dinner. I sat out in the garden in the sun, then, when Mrs. Hernandez called me, I sauntered in to dinner.

When I entered the dining room, I was surprised to see Harry there, decanting a bottle of 1985 *Château Mouton Rothschild*.

"Hey, Jeremy," he said. "I got my second wind and decided to join you for grub, and I thought you might like a nice wine."

"I would indeed," I replied. "It's a long time since I've had Mouton."

"1985 is what I would call a polished, elegant, balanced drop, not the usual powerhouse you expect from Mouton Rothschild."

"I shall enjoy it, I'm sure."

"If you've got your machine handy, I thought we might have another session while we eat. It might be a bit disjointed, but we should try to get it all while we have the opportunity. That okay with you?"

"Sure, if you feel up to it."

"I think I'll be okay for a while, anyway. Oh, here's Mrs. H with soup. She tells me all ingredients came from my garden. Hernandez picked them less than an hour ago."

"Wonderful."

"Then she tells me we're going to have roast duck. That didn't come from my garden, but from the farm up the road."

Sixth taped interview with Harry Posen,
Zulla, Virginia, May 29th, 2019

I was feeling pretty worn out the next day, but I had to get over it because I knew there would be many more rough days ahead. It seemed as if almost all the work relating to Sollows' disappearance fell to me, or at least to me to organize. It was a hard grind, I can tell you.

When all other avenues had been exhausted, I thought I might have one last ace in the hole. I knew that re-checking the same old networks all over again would only come up with the same result, but there was one last option.

For several years we'd had a very highly-placed secret source, almost as good as Kimberly. He was little-known in the Agency, but had delivered remarkable material over the time he'd been with us. But his position was extremely precarious and we used him very sparingly so as not to risk blowing his cover.

His code name was "Sphinx". I'd never had cause to use Sphinx—until now—but what I'd heard of him and his product came from my bosses or from the folks at Central Records. Apparently, they had not even been told who ran Sphinx, and the general belief was that it was the Director himself. The lines of communication were carefully and clearly set out within certain parameters, and in extraordinary circumstances anyone above a certain security clearance could use Sphinx.

So, I thought, what the hell, let's give him a try. It took some time, but eventually his response was brought to my office. It was disappointing. It said:

> *Uncle: Have your inquiry. Sorry, nothing helpful except slight whisper. Will follow up and contact. Three days soonest. Sphinx.*

So when the Director called us all in again I was pretty despondent and more than a little desperate. As Phil said, it was like punching a bowl of rice pudding: It got you nowhere and left you dirty and feeling like a fool.

"Well?" Casey demands as I come in.

"There's still nothing, sir. Sphinx responded not long ago to an inquiry I put down the pipeline last night. He said all he has heard is a whisper."

"A whisper? What kind of whisper?"

"He didn't say, sir, but said he would contact us again later."

"What does 'later' mean?"

"I don't know, sir, but it could be as much as three days."

"This isn't very helpful, Posen," the Director says like he's talking to a small child whose report card is disappointing,

Casey was a nice man, but sometimes he could get under your skin in a most irritating way, and I lost my rag,

"I'm sorry, sir, but that's all we've got! Sollows has vanished from the map—apparently along with this Repnin—and nobody knows why his contingency file is empty. If Sollows prepared one—as protocol required him to do—he must have removed it himself before he left. Then again, taking it with him makes no sense. Sir, we've searched high and low and can't find it anywhere."

"Alright, alright, Harry, calm down," Casey says, and turns to LaCusta. "Tell me, Phil, when an operation is set up and its master file is opened in the computer, does the machine automatically open up a contingency file for that operation?"

You gotta remember, Jeremy, that this was 1985 and computers weren't what they are today. Anyway Phil answers, and says, "No, chief, because so many operations are piffling affairs which don't need contingencies. With major ops the file is only opened when it has been registered by hand with the stockholders."

"You mean Central Records?"

"Yes," said Phil.

"So," says Casey, looking up at the ceiling like he's expecting to get help from the angels, "when I open a file—a major file—the computer logs it. If I then open a manual file—for want of a better word—and lodge it with the stockholders, they somehow tip off the computer, which then opens another file in its own unfathomable intestines. Have I got that more or less right?"

"More or less," says Phil.

"Now, bear with me," says the Director, like he's addressing a classroom full of students. "Do the stockholders merely convey to the computer that a contingency file has been lodged or do they also convey the contents—or in this case, the lack of them?"

"Not unless specifically asked to do so," Phil says. "Most op leaders do it themselves, because it's their lifeline and they want to make double sure the system has the correct poop."

"Hmm." Casey stares at us. "Is it conceivable that the file with the stockholders may contain something which the file on the computer did not?"

"Jesus Christ!" says Phil. "Fuck me, why didn't we think of that before?"

"Yeah, Edgar could have been so rushed he forgot to transfer his extraction plan to the computer," I said.

The Director raised his eyebrows in a pityingly way and very condescendingly says to me, "Don't you think you'd better trot down there, Harry, and fetch the file?"

Well, of course, I did like I was asked, and brought it back. God knows, I wish it had been good news. It would have been nice to bring the boss something useful.

"What is it?" Casey asks, his smile fading from his face.

"There's only one small piece of paper in the file."

"Let me have it."

It was a torn-out page from a book of children's nursery rhymes. I handed it over like it was radioactive.

Phil came round and stood behind the boss, and MacMahon peered over his shoulder.

On the page there was a brightly-coloured picture occupying one side, showing a brown figure leaping over a hedge with a farmer, police and villagers in hot pursuit. The trees were a brilliant emerald green and the sky a deep azure blue. The fugitive wore a red blazer and a straw hat with a striped band. In his hand he waved a gaily-painted candy walking stick. Underneath the picture was a caption:

> RUN, RUN AS FAST AS YOU CAN
> YOU CAN'T CATCH ME
> I'M THE GINGERBREAD MAN

"What the fuck does that mean?" Phil shouted.

"What indeed?" said the Director, scowling.

20

32461/02/06/85/3.23 EST AMERICAN NEWS SERVICE INTERNATIONAL /ANSI PRESS. NETWORK TERMINALS COPY IMMEDIATE RELEASE

A mysterious plague has struck the Sudanese village of El Kamier, 40 miles NW of the town of Nyala. 40 have died within 12 hours and 100 plus are currently critically ill. The outbreak has caused widespread concern in the region and the government is expected to take action since the president, General Abdel Rhaman Swar-al-Dahab, said he will introduce martial law if necessary.

The unknown killer struck with sudden and extraordinary virulence. Victims have experienced the onset of blinding head pain, high fever, nausea and delirium. Many of the initial casualties were young children who died from severe dehydration. Older people suffered heavy hemorrhaging, kidney collapse (ESKD), and respiratory failure.

Of 260 residents of El Kamier, 150 are estimated not to survive until tomorrow.

Sudan's Health minister Dr. Amal Waseef has appealed for calm, saying he has called upon the United Nations (WHO) for assistance. Waseef says if disease is caused by contaminated foodstuffs many villages and thousands of people could be affected.

El Kamier has one of the country's most prosperous poultry producing co-operatives, serving as a distribution center for Al Istiwai province. Local militia has been dispatched to the area to retrieve livestock and grain for testing.

Sudan is no stranger to natural disasters as floods and droughts routinely ravage vast areas of the countryside while the low level of medical care and hygiene contribute to the rapid spread of infectious diseases.

Some sources in Khartoum say that the outbreak is nothing more than an unusually virulent form of influenza and that many of the symptoms are being exaggerated by an undereducated, disadvantaged populace. Others say the problem is likely a resurgence of equine fever, the ancient scourge of the region.

Until diagnoses can be confirmed and appropriate protocols initiated, the residents of El Kamier and surrounding areas will continue to die.

--30--

21

It was at least a year after I had carried out my recording sessions with Harry Posen that I heard about Barry Carrick. And it was another year after that before I could afford to go to Europe and see him and others connected with Operation Renegade.

The World Health Organization, which was created in 1948, operates in not a little degree of secrecy. Although they spend a lot of money publicizing themselves and blowing their own trumpet, it is not easy to penetrate the middle ranks to see who performs what functions. If I had not, quite by chance, met someone who knew Carrick, I should never have known he was the one whom the WHO sent to El Kamier in 1985.

I tracked him down to the little town of Aghavannagh in Ireland, in the foothills of the Wicklow Mountains. I gathered he had been born in the vicinity and moved back there with his wife, Kitty, when he retired. I knew there were subjects I could not cover with Dr, Carrick because of a promise of confidentiality he had made to the CIA in June of 1985, but nonetheless I needed to meet him in the flesh and get his first hand impressions of El Kamier.

He was reluctant to speak to me, and was clearly still somewhat traumatized by his experience, but his wife persuaded him to put his story on the record. So, we sat in his rather wild garden—quite unlike Harry's—with its wonderful view of Lugnaquilla Mountain. As Kitty laid out glasses and bottles of Beamish stout, I set up my recorder.

Taped interview with Dr. Barry Carrick
Aghavannagh, Wicklow, Irish Republic, July 15th, 2022

I was educated not far from here and studied medicine in Dublin, and at Queen Mary University, London. Then I did two years at the School of Hygiene and Tropical Medicine there. I went to work for the WHO in 1978, and by 1985 I was the Chief Physician of the medical unit for communicable diseases in the Eastern Hemisphere.

Together with a small team, I was sent to El Kamier in early summer of 1985. It was a ghost town, a perfect microcosm of purgatory. Medical attention from the provincial or Sudanese government had been rudimentary at best, and there were wasted, contorted bodies everywhere. And drought. I think it had been months since they'd had any rain.

Very few crops remained because most had been burned by militia units from Kambal, in the mistaken belief that they harboured a bacterium which had caused the outbreak. So in addition to the disease, you had famine as well, so the people who were not already dead from the disease starved or had staggered off into desert areas to die there.

There were huge pits, hastily dug by Komatsu excavators, but these were filled to the brim with corpses, so they had simply left others where they found them and the operators had hastily retreated to their bases.

I saw eleven children die in one hour. I tried to think straight in order to review the treatment protocols. I ruled out Q fever, cholera, and ergotamine poisoning. Although the living patients showed signs of all three afflictions, there were no traces of the corresponding bacteria or viruses.

In sheer desperation, I ordered my physicians to treat for hemorrhagic fever with mild saline drips. Miraculously it seemed to work, but only temporarily. As the fevers dropped and kidneys began to function, the patients just died of respiratory failure. They were cooler, they were calmer, but they died all the same.

The most horrible feature of this nightmare was the silence. The living were so utterly exhausted by their suffering they were too weak to react to their own pain. But the eyes! The eyes followed me, waiting for me to perform some miracle. Towards the end, when motor impairment had become acute, the eyes lost their focus.

I'm afraid, Mr. Akerman, I prayed for them to die, and my prayer was answered time after time after time.

There was one little girl who I thought might have a chance of surviving, so I picked her up—she was just skin and bone—and carried her to the hut we called a clinic. She tried to speak through her bleeding mouth, but only a gurgle came out. I didn't have anything left to offer her. I didn't know what to do, so I sang *Too-Ra-Loo-Ra-Loo-Ra* the way my Mother did to me. She died in my arms before I could get to the chorus.

There was nothing to be gained by my staying there any longer. Those who were left towards the end of my time were dying like flies and I could get no sense, or co-operation, out of the few Sudanese officials still hanging around the fringes.

So we packed up and headed back to Geneva, where, after getting all the info I could from my team, I wrote my report. There's nothing more I can tell you.

~

Dr. Carrik's report was seven pages long and I read it, as best I could, on the plane from Dublin to Heathrow. It was extremely technical, as you might expect, and there was much I did not understand, but I can quote relevant, comprehensible sections:

> Total population of El Kamier 263
> Total affected 263
> Total deaths 263
>
> Etiology:
> Violent headache and fever.
> Convulsions, nausea, diarrhea.
> Mental confusion, hemorrhaging, renal failure.
> Respiratory failure.
>
> Testing ruled out the following:
> Typhus, Cholera, Q-fever, Hemorrhagic fever, Equine encephalitis, Ergotamine poisoning, Lassa fever, Smallpox, Tularemia.
>
> Protocols advised (Strong likelihood they will be ignored to one extent or another):
> Cordon 1.5km around the village.
> All personnel, military or civilian to have level V immunity of the Rome Protocol 1979, and observation of sanitary proced-

ures as outlined in Directive 21A.

Surviving livestock within the cordoned area to be strictly quarantined or destroyed.

All human remains to be buried in canvas shrouds and burial pits to be saturated with lime chloride.

Conclusions:

El Kamier's disease corresponds to no known organism.

The pathology responds to no known treatment.

The disease does not appear to be communicable.

The disease is invariably fatal.

22

Reconstruction of events in Russia in the early summer of 1985, based on news reports and conversations with family members of former Kremlin officials who cannot be named.

At some point following the CIA viewing the contents of Sollows' contingency file, General Secretary Mikhail Gorbachev must have sent for Chebrikov and demanded a report. He must have felt at least a little insecure because there were several hawkish members of the Politburo who were giving him a hard time. Some of them were suggesting that any kind of collaboration with the United States was tantamount to high treason, and if the Repnin-Sollows mission went sour, as it now appeared, they would surely blame him.

"Viktor Mikhailovich," Gorbachev might have said, "are you telling me that none of your thousands of agents and informers can tell you anything?"

"That would seem to be the case," Chebrikov would have replied. "Valentyn Andreivich did not even contact our man in Cairo. The poor man sat up all night waiting for him."

"Incredible! What about the American?"

"Sollows. One of their most senior people. We do not know for certain that he and Valentyn Andreivich even established contact with each other."

"What is your opinion?"

"It is difficult to know, General Secretary, but my guess is that they got into Iran and, maybe, reached their goal. What happened then is anyone's guess."

"But...?"

"Well, the Libyans tell us that Tehran officialdom was in an uproar on the night in question and for several days following."

"Hmph. Do you think they actually got the stuff?"

"I do."

"And then?"

"I hesitate to suggest this, Comrade, but it is possible that the American waited until Repnin's guard was down and then assassinated him. By now he could be safely back in Washington."

"*Ye-bat*! That cannot be! What would be the point of that? Would it not jeopardize Reagan's new so-called 'peace initiative'?"

"I cannot say."

"Tell me candidly, Viktor Mikhailovich, is there anyone here capable of mounting such an operation?"

"Here? In the *Soviet Union*?"

"Precisely."

"*Svyatoye der'mo*! Er...you mean without my knowing about it?"

"Yes."

"Well...er...I should think it highly unlikely, unless, of course..."

"What?"

"That whoever it is, is plotting against me, too."

"Indeed."

"Well, Comrade, it would have to be someone in the Politburo itself or at least a member of the Central Committee..."

"Yes...?"

"And with considerable influence in the party."

"Does anyone you know fit that description?"

"Well...oh...yes...Yegor Kuzmich"

"Yes, Ligachev. That is who I was thinking of, too. Keep this conversation to yourself, Comrade."

"I certainly will, General Secretary."

When the Politburo met later that day, the reaction to the news must have been greeted hungrily by Gorbachev's rivals. When the roll was called, the following members answered their names:

> Geidar Aliev, Vladimir Vorotnikov, Viktor Grishin, Andrei Gromyko, Dinmukhamed Kunaev, Grigory Romanov, Mikhail Solomentsev, Pavel Demichev, Vladimir Dolgikh, Vasily Kuznetsov, Boris Ponomarev, Viktor Chebrikov, Eduard Shevardnadze, Mikhail Zimyanin, Ivan Kapitonov, Yegor Ligachev, Konstantin Rusakov, and Nikolai Ryzhkov.

Nikolai Kunaev was not present, probably because he was recovering from a hospital operation. Gromyko, who had been foreign minister under Bulganin, Krushev, Kosygyn and Tikhonov, was now 76 and in poor health, and seemed inattentive. Geidar Aliev, and a few others could be relied upon to give the General Secretary a hard time, while Eduard Shevardnadze, Nikolai Ryzhkov and Alexander Yakovlev were always his strongest supporters.

Although no actual vote was taken on his personal position, of the nineteen members present, Gorbachev sensed he was secure in that he could count on thirteen of them unless things got much worse, and only about five who would stick with him if they did.

The matter came to a head when Grishin proposed that the Paris talks not be resumed, that no further co-operation with the Americans be undertaken, and that a *Krasnaya trevoga* be issued. Gorbachev and Shevardnadze argued it was too soon for such precipitate measures, but were overruled.

Consequently, much against his better judgment, Gorbachev instructed Chief of the General Staff, Marshal of the Soviet Union, Sergey Akhromeyev, to put the Soviet Military on high alert and to order troop dispositions accordingly.

23

RESTRICTED.
Transmit In cipher base commander Schweinfurt to
C-in-C Washington 77X211J4 49102 4/6/85 "spider"
Sit Rep/Soviet Troop movement.

Soviet build up continues to accelerate at key
positions across the line.

Est additional 25,000 ground troops in place. Low
flying rec not possible due to alert scramble
status of MIG force.

Reliable info indicates domestic train traffic
curtailed & rail cars missing at 3 points.[Map to
follow]
Indications bulk of troops moved to forward
positions in SU & Czecho. GDR being marshalled to
interior.
All leave cancelled & dependents ordered on
standby status. Base on 24 invasion alert.

Preps taken for chemical attack possibility.
Schweinfurt limited protective gear only.

Please advise soonest.

Colonel Michael R. Evans
Commander U.S. Army Garrison Schweinfurt.

24

To: General John W. Vessey Jr. Chairman of the Joint Chiefs of Staff
From: The President
June 5, 1985

Dear General:
Please proceed forthwith to place the armed forces of the United
States of America on Defense Readiness Condition 3 and await further
instructions.

Ronald Reagan

25

I had breakfast alone the next morning. Mrs. H prepared poached duck eggs with ham, which I greatly enjoyed. I drank my last cup of coffee and went out onto the back lawn.

I was surprised to see Harry at the bottom of the garden, leaning on a fence and looking into the nearby field.

"'Morning, Jeremy. Do you ever study cows?" he asked as I joined him.

"Not in detail."

"All day long they munch the grass and only look up once in a while. They walk very slowly, following the grass. Do you suppose they experience anxiety?"

"I have no idea," I said. I noticed that Harry was speaking almost as slowly as the cows were moving.

"I wonder if they know they're going to die."

"I shouldn't think so."

"If they did know they were going to die, I think they would gallop around, organize races, go to new places in the field, and make more noise."

"You're in a funny mood today, Harry."

"Yes." He grabbed my arm. "I think we should take the whole day to get stuff on tape. I don't know when I'll feel this unbad again."

"If you can do it."

"I'll try."

Seventh taped session with Harry Posen
Zulla, Virginia, May 30th, 2019

The week following the discovery of the page bearing the gingerbread poem was one of the worst of my life. Not only was work a nightmare, but my personal life was reduced to zero and I put on weight because I had no time to exercise. And I wasn't sleeping well, so I felt sluggish most of the time.

To make matters worse, much worse, was that on one of the few occasions on which I did get out of the office—I had an errand to run to the Capitol—I ran into that bullheaded old bastard, Senator Moran, my ex, Marjorie's, father. He couldn't have known that Marge had broken up with me, and dragged me off to a wretched lunch during which he never stopped yakking about the grandchildren we would give him. Give me strength!

Anyway, back to the day after we found the page from the children's book. Overnight, Phil and Clayborne—whether independently or jointly I can't say—came to the conclusion that the presence of the page in Edgar's contingency file had to mean that there was a traitor in our midst. And by the time I got to the director's office it seemed that they had convinced him, too.

"What do you think, Harry?" MacMahon asked me. Apparently, he was skeptical.

"Well, if there is a mole, who is he working for?"

"KGB," Morse said instantly.

"I don't buy that," I said. "It makes no sense."

"Get Cathcart in here," said the Director. "I want the opinion of Internal Security."

"Oh, Chief, no!" John cut in. "He will undoubtedly want to declare a Code Red."

"Yes, as soon as Larry Cathcart is brought in, the whole place will be chaotic," I said, "Everyone will be under suspicion. We won't be able to do our work without looking over our shoulders."

"Tough tit. Do it," Casey said gruffly.

It turned out that MacMahon and I had been right. As soon as he was told, Cathcart announced that he was empowered to initiate security screening even if the Director demurred. Casey nodded sagely, and we were plunged into a terrible, unsavory atmosphere like that which existed when Angleton was Head of Counter Intelligence before 1975.

I don't know who it was, but someone once said that if John le Carré and Graham Greene had collaborated on a bizarre, obsessive superspy, the result might have been James Jesus Angleton. Angleton saw a 'red' under every bed and, sadly, we were back into that kind of mindset.

For one thing, it meant that I hesitated and second-guessed myself before I did anything. It limited my actions and considerably slowed me down in my search for Sollows.

My next step was to go down to Susan Masters, Head of Cryptography, to see if her unit could make any sense of the gingerbread rhyme. I wondered if it was a message in code, and, if we could crack it, what it might say. To cut a long story short, the analysts spent days turning themselves inside out, and could come to no conclusions.

"Sue, please give me some good news," I begged her. "Tell me what the rhyme means."

"Harry," she replied, "my opinion is that it doesn't mean anything at all."

What really bugged me was the silence from all the networks. Initial talks of "whispers" didn't materialize. The Tehran government not only said nothing about having two dangerous spies in custody, we could get no indications that any of the Iranian prisons had recently admitted important captives.

I think there's another saying, Jeremy, that desperation drives men to extreme measures. I was fresh out of ordinary measures *and* extreme measures, except one. It never even crossed my mind until I was passing Bill Chalmers' office and saw him watching CNN showing some Arab in full headdress. It came to me in a flash, "Sheik"!

"Sheik" was the code name for a source we had not used for years because we were sure he was unreliable. We cut him loose after we got clear evidence that he had taken his exorbitant fee for giving us a pack of lies.

The only thing stopping me from trying to make contact with Sheik was Larry Cathcart's witch hunt. Of all the times not to do anything unusual or suspicious, this was it. So, what I did was go to Larry and lay my cards on the table.

"Run that past me again," said Larry, frowning.

"I've run out of leads on a very big case—it relates to the night you opened that safe for me—and this contact is the only idea I have left."

"Hmph. This contact. Is he Russian?"

"No, Iranian."

"High up, is he?"

"Yes."

"So, what's your problem?"

"Trouble is, I can't trust the guy. If I even get him, he could feed me lies."

"Then why do it?"

"I may get something from the way he reacts to my call."

"Ah."

"So, what do you think?"

"About what?"

"Can I do it?"

"If you want to. Sure."

Feeling that my back was now protected *vis-à-vis* Larry's witch hunt, I withdrew to my office to make the call. I was not even sure his contact phone number would still be operative. Still less was I sure that, even if I did establish contact, he would be honest with me. But what the hell, what choice did I have?

"Yes?" came the low, almost ghostly voice.

"It's 'Toolmaker'. It's been a long time."

"It is not advisable to converse."

"I just want to know one thing."

"What?"

"Did you lose anything important lately? Anything stolen?"

"*That was you?* You people are insane!"

The line went dead, but I had my answer. Sollows, either alone or with Repnin, did get the Cephalinol, and he or they had not been captured by the Iranians.

But where the hell were they now?

26

Harry was as good as his word and we carried on recording until dinner time. He was even able to continue through the meal and for a very short time afterwards.

However, at the point in history which Harry was then discussing, a number of other related events were taking place. Accordingly, I have inserted relevant items, and the resumptions of Harry's narrative, where chronologically appropriate even though I recorded them at different times.

I needed to fill a lot of gaps in the story; which had become apparent from what Harry had told me. Some of them, I now realized, could be filled by further information from Peter Roussel.

I called him in June of 2019 but was informed, I don't know by whom (a housekeeper?), that he was away and would not return for several weeks. I phoned again in July, but was told by the same person that he still had not returned. Finally, in August I was successful in making contact.

Telephone conversation with Peter Roussel,
former Deputy Press Secretary to
President Ronald Reagan, August 3rd, 2019

AKERMAN: Mr. Roussel, it's Jeremy Akerman. You may remember we spoke in Houston about my prospective book, *Operation Renegade*.

ROUSSEL: Oh yeah. I remember. I didn't expect to hear from you again. To be frank, I would have preferred if you hadn't.

A: I appreciate your concern, sir, and again I promise not to reveal the identities of any of my sources during their lifetimes.

R: Well, that's something, I guess.

A: Mr. Roussel, don't you think it would be better if my book had the facts from those with firsthand knowledge, rather than second hand material or pure speculation?

R: Take your point. [A long sigh] Alright, what do you want to know?

A: In June 1985 there were huge Soviet troop movements and the US responded with DEFCON 3—

R: How do you know about that?

A: From other sources. Were you with the president at that time?

R: Not when he signed the order to General Vessey, but later that day.

A: Do you know why the Soviets took the action they did?

R: No. We could only speculate.

A: How seriously was the Soviet threat taken?

R: Very seriously by Cap Weinberger and Don Regan, and, of course, myself.

A: And the President?

R: Not so much. He took everything seriously, but he had an inner calm and good judgment. I don't know if he was privy to information we didn't have, but he was quite measured in his analysis. His instincts told him the Soviets were only trying to send a message.

A: What kind of message?

R: He didn't say, and it wasn't our place to ask.

A: After the initial flap—

R: I've told you, President Reagan didn't *flap*.

A: Sorry. I mean, did the subject take up the whole day? Were you dismissed from the Oval Office, or what? How did it go down?

R: We stayed and the president calmly said, "What's next?"

A: And what was next?

R: Oh, Faith Whitlesey reported on the Fourth of July plans.

A: Oh yes, the balloon.

R: The balloon was part of it, yes. [laughter] She and Larry had been working hard on the program.

A: Do you recall what the program involved?

R: Ah, I see where you're going with this. Because of subsequent events.

A: Yes.

R: Well, sure. There were four separate rallies tied together with the president's peace theme. DC, Philly, Boston and New York—

A: Excuse me, why those cities? They were not GOP strongholds.

R: This was 1985. Then the Democrats didn't have the Northeast in their back pockets the way they do today. The year before Reagan, had taken every state except Minnesota. And remember that, thirteen years before, Nixon had also won forty nine of the fifty states.

A: Oh yes, I wasn't thinking.

R: No, the real reason those cities were picked was because you could get from one to the other in a day.

A: Ah, in the balloon?

R: Yeah. It looked like a real winner. The boss would land amid huge crowds like Zeus descending from Mount Olympus.

A: I can see how that would be impressive.

R: It sure was. ABC had booked for continuous coverage from noon until nine at night. So, one way or another, the president would visit pretty much every home in America.

There were going to be all kinds of performers at these events, both professional and amateur. We even had Sinatra and Whitney Houston. They agreed to accompany the president and sing *That is America to Me* and *Saving All My Love for You* at each location.

[Throat being cleared]

There was even a proposal to show off the Marines, but Reagan nixed that idea. He said the optics would conflict with the peace theme.

A: He must have wondered if all that could really go ahead in light of the Soviet troop movements and DEFCON 3.

R: If he did, he didn't show it. He seemed very interested in the balloon. He used to joke that he was a latter day Phineas Fogg.

A: Tell me about it.

R: About what?

A: The balloon.

R: Well, it wasn't really a balloon. It was a bit like the Goodyear blimp. It was painted navy blue with white stars. I went with Faith to Fort Belvoir to inspect it when the army was getting it ready. Really impressive."

A: Yes, I remember seeing it on television.

R: Yes, you would have. That it? Any more questions?

A: Just one.

R: Shoot.

A: During the early part of that year, did you hear anything about a senior CIA man going missing? Or anything about a substance called Cephalinol being stolen?

R: Later, but not then, no.

A: Thank you very much, Mr. Roussel. May I call you again if I need to?

R: [Very long sigh] Yeah, I guess so, if you have to. Just don't make a habit of it.

A: I'll try not to. Goodbye, sir.

R: Yup.

27

3286701/6/6/85 16.53 EST/AMERICAN NEWS SERVICES INTERNATIONAL (ANSIPRESS) NETWORK TERMINALS COP IMMEDIATE RELEASE.

Despite denials by the Casa Rosada, reliable sources in Buenos Aires confirm that a mysterious disaster has struck the town of Port San Julian, 900 miles south of Argentine capital.

Reports of the incident surfaced early this morning when the army detachment at neighboring Port Santa Cruz was placed on stand-by alert, and when domestic passenger flights were suspended without explanation.

A senior official at the Interior Ministry who would not be identified privately confirmed that near panic had set in at the small Atlantic port. Scores of individuals have fallen ill with a variety of symptoms ranging from severe influenza to pneumonia and high fever. Health professionals say that a virulent strain of encephalitis may be responsible for the outbreak.

Within hours, Port San Julian has become a virtual ghost town as shops, schools and essential services have been forced to close because of ailing staff. Attempts to fly in additional medical personnel have been hampered by the severity of storms. Heavy winds and driving rain have prevented an airlift, but weather forecasts suggest the weather will improve in the next few days.

Consistent with its policy of media censorship the Argentine government will not allow local media to report news of the Port San Julian disaster. But rumors have been sweeping the capital and food hoarding has begun in some areas of the city.

Although the incidents would appear to be unrelated, the disaster at Port San Julian has some similarities with an earlier outbreak at El Kamier in Sudan which claimed over 300 lives.

-30-

28

Interview with Denise Savoie,
former assistant to Bernard Roy,
Principal Secretary to Brian Mulroney,
Prime Minister of Canada
August 7th, 2019

AKERMAN: Originally you refused to let me interview you. Why have you changed your mind?

SAVOIE: I thought that if I didn't, you would publish a whole bunch of lies.

A: Why would I do that?

S: All you journalist do that. At least they did when Mr. Mulroney was Prime Minister.

A: I'm not a journalist, and the reason I want to talk to you is to get the facts straight.

S: Okay. If you say.

A: I promise I will only reproduce what you tell me.

S: Okay.

A: Are you sure?

S: Yes. Go ahead.

A: The date would have been sometime in early June of 1985. You were working for the Prime Minister then?

S: I was working for M. Roy.

A: That would be Bernard Roy. He was the Prime Minister's Chief of Staff?

S: No.

A: No?

S: No, it wasn't called that until later. Then it was called 'Principal Secretary'.

A: And you were Assistant Principal Secretary?

S: There was more than one. I was one of them.

A: I see. Now, sometime in early June, I understand that you were shown a letter by Mr. Mulroney's Correspondence Secretary. Do you remember that?

S: I cannot forget it.

A: Please walk me through what happened.

S: I was at my desk and Lisette—that's one of the secretaries who deals with the correspondence—and she say to me, Denise, take a look at this. So she give me this letter and I read it.

A: What did it say?

S: *Je l'apprends par le coeur*, like you say. It says:

> Dear Prime Minister, unless you deposit $100 million in account 178512 Limmat Kreditverein, Limmatquai 17, Zurich by midnight tomorrow we shall destroy a small Canadian town.

We have Cephalinol. Consult your friends in Washington. This is no idle threat.

That was it. I remember it word by word.

A: Was it signed in any way?

S: No.

A: What did you do with it?

S: I take it straight to M. Roy.

A: And what did he do?

S: He sent for M. Doucet and they talk about it.

A: That was Fred Doucet, the prime minister's Senior Advisor?

S: I guess so. He was the Prime Minister's *copain*.

A: They discussed it in front of you?

S: Yes, why not?

A: What did they decide to do?

S: They put in a big envelope and call Angela and tell her to take it across to the RCMP right away.

A: And then what happened? Oh, please, Ms. Savoie, don't cry. Please don't cry.

S: It was so terrible.

A: It must have been—even all these years later.

S: Yes.

A: Do you want to stop?

S: No. *De toute façon*, Angela left and I don't know how it happened, but she was killed by a truck on Wellington Street.

A: That was awful. What happened to the letter?

S: The ambulance men put it in her purse and took it to the morgue.

A: So the RCMP never got it.

S: No.

29

Glengarry Times

June 8, 1985

MYSTERIOUS SICKNESS SWEEPS ALEXANDRIA
By Eduard Alain

Sylvie Grenier was having a good day yesterday until around noon. Sylvie ran the Alouette Lunch on Main Street. She had a large number in for breakfast and was clearing the tables when suddenly she felt hot. Then her vision became blurred, which was followed by deep chills. By one o'clock she was dead.

Lionel Martin was about his business in the drug store when he started throwing up and gasping for breath. This happened around 12:30, and an hour later he died.

Dr. Marc Beaubien had just told Mrs. Ida MacDonald not to worry about her son, Justin, and that he was probably suffering from a mild flu. By 3 pm all three were dead.

These were just a few of the town's 2,800 people who were stricken by a mysterious sickness which swept through Alexandria yesterday with devastating effects. Allowing for residents who commute and work in Ottawa or were away from home for other reasons, authorities estimate that approximately 2,000 people died here in the space of three hours. All hospitals within a 100 km radius took live patients, but according to reports none of them survived.

The Times cannot get additional information about the disaster because most of the medical and political establishment are being tight lipped. Whether this is because they do not want panic to spread through Glengarry County and beyond, or because they simply do not know and understand what they are dealing with.

I asked Dr. Jennifer Cardin of Chesterville, who has recently returned from the Congo and has qualifications in tropical diseases, if she had witnessed anything like the Alexandria outbreak. She said the symptoms, as described to her, did not match anything in her experience, but she said there seemed to be similarities between the Alexandria event and recent epidemic-like disease eruptions in Argentina and Sudan.

By the time of our next edition in two weeks, we should be able to provide a complete and detailed update of the fallout from these catastrophic events.

30

Continuation of seventh taped session with Harry Posen
Zulla, Virginia, May 30th, 2019

I guess it was two or maybe three days after I reported "Sheik's" news to the Director, John and Phil, that we were sitting around, feeling sorry for ourselves, when Bill Chalmers timidly tapped on the door.

Phil went and opened it. "Not now, Bill. Can't you see we're busy?"

"I know, Phil, but I really think you ought to see this." He held up a copy of the *Washington Post*.

"What is it? What am I looking at?"

"This item at the bottom of page six," Bill said, pointing.

"Jesus, Bill," Phil said, struggling to find his reading glasses.

"Come in, Chalmers," the Director called out. "If you think it's important, we should all know about it."

Bill crept in hesitantly—I was put in mind of Sandburg's poem: 'the fog came in on little cat feet.'"

"Whatever it is, put it on the desk so we can all see it."

Bill spread the paper on the Director's desk—it was huge so there was plenty of room for it—and put his finger on a smallish news item.

"What is it?"

"This," said Bill. "'Recently suspended WHO doctor to lecture at Johns Hopkins.'"

"What about it?" asked John. "Who is he?"

"Dr. Barry Carrick. He's the Irish guy the WHO sent to Sudan to study the outbreak at El Kamier."

Suddenly, the whole room perked up, huddled around the desk and soaked up the *Post* story.

"Pick him up," said Clayborne.

"'Pick him up'?" The Director echoed mockingly. "The man's a foreign national who has broken no laws."

"Sorry, Chief," Clay spluttered. "I meant let's politely invite him to lunch."

"Good idea," Casey said. "Why don't you arrange it? It's 9:10 now. See if he will join us at Schlesinger's Chop House at one o'clock. Tell Chris Schlesinger we want the back room."

So, come 12:30 we all piled into the Director's bullet-proof limo and drove to the restaurant.

Casey arranged the seats so that the Irishman would be directly across from him. To the boss's right was John MacMahon and to his left was Phil. I was sitting next to Phil and Clay was next to John.

When Carrick arrived, we could hear him before he entered the back room. Clearly he was mad about something, and when he came in we could see what it was. Two Agency heavies were escorting him—almost frog marching him—like he was a terrorist.

"Am I under arrest?" Carrick demanded.

"Guys, get out of here," said the Director to the heavies. "No, Doctor, you are not under arrest, and I apologize deeply for the way you have been treated."

"Why am I here?"

"We have invited you—"

"It didn't feel like an invitation."

"I appreciate that, Doctor. Please sit down. We were just about to order lunch. Have you eaten yet?"

"No. I didn't get a chance. I was going to find a restaurant when your dogs grabbed me."

"Please join us. Order anything you like. Harry, pass Dr. Carrick a menu."

Carrick glanced at the menu and ordered something simple like a burger—I don't remember what, exactly—while I had a salad—my damn waistline again—and I think the others had filet steaks or rack of lamb. The Director had Chris, he was the owner, bring us bottles of Claret, Château Canon, if I recall correctly.

"I'm still waiting to be told why I am here," Carrick said.

I can still hear his voice—the 'I's came out like 'oi's and he dropped some of his 'g's. I could tell the Director liked the guy instantly because, you know, Casey was Nassau County Irish.

"Before I start," the Director said, "I have to tell you that anything you say to us will be kept in the strictest confidence. Of course, we have no authority to bind you similarly, but we hope you will voluntarily respect our confidences."

"Alright. You have my word."

"Good. I'll come straight to the point. We are in some confusion with regard to the outbreaks in Sudan, Argentina and Canada, and it occurred to us that you might have some ideas on the subject."

"Indeed I do!"

"We thought so."

"How did you find out about me? Obviously not by my reports to the WHO. They've been buried so deep nobody could ever find them."

'Yes, we understand that you are on 'temporary reassignment'. Does that mean what I think it does?"

"Yes. I've been suspended. Canned. The brass felt I was too outspoken about the immensity of the potential risk and that I would start a panic which would upset the world's equilibrium."

"You have my sympathies. Please tell us what conclusions you've come to."

"Okay." Carrick pushed aside his plate, took a swig of his wine, and leaned forward with both arms on the table. "Understand that I have closely compared notes with the physician who investigated the Port San Julian event, but I want that kept secret. I don't want him to lose his job."

"Understood."

"Basically, I noted these salient features: In each occurrence the mortality rate was staggering. Even aggressive treatment could not stop the spread, despite the fact that a variety of otherwise treatable symptoms were exhibited. In both cases, the period of infestation, for want of a better word, lasted no more than three hours. Neither town had any irregularities with water or food supply, nor had there been any suspicious newcomers—whether animal or human—which might have been carriers."

"What about the Alexandria outbreak?"

"I haven't been able to find out about the Canadian incident. I'm no longer able to access that level of official information. Anyway, to continue: In both cases blood was checked and none of the known pathogens or substances were confirmed. In neither case were any fixing agents or precipitants found. So, what we have, at least in those two outbreaks, is some *thing* with a super-inflated mortality quotient that leaves no chemical or biological traces."

"Doctor, aren't you describing something which is impossible?" I asked.

"I don't think so. This is similar to 'Yellow Rain', which I encountered when I was working in Laotian refugee camps in Thailand and, although 'Yellow Rain' had a lower mortality rate, the symptoms were almost identical."

"But doesn't 'Yellow Rain' leave chemical traces?"

"Yes. And this is why my superiors in Geneva thought I was a dangerous lunatic. Mr. Casey, I believe that somewhere there is a 'fourth generation' of chemical weapons."

Carrick saw us exchanging glances. "Ah, I see you agree with me. I won't ask you why, because I know you couldn't tell me. Anyway, I think they are, in effect, chemically-boosted organisms functioning as both chemical and biological agents. The first would account for the mortality quotient and the second for the lack of a precipitating agent."

"Does that mean they can breed?" Clayborn Morse asked.

"Certainly, in theory, but only under the right conditions would these strains be self-replicating. These super-charged bugs wouldn't be like cockroaches which are said to be able to survive a ground zero nuclear blast. Too much heat and dryness or too much cold and wetness and they would die."

"I see," said Casey, placing his hands under his chin.

"Of course, I'm guessing to a considerable extent and I don't know the precise weather conditions in all three locations, but I think that if those conditions had been even slightly different the deaths could have been infinitely greater, maybe in the millions."

"Jesus!" Phil exclaimed.

"The bottom line is that I believe if this stuff, whatever it is, gets going under the right conditions, there'll be no way in God's green earth that it can be stopped until it stops by itself."

31

Reconstruction of events at the Lubyanka Building (KGB headquar-ters), Dzerzhinsky Square, Moscow, June 9 or 10 1985, based on conver-sations with former middle and lower rank officials, all of whom in-sisted on anonymity, and the document described below.

We know that sometime in the mid-morning of June 9th or 10th, Major Zina Varenko left her office and took the elevator to the top floor, pre-sumably because she had been summoned by the Chairman. She was seen leaving the elevator and entering the outer office, which housed Viktor Chebrikov's personal staff.

Major Varenko did not reappear until at least twenty minutes later. It is difficult to imagine that the discussion of any matter between Varenko and any of the staff would have taken that long, so it is fair to assume that she was with the Chairman in the inner office.

I have a copy and a translation of a document purporting to be a rudimentary transcript of a meeting between Varenko, Chebrikov and one Colonel Olga Malashenko, but, for some reason, it is undated. Therefore, I cannot absolutely state that the document applies to this occasion. However, all things considered, I think it a reasonable infer-ence and I present the following reconstruction with some confid-ence.

> After initial greetings which, knowing Chebrikov, were likely to have been brief if not curt, Varenko was introduced to Malashenko, whom she said she already knew because the former had given instruction to her at the Khorino Academy.
>
> From all accounts, Malashenko was a squat, grey-haired woman with thin, compressed lips and eyes devoid of any warmth.

"Over the past several weeks there have been three mysterious episodes around the world causing many deaths," Chebrikov said, sitting behind his desk. "Typically the western capitalist media report such events in an irresponsible manner, unlike our own, which have been carefully crafted so as not to alarm our populace.

"Naturally, at official levels, our concern has been considerable. Colonel Malashenko has been monitoring the situation very closely from her research station at Blagoveshchensk. It is on her advice that I now proceed to instruct you to devise special emergency plans. The Politburo is of the opinion that the fewer people who are party to those plans, the better. Normally, I would be directing this to Colonel Repnin but in his... er...absence, it falls to you."

"I can tell you, Major," said Malashenko in her contralto voice, "that neither we nor the Americans possess any substance which produces effects as drastic as those we have seen recently."

"That is the truth," Chebrikov asserted. "Please continue, Colonel."

"In the case of the Sudanese outbreak, the Committee for State Security had an agent not far away who transmitted reliable data which enabled us to develop a reasonable hypothesis before the other incidents occurred. From subsequent analysis, and data we have stolen from the WHO, there seems little question that the three incidents are definitely related.

"Some time ago I prepared a major study for the leadership of the party which examined the state of trichothecene weapons, the two major drawbacks of which are unreliability and inefficiency. However, information came into our possession that scientists for a major chemical corporation in Sicily had accidentally stumbled onto a trichothecene hybrid which was hardier and which offered a much higher mortality quotient. Some of this you will already know."

"I do."

"What puzzles us is the strange concentration on specific areas. A member of my staff has been looking into the meteorological history of the affected places, and she found that in each case there was a variation from the norm."

"But Colonel," said Varenko, "Does—?"

At this point the document is badly stained and I can only assume that Varenko was making the case that chemical weapons usually affected only finite areas, and that Malashenko replied that in this case the weapon was a biochemical hybrid.

The next passage which is legible is, presumably, also Malashenko.

"—mortality rate. Only one substance displays all these features and that is the one called Cephalinol."

"Thank you, Colonel," said Chebrikov. "We will take it from here."

Malashenko then left the office.

"Thank you for not saying anything about Valentyn Andreivich's disappearance," Chebrikove said. "That is strictly on what the Americans call a 'need to know basis'. So, you have your mandate to form an emergency plan, although, by the sounds of this Cephalinol, there is not much defense against it."

Varenko went back to her office. Chebrikov also left but was stopped in the corridor by a corporal with a manila envelope. The conversation was overheard by cleaning staff.

"Excuse me, Comrade General, but we have just received this. The instructions were that it is for you to open personally."

"Yes? Well open it, comrade."

The woman slit the envelope with her thumbnail and a piece of paper fell out and fluttered to the floor.

Chebrikov bent down, picked it, and read it. "Go!" he yelled at the corporal. "Have my car brought round immediately and call the General Secretary's office and tell them that I am coming to see him."

None of the staff nearby saw what was on the paper, but in his unpublished memoirs (now in the National Library in Kiev, and only recently discovered), a Ukrainian Politburo member, Vladimir Antronovich Ivashko, mentions that Chebrikov waved the message around at that afternoon's meeting of that body. On page 198 on the manuscript he says:

> Chebrikov was very excited and some of us laughed, but Mikhail Sergeyevich said it was a very serious matter and read it out to us. As far as I can remember, it said that we had to deposit ten billion American dollars in a Swiss bank, or Pokrovkse, near my home town of Poltava, would be infested with a deadly poison.
>
> Few of us took it seriously at the time, and we gave Gorbachev full authority to deal with the threat accordingly. I believe he paid them off, because the infestation never happened.

32

Continuation of seventh taped session with Harry Posen
Zulla, Virginia, May 30th, 2019

The next day I was lounging in my office, dazed and puzzled by the unfolding events, and wondering which of the United States' lesser enemies had both the ability and the motive to undertake such a daring and risky enterprise.

I remember looking out of the window and watching a red tailed hawk slowly circling, and then drop and settle on a utility pole. It seemed to have its eye on some poor creature on the ground inside the CIA compound.

Before I could see whether the hawk dived and got its prey, the phone rang. It was Ivor Richards from Data Control.

"Hello, Ivor. It's not often I hear from you."

"No, Mr. Posen, you don't."

"What's up?"

"I have a Time Lock for you at 10:30. Will you come down? Or if I give you the gate code you can punch it up on your terminal."

"A Time Lock? What is it? Who's it from?"

"I have no idea. It's been in the works for some time, but Archie—that's our master computer—only flashes a warning an hour ahead of scheduled release."

"Jesus Christ, Ivor, what the hell is going on? Who put this into the system?"

"I don't know, Mr. Posen. It could be anyone with access."

"That means almost anyone on this floor."

"That's right."

"All right, give me the code and I'll look at it here."

Two minutes before 10:00, I entered the gate code along with my own ID. A large green W-A-I-T came up, followed by a clock. When the hands of the clock reached the top, a long, loud beep occurred, the clock vanished and MESSAGE FOLLOWS appeared.

Well, I have to tell you that at first I thought I must have been dreaming. I sat there stunned for a minute, then shouted to Phil to get John.

They came running in and crowded around my chair. Then I saw the Director, still looking pale, standing in front of me.

"What's going on, Harry?" Casey asked.

"I just got a Time Lock. It's a message demanding $10 billion and threatening release of Cephalinol in an unspecified city on the Eastern Seaboard—"

"When?"

"Sometime in July, it says."

"Let me be clear," the Director said. "This message comes from within our own system?"

"Yes, sir."

"Who the hell sent it? Can we find out?"

"Oh God! No!" I exclaimed. "Look at the bottom, sir."

"What am I looking at, Harry?"

"This number: 566-c/AS-1."

'It looks like a personnel number," said John.

"I wish it wasn't," I said, "but it is."

"For God's sake, whose number is it?" Phil yelled.

"It's Edgar's. He signed the message with his own number."

There was a deathly silence for several seconds as they looked at each other in disbelief. Then the cursing and shouting started as each of them competed with each other to express their surprise and disgust.

"That slimy, traitorous bastard," said the Director. "I think we have to assume that the Russian—what's his name?"

"Repnin," said John.

"That this Repnin is in this with Sollows."

"It's logical," said John.

"I'd better put out a feeler to Chebrikov. If they stall, it likely means this Repnin has been killed by Sollows. If they agree to a phone call with me, it means they got a similar message and are in the same boat as us."

"And if they are?" John asked.

"We'll have to set up a joint operation with the KGB to find these bastards and treat them with extreme prejudice."

"Who will you name as our rep?" Phil asked.

The Director looked around the room and his eyes settled on me. "How about Harry? Can you do it?"

"I guess so, sir."

"Good man."

"Do you have a name for the op, sir?" I asked.

"I surely do. If the Ruskies agree, it will be *Operation Renegade.*"

~

We have no eyewitness account of the Russians receiving a similar message to the one sent by Edgar Sollows, but from subsequent events it became clear that they must have done so about the same time that Harry got his message.

Casey spoke with Chebrikov later that day and concluded that Sollows' and Repnin's outrage must have been worked out long in advance, that its execution had been carefully planned, and that they must have recruited a number of persons to assist. Whether these were, or had been, either CIA or KGB agents was unknown, but was feared.

We know that Gorbachev talked with President Reagan early the next day and that they approved a counter-offensive to be named *Operation Renegade* or *Операция Ренегат*, and that it should be jointly headed by Harry Posen of the CIA and Zina Varenko of the Committee for State Security.

33

Much to my surprise, Harry joined me for breakfast the next morning and appeared fit, if not jaunty.

"Good morning, Harry. I thought our sessions yesterday might have tired you out."

"It's a funny thing. This disease is not relapsing or remitting like some forms of MS, for instance, but its impact varies from day to day."

Mrs. Hernandez brought in plates of sizzling bacon, eggs, toast and sausage and fussed over setting them out on the table. Then she poured coffee while we watched patiently.

"At least that's the case in the early stages," Harry said when Mrs. H had left. "It's characterized by a gradual, continuous decline in language skills—of course, you've seen plenty of signs of that, with no clear periods of recovery or distinct attacks or relapses. It's slow and steady."

"What will happen when you can no longer speak? Did the doctors say if you could still communicate?"

"Yes, they said a person with PPA who can't speak might still communicate through methods such as gestures, pointing, or visual aids like pictures and writing."

"I'm guessing that, while it gradually lessens language skills, it doesn't remove your need or your wish to communicate."

"No, that'll be the worst part. Wanting to, but not being able to. But they say if I can take more time, reduce distractions, I might be able to communicate in a rudimentary way."

"Would you be able to type, if you couldn't speak?"

"They say it's possible, but not guaranteed."

"Well, I hope it'll hold off much longer." Harry's explanation made me inordinately sad. "Are you up to recording more stuff today?"

"You bet. There's an awful lot yet to do, and we must press on in case this thing catches up with me faster than expected."

The breakfast was very good indeed and we both tucked in, although Harry took much longer than I to eat. He explained that this was caused by something called dysphagia, or difficulty in swallowing, which made eating take more time.

When he had finished, Harry got up and went to the window. "There's a heavy dew this morning, so the grass'll be wet. Although later on it should be nice. So we won't go out yet. Bring your tape recorder into the study."

Eighth taped session with Harry Posen
Zulla, Virginia, May 31ˢᵗ, 2019

Casey briefed John, Phil, Clayborne and me not long after his call with Chebrikov. He didn't attempt to give us a blow-by-blow account of the conversation, but outlined the points on which agreement had been reached, and subsequently ratified by Reagan and Gorbachev.

Casey said that Chebrikov had hinted at some disagreement between him and the General Secretary on the choice of Zina Varenko because there were men in the KGB more senior than her. Gorbachev had decided the issue in her favour because he said that, having been Repnin's lover, she would know him and his weaknesses better than his wife or his mother.

The Director added, rather gratuitously I thought, that neither Chebrikov nor Gorbachev had ever heard of me, but they'd go along with Casey's choice for joint operation leader.

Because of the scope of the operation, both leaders had agreed that each nation's allies should also be brought into the act. That included the MI6 from Britain, the MfS from the GDR, the DGSE in France, the MPB in Poland, the BND in Berlin and the StB in Czechoslovakia.

The operation was to have unlimited funding. Whatever, wherever and whenever, Varenko and I were to get what we needed to do the job.

They agreed that Varenko and I should meet in London and then proceed to Vienna, where we would set up our headquarters, something which Casey said had already been cleared with Austria's AbwA and Ministry of Defence, who were going to provide clerical and technical personnel. Also, they agreed that I should pack my bags and get out there as soon as possible.

One other point, which the Director told me in private at the end of the briefing, was critical. "Harry," he said in a low voice, "if you find Sollows or Repnin, or both, there's to be no nonsense about bringing them home to be put on trial. Do you understand me?"

"I think so, sir."

"Kill them on sight."

With that sobering thought, I went home, packed my bags and took the first flight to Heathrow. It was kind of a bumpy ride—headwinds or something—and I arrived tired and out of sorts.

For whatever reason, our masters had arranged that Varenko and I would have our introductory meeting at the Canadian High Commission in Trafalgar Square—Canada had been brought in because of the Cephalinol attack on Alexandria.

I was conducted to a room on an upper floor and given a magazine to read, but instead I looked out of the windows at the Square and Nelson's column, and speculated on how the hell they built something 170 feet high back in 1843. I stared at the pigeons and the tourists, and wondered if it was true that if you waited three hours at the foot of the column you were bound to see somebody you knew.

I was snapped out of my reverie by a voice calling my name. It was a woman's voice, with a British accent, and I turned and saw this gorgeous girl. I thought she must have been an employee of the embassy, but she made a beeline for me with her hand stuck out.

"May I call you Harry? I think it will be easier that way. I am Zina Varenko"

This was the woman I had travelled 3,000 miles to meet—a KGB agent! And the lover of the villain we were sworn to track down and kill. I don't know what I imagined she'd be like—a cold, dumpy, woman with her hair in a net, I guess—but it wasn't this. This one didn't look at all like a Russian, let alone a colonel in the KGB. She was a bit thick in the hips, maybe, and not all her parts were perfect but they all went together in a wonderful way, if you take my meaning.

Jeremy, I think I must have fallen in love with her at that very moment, and I just stared at her in pleased amazement.

"Perhaps you were expecting a stout peasant in a tent frock and army boots, smelling of boiled cabbage?" she said with a lovely smile. Oh those lips!

"I'm a bit jittery. I've never worked with the enemy before."

"First for me, too. Shall we sit down?"

While we exchanged details of the case, I could see that while I was sizing Zina up, she was sizing me up. It was a curious feeling, and not at all unpleasant, because I saw it as a sign that something might develop between us. She never confided exactly what she saw in me that day, but one thing I could tell we had in common was that we both had problems with our weight.

After we had dispensed with the formalities and agreed on our approach to the operation, Zina suggested we go out for dinner. I agreed with alacrity because I was starving.

Much to my surprise and delight, when we got out into Trafalgar Square, she took my arm and led me over to Piccadilly, up Regent Street and along Oxford Street, thronging with humanity, and then up Duke Street, next to Selfridges, to a tiny Indian restaurant.

There were fewer than a dozen tables and we took the only one vacant. Not that I minded, but without consulting me she proceeded to order deep fried onion bhajis, curried eggplant, shrimp biryani, Murgh Shahi, bowls of raita and bottles of beer. I sat back, amused by her presumption, but approving her choices. I wondered what the caloric levels of the food would be, but I figured if one weight watcher could eat the stuff, so could I.

"I got to like this place when I worked as an attaché at the Soviet Embassy," she said with a delicious laugh. "Since it was a good half hour walk back to Kensington Palace Gardens, I thought I might be able to burn off the calories."

Doing my best to avoid giving away any inside information about the Agency, I told Zina everything I knew about Sollows, following which she made an unexpected, but, as it turned out, shrewd observation.

"This man is diabolically clever. He is extremely devious and very dangerous. I don't think Repnin is much like him, so I wonder where and how they got together."

"Why do you say that? Please tell me about Repnin. I understand you and he were…er…quite close at one time."

"Yes, yes." She blushed, and the resulting pink in her cheeks and the end of her nose was quite entrancing. "Valya is a reckless man. It is somewhat surprising that he rose so high in the KGB, given that he is restless and consequently unreliable. He is cultured but not sophisticated. In that, I sense he is not like your Sollows. Valya is selfish, un-principled and completely ruthless."

"Not a man to turn your back on," I said.

"What are you saying?" she snapped.

Suddenly I felt embarrassed. I guessed she had somehow interpreted my perfectly innocent remark as some kind of comment on her and Repnin's sexual life.

"Nothing. It's just a western expression, meaning you can't trust someone."

"Really?" She stared at me coldly, as if trying to make up her mind if I was lying, then relaxed. "When should we go to Vienna?"

"Whenever you wish. We have to meet with MI5 and MI6 people tomorrow to work out some details and to find out who they will lend us. Incidentally, Zina, your English is near perfect. I regret that my Russian is so poor."

"Ah. Do you know ya platuyoo?"

"No, I don't think I do."

"Say it after me: *Ya platuyoo.*"

"Ya platuyoo."

"Thank you very much, Harry!"

"What for?"

"You have just offered to pay for dinner!" Her peals of laughter rang through the restaurant.

At that moment I knew I was a goner.

34

VINGT-QUATRE HEURES
Au service de Lausanne et du Quartier.
10 Juin 1985

Le meurtre mystérieux de chirurgiens locaux laisse la police perplexe
Par Michel Bonnet

Translation

Two murders, within as many hours, in the Pully district have the local police puzzled, according to informed sources. Inspector Romuald Griffe told reporters that he could not yet reveal the motive for killing Dr. Thierry Raymond and Dr. Axel Scheel, but an extensive manhunt was underway to find the killer or killers.

The sequence of these unfortunate events appear to have been as follows:

Dr. Raymond, reputed to be one of the world's best plastic surgeons, left his office in Lausanne at 6:12 pm, got into his silver Alfa Romeo and drove to his home in Pully. According to his secretary, Madelene Boisson, who has just returned from visiting her mother in Geneva, the doctor had a busy week and had completed two intricate pieces of surgery on which he had completed preliminary work several months ago. He had commenced more extensive work some weeks earlier, on which he had received the expert assistance of Dr. Scheel.

While Dr. Raymond was driving along the north shore of Lake

Geneva to Pully, a violent explosion rocked his offices in Lausanne, destroying the entire administrative wing of the establishment, including all its records. Fortunately, the surgery itself was virtually untouched.

Unaware of what had occurred to his medical establishment in Lausanne, Dr. Raymond reached his home, a split level dwelling in the upmarket area of Pully, kissed his wife, Lorette, and walked down towards the lake to have his regular evening glasses of pre-dinner Pernod with his friends, Mayor Henri Cleroux, local dentist Placide Meyer and Douglas Stewart, vice president of the Seagram empire whose offices are nearby.

Around 7:35 Mayor Cleroux and the others became worried that Dr. Raymond had not joined them, and went walking up from the lake to try to find him.

When they reached L'Avenue des Desertes, they saw the doctor on the other side and waved to him. Dr. Raymond waved back and stepped into the road, whereupon a black Peugeot travelling at extremely high speed hit Dr. Raymond and splattered his limbs against the wall of the nearby Magazin du Vin.

Mayor Cleroux told *Vingt-Quatre Heures* that they were in no doubt that the doctor was dead, but that they did not have time to see the Peugeot's number plate.

Meanwhile, about five miles away, above the Number Nine Motorway, Dr. Scheel's wife, Magda, said the doctor was stretching wire across his garden pond to prevent a heron from eating his goldfish. A few minutes later, Mrs. Scheel heard a loud crack and saw Dr. Scheel fall forward into the water. She called the police and an ambulance, but Dr. Scheel was pronounced dead at the scene. Police told *Vingt-Quatre Heures* that the doctor was killed by a single shot from a .303 rifle.

Dr. Scheel, 33, was considered one of the most promising up and coming plastic surgeons in Switzerland. Police say the investigation is ongoing and may take some time to complete.

-30-

35

DAILY EXPRESS

WAS ZATO A SPY?

A Czech diplomat lived high on the hog. How did he do it? Was he working for us? Pincher investigates a strange death.

Chapman Pincher
June 11 1985

Few people realize that within a 30 minutes train ride of London's sprawling, noisy, dirty, crowded streets lies a beautiful, peaceful, unspoiled patch of English countryside.

It is called Blackheath in Surrey, where twisting, narrow, leafy lanes, quiet ancient churches and tiny, half hidden estates and houses are comforting and reassuring. But it is a place only for the rich.

Life among forests and moorland, abounding in wildlife and bursting with bracken, campion, yarrow, and honeysuckle, does not come cheap. In fact, the call of the wood pigeon, magpie, rook and jay in this neck of the woods require very deep pockets indeed.

Those who can afford to do so, mostly work in London. They are Permanent Secretaries of government Departments, bank presidents, stock brokers, the occasional rock star, and property speculators. They park their Jaguars and Rolls Royces at the little station of West Clandon and travel to the City or Westminster first class. In the evening they return, roll their *Times* into a baton to flick at impertinent flies, hop in the car and then home to G & T or Muscadet on the terrace or back lawn before facing elegant dinners (prepared by wives called Tessa, Bunty, Felicity, or Samantha) of quiche and fresh veg while listening to accounts of meetings of the Women's Institute.

It is as English, and Tory, as roast beef and Yorkshire Pudding on Sundays, pints in the pub at noon on Saturday, golf at the club, walking the dog (called Sebastian, Trizer, or Bouncer) or the Queen's Christmas Message. But there was nothing English (except his ostentatiously adopted mannerisms) about the man from Czechoslovakia who lived among the British Brahmins in this bucolic paradise.

Deepdene, the house belonging to Antonin Zatopek (known to his pals as "Zato") was valued at 480,000 pounds in 1984. Just along the leaf shaded road is Aston House, the home of the widow of renowned Belgian educator Joseph Lauwerys (one of the founders of UNESCO and the Japanese academic study Moralogy). Like the Lauwerys establishment, Zatopek's large house is of grey stone and has extensive grounds with a pond and stream. And a large, stone carving of a pelican.

The other night something happened in Blackheath to mar its usual bliss. Zato was murdered.

I first met him years ago when he was first appointed Deputy Ambassador of the Czechoslovak Republic to the Court of Saint James. Few of us believed he was really a diplomat. His appearance told us that in all likelihood he was one of Alojz Lorenc's thugs from the *Statni Bezpecnost*, the secret service of that benighted Warsaw Pact nation. When he remained at the post year after year, we knew he was Prague's Head of London Station.

What made Zato something of a puzzle was that he did not at all act like a devout Communist, wear a hairshirt and live on vodka and black bread. He liked the capitalist high life too well, drove an Aston Martin, and acquired *Deepdene*. By no stretch of the imagination could any sensible person see the puritans in Prague shelling out the kind of money needed to buy, upkeep and pay the rates on the place. So, the question a number of us kept asking ourselves was: How did he get it?

One answer which kept popping up was that Zato was a double agent. For whom, we couldn't say. I drew a complete blank with my regular contacts in MI6 and I think I believed them that Zato was not on the British payroll. If indeed he was double crossing his handlers in Prague, while he might have been doing it on our turf he was not doing it at our behest.

126

Fast forward (as the Americans say) to Wednesday night. Probing—if that is the right word—the local constabulary and Special Branch who arrived quickly thereafter (you can smell them a mile away) produced the following extraordinary, and as yet unexplained, scenario.

Zatopek left his office at 5 pm. This was not his "show" office at the Czech embassy in Notting Hill Gate, but the one where the StB did its dirty work, a discreet Georgian house in a *cul-de-sac* just off Grosvenor Square. He was under observation by MI5 and was recorded strolling up Brook and Davis streets and catching the Underground at Bond Street to Waterloo. From there he caught a train to Guildford and then a connection to Chilworth, a charming, red brick village which fringes the wooded and more exclusive hills.

He walked from the station (it is not currently known why he did not use his car) and began the short climb to the Elysian Fields of Blackheath, past the Franciscan monastery to a narrow, unpaved road to Deepdene. There he was greeted by his two massive Dobermans and unchained them. It is assumed he went inside and, as was his custom, had a very large *slivovitz* and cooked his dinner.

The police think that some time before retiring for the night, he would have gone out to conduct a security check, rounded the south corner and seen the bodies of his dogs, obviously poisoned and prostrate on the stone flags of the terrace. It would have been at that point that Zatopek was murdered by someone wielding the stone pelican which smashed his skull and instantly killed him.

Who did it? The police admit they have no idea who could have done it or what the motive could have been. An examination of the house revealed that nothing had been taken, even though there was a large number of valuable pieces of silver, china and several highly collectible paintings.

Was this a revenge killing? Did his masters in Prague finally discover his treachery and eliminate him? Did the secret service of the country to whom Zatopek was betraying the Czechs tire of his demands for more money? Was this the random act of a madman on the loose?

One curious item listed in the police inventory of Zato's possessions was a picture of no monetary value whatever. It was a faded photograph of a mine in South Africa. Since he was not known to have ever visited or have any connection with that country, its significance, if any, is unknown.

As of now, in the mysterious matter of the murder of Antonin Zatopek there are no answers, only more questions.

36

Continuation of eighth taped session with Harry Posen
Zulla, Virginia, May 30th, 2019

The next morning was sunny and warm, so Zina and I decided to walk to our meeting. We'd misjudged the distance from our hotel in St James to the SIS building on the embankment on the other side of the Thames near Vauxhall Bridge, so we arrived quite late.

After going through some of the tightest security I'd ever seen, we were ushered to an upper floor and into a large room where there were a bunch of people, all looking at their watches.

A distinguished, grey-haired guy in his late fifties, who spoke as if he had a plum in his mouth, introduced himself as Christopher Curwen (who we later learned was "C"), then turned the meeting over to us and departed. In case anyone there didn't know why we had come, Zina outlined our problem and said we needed at least two experienced Brits to come to Vienna and be part of our team.

There were five people who were suitable and, after having a chat with each of them, we decided on two permanent members and a reserve. Gordon Rattenbury was an ex-army major who had service in the Metropolitan Police Special Branch before being recruited to MI6, or SIS as they call it. He was a bit old for active fieldwork—I guess he was about 50—but his knowledge and demeanour impressed us.

The other permanent member was a rather plain-looking woman in her late thirties called Heather Milton-Jones, whose resumé of action and training was positively scary. I couldn't help staring at her hands, because she told us she had once strangled a terrorist with them and on another occasion had killed an enemy agent with a one-handed rabbit punch to the back of neck.

As Heather was stepping away from the table, Zina whispered to me,

"008, license to kill."

The stand-by we chose was a burly young fellow called Julian Clarkson. He would come to Vienna later, as and when needed.

Just as we were winding up the meeting, Sir Christopher came back in and said he had been taking to the Austrian Minister of the Interior, Karl Lausecker, who had set aside an entire floor of the Ministry at Herrengasse 7, 1010 in Vienna, and had appointed an administrator and three assistants who were waiting for our arrival.

Sir Christopher said a department car was waiting to take us to Heathrow, so Zina and I, together with Gordon and Heather (who, along with the other candidates, had been told by Curwen to have their packed bags and be ready to go) thanked him and left.

When we got to Vienna we went straight from *Flughafen Wien-Schwechat* to the Herrensgasse by ministry limousine. It took the best part of an hour to get into the city because of traffic and some road-works along the way. As the others chatted, I looked at the passing scenery and wondered how many of our other agents would have arrived yet. The agreement between Casey and Chebrikov, and ratified by Reagan and Gorbachev, was that, in addition to our own agents, we would each call on the services, and agents, of three of our allies.

I looked at my list to remind myself. I have to tell you, Jeremy, I still don't know how to pronounce some of these names, and don't ask me to spell them. Anyway, I had Matt Smith and Tony Aprile from the CIA, Gordon and Heather from MI6, Marcel Labelle and Louise Lemelutier from the DGSE in Paris, and Karl Mauser and Henrick Bach from the FRG.

Zina had Nikita Balakin and Sergei Ivanov from the KGB, Maytyas Cerny and Jan Prokhazka from the StB in Prague, Marcez Kowalksi and Jakob Wencell from the Polish SB, and Gerd Mueller and a person yet to be named from the GDR's MfS or *Stasi*.

Zina had called the Interior Ministry from the airport to let them know we were leaving, so as soon as the limo pulled up outside the building on Herrengasse, we were greeted by a large, smartly dressed, older woman and three of the prettiest girls you ever saw. Apparently, this was to be our administrative support team.

The older lady introduced herself as Frau Dorothea Becker. She told us she had worked as Principal Assistant to the Minister of the Interior for twenty-two years, and made a point of telling us that she had delayed her retirement especially so she could work with us.

The assistants were Johanna, Lena and Annika.

On the way up in the elevator, Dorothea told us that the third floor had tight security installed and was secure from the remainder of the building, that bullet-proof glass had been recently been put in, and that our sixteen agents were assembled in the conference room on the third floor.

"The GDR sent two people?" Zina asked.'

"Yes, they are both here."

"Oh, I only have Gerd Mueller on my list," I said.

"The second man arrived just before you did."

When we walked into the conference room we were greeted with unexpected applause. Almost blinding sunlight streamed through the huge windows, apparently unimpeded by the bullet-proof installations.

We dropped our suitcases by the door, took our places at a large raised desk opposite the windows, and gazed at the sea of faces. I was settling in my chair when I noticed that Zina had gone white.

"What's wrong?" I whispered.

"What the fuck is *he* doing here?"

"Who?"

"Third from the left. Next to Mueller from the MfS," she hissed. "He's not German. He's KGB, currently attached to the *Stasi*."

"So, what's the problem?"

"He's a fucking colonel and I'm only a major. If he's going to try to pull rank, there could be all kinds of complications."

"Who is he?" I looked over at a rather slight figure with a pouting, insolent face and dead eyes.

"Vladimir Vladimirovich Putin," she said through her teeth.

37

I did not see Harry at breakfast the next day. I waited for a while after finishing my second cup of coffee, then, when he did not appear, went out of the house, intending to take a walk along the roads.

However, the day was dark and windy and it felt as if rain was on the way. So I went back and mooched about in Harry's study, reading snatches of one book after another.

He had quite an extensive library, and I was surprised it contained so many works on esoteric subjects. *The Art of the Wagon Maker* stood next to *The Encyclopedia of Mushrooms* and *Hats throughout the Ages*, along with more conventional works you would expect to interest him.

Shirer's *The Rise and Fall of the Third Reich* and *The Collapse of the Third Republic* looked as if they had been handled many times, as did Mitrokhin's *The Sword and the Shield* and Earl Haynes and Harvey Klehr's *Venona*, an expert analysis of Soviet espionage.

At 12:30, Mrs Hernandez poked her head around the door and asked what I would like for lunch, but I told her I wasn't hungry and would wait until dinner.

Then, about an hour later, Harry shuffled in. "Sorry, Jeremy. I had a bad night."

"I'm sorry to hear that. Would you prefer we didn't do any work today?"

"No, I must try, although I doubt we will accomplish as much as we did yesterday."

He told me that there were 50 million people in the world with dementia, and of those about half a million suffered from Primary Progressive Aphasia (PPA), of which there were three internationally recognized variants, each presenting with a distinct neuroanatomical distribution of atrophy and underlying neuropathology.

I confess this was all a bit too technical for me, and I was afraid that Harry might wear himself out and not be able to record his Operation Renegade reminiscences.

Again, he told me he was glad he had no wife or partner, as spouses of people with PPA reported a long trajectory of change, even prior to diagnosis, often resulting in feelings of loss of relationship and meaningful social interaction and, of course, increasing dependency on them for communication.

"Well we better get started," he said with a long sigh. "Where do you want to do it? Here or in the living room?"

"Here is fine."

At this point, I should point out that the transcripts I made from these recordings were edited for repetitions, wrongly used words and expressions, and for silences during which Harry was groping for words. So they give a false impression of fluency and lucidity. What may take the reader only five minutes to read, took Harry many hours to communicate.

Ninth taped session with Harry Posen
Zulla, Virginia, May 31ˢᵗ, 2019

I called the meeting to order, and when everyone had settled, I got up and outlined the task ahead of us. I explained how it had all started, the dire events which had occurred to date, and the decision made by Reagan and Gorbachev to cooperate and set up Operation Renegade.

I said we were all the same team, that we were not going to be stuffy about observing rank or station, but that whatever any of us discovered anywhere had to be fed back to Zina and me at central control. Any administrative matters were to be taken up with Frau Becker.

I asked Gordon Rattenbury of the UK if he would make contact with the justice ministers of various countries and then with major police forces around the world so as to get wind of anything unusual occurring in their jurisdictions. I told them that the remaining agents would be dispatched to investigate any and, I hoped, all leads.

I said we had no idea what these leads might be, or indeed how credible they would be, but we had to check out everything possible. It was inevitable, I said, that many of these would prove to be a waste of time, and that we should expect that some, if not many, might be red herrings deliberately put up by Sollows.

"To emphasize or cement the notion that this is proper team work," I said, "as often as possible we will send two agents to investigate each lead, one from the Warsaw Pact and one from NATO. You are not, any of you, here to uphold your nation's pride or to advance any ideological position, but to hunt down these rats and deal with them."

"What do we do with them if we find them?" asked the sallow man Zina had pointed out to me.

"I think, Colonel Putin," I replied, "that you will know what to do if the time should come. I imagine you have some experience in the field of eliminating problems."

There was a loud ripple of laughter around the room, but his face showed no emotion. He just sat there staring at me with those dead eyes. I decided that was a good point at which to break for coffee.

"My God, he's a cold fish," I whispered to Zina. "Tell me about him."

"He's currently stationed in Dresden, using a cover identity as a translator. He's really the KGB's liaison officer with the Stasi. The East Germans love him, so you can imagine what he is capable of!"

"Why is he, a lieutenant-colonel, here, Zina?"

"There are only two reasons I can think of. One is that he heard of this operation and its possibilities for honours, and used his rank to horn his way in as one of the East German reps."

"What's the other reason?"

"Chebrikov sent him to spy on me."

"You really think?"

"If Gorbachev overruled Chebrikov over my appointment, his nose could have been out of joint."

"Hmm. We'll have to keep a close eye on him."

"Maybe send him to follow leads in Outer Mongolia!"

The agents were wandering back to their seats, carrying mugs of coffee and tea. I got up to stretch and accidentally kicked one of my suitcases.

"Do you have anywhere to stay?" I asked Zina. "We came straight from the airport. Did you make a reservation anywhere?"

"No, I forgot. Let's ask Frau Becker." She turned and beckoned to her.

"Dorothea, Is there a good hotel not far from here?" I asked.

"There are lots, but not many close by. You want to walk to work each day?"

"Preferably."

She rifled through a file, pulled out a sheet of paper and handed it to Zina. "One of the girls gave me this. It's a very old hotel on a street behind this building. It's called *The Monaco*. Not very big, but it's been recently renovated by a new owner. Annika told me they have a new chef and his cooking is out of this world."

"That sounds perfect," said Zina. "Please call and book two good rooms for an indefinite period."

"Together?"

"What?"

"Do you want the rooms to be next to each other?"

Both Zina and I blushed like two kids. She started giggling.

"Why not?" I said,."Please do that."

"*Jawhol!*" said Frau Becker, almost singing. "*Je mehr wir zusammen sind, desto glücklicher werden wir sein.*"

~

By this point Harry was thoroughly exhausted and could not continue, so he went back into the house.

I put on a jacket and set out across the wet fields towards some small woods in the distance. Despite the weather, a red bellied woodpecker was ferociously attacking a tree as I passed by.

38

Much to my surprise, the next morning Harry was already up and about when I went down for breakfast. He recommended some Virginia ham, which he hauled out the fridge and plonked on the table.

"Have some of this with bread and butter. Apparently Mrs. H. is sick, so no cooking today. If I'm up to it we'll go out for dinner tonight. They do a fair steak at the Red Horse in Middleburg."

"Okay. That ham looks delicious. Have you eaten?"

"Yes, I had some earlier. I'll see you on the back lawn when you're done. I have a feeling we might be able to make some progress today."

And so it proved.

Tenth taped session with Harry Posen
Zulla, Virginia, June 1st*, 2019*

As soon as we had wrapped up our meeting, Zina and I dragged our cases up the Herrengasse, past a huge museum and, as Dorothea had directed us, took a left on Leopold Figil Gasse and then left again on a strange street named after Bruno Kreisky, who had been Chancellor of Austria until a few years before. There we found *The Monaco*.

We almost missed it because it was one of those establishments which is very narrow at the front facing the street, with a plain door and a small flight of steps. It was quite unlike most hotel entrances and there was no top-hatted doorman to welcome us or take our bags.

I looked at Zina and could tell she was bitterly disappointed, especially after having received rave reviews of the place. The sign, which was no bigger than a large book, had gold lettering on a bottle-green background and was set into the brown stonework.

"It looks like a dive," she said.

"Do you want to find somewhere else?"

"No, let's try it for a day. If it's no good we can make our excuses and leave."

Inside there was a long passage which eventually opened out into a larger space containing a modest reception desk and the entrance to a small bar with maybe three tables. There was a curving flight of stairs, richly carpeted, and further on down a hallway I could see the entrance to what looked like a dining room. I don't know much about hotels, furnishings and all that kind of thing, but here it looked amazing, and I could tell Zina was impressed with the wood panelling, velvet hangings and very good paintings.

On a table in the middle of the hallway, if I can call it that, were two vases—Zina said they were Meissen—full of yellow roses. Very much in contrast with the exterior, the inside was the height of luxury. The only thing missing was an elevator.

The place seemed deserted and I was about to give a shout, when Zina found a tiny bell embedded in the surface of the desk. She pressed it and from nowhere an elderly man appeared, wearing a white shirt and neck cloth, half-moon specs, and black breeches.

"Fraulein Varenko and Herr Posen." It was not a question but a quiet, almost sepulchral announcement. "I am Adalbert. Please to follow me. I am to carry your bags."

How the poor guy managed to carry all the cases and stagger up that staircase was a miracle, but he wouldn't let either of us help him.

Fortunately our rooms were on the second floor—what in Europe they call the first floor—so poor, old Adalbert did not have far to go with his ridiculously heavy burden. He threw the doors open and I let Zina go ahead to examine them and pick which one she preferred.

Both rooms were amply supplied with the finest crystal glasses and decanters, bottles of Rémy Martin cognac and Macallan sherry cask whisky, boxes of Monte Cristo Number 3 cigars and Balkan Sobranie cigarettes, and stacks of embossed, crisp, cream notepaper and envelopes.

When I followed Zina into the first room, I noticed her looking at a door in the wall. When we went into the second room she stared at a similar door. Neither of us said anything, but I knew we were thinking the same thing: This was a door which adjoined the rooms and, presumably, could be opened from either side. This gave me a shiver of excitement.

There wasn't a lot of difference between the rooms, but Zina chose the one with a slightly bigger tub and a few more flounces around the bed.

"Would you want I should reserve you a table for dinner?" Adalbert asked.

"Zina?"

"I was thinking of going to *Die drei Husaren*—the food there is fabulous—but it is getting late, so let's eat here."

"Adalbert, please could you arrange for us to have a table in thirty minutes—will that be enough, Zina?"

~

The dining room was like something I imagined might have existed at the time of the Emperor Franz Joseph, with ornate chairs, starched white tablecoths, heavy silver utensils and candle sticks on the tables, and subdued lighting.

"I like this place," said Zina. "I hope the food is good."

Just then a tall, imposing, man with a full head of dark brown hair, looking a bit like a middle-aged Beatle, materialized beside our table and introduced himself as Oskar Weiler, the proprietor. From a trolley behind him he produced two flutes and a bottle of *Bollinger RD* 1975.

"Will the *Fraulein* partake?"

"Yes, the *Fraulein* most certainly will," said Zina eagerly.

"And *der Herr*?"

"Yes, please."

While we were sipping the Champagne, I glanced through the enormous wine list, on which the very best of the world were represented. Rather than give us a menu, Oskar said he would choose for us, if we allowed him.

The meal was outstanding in every respect. Beautiful oysters to start, followed by roast guinea fowl with asparagus, morels, and a Madeira sauce. While Zina enjoyed a dessert of cherries and ice cream, I had a cheese board with *Alpkase*, *Bergkase* and the so-called Hay-milk cheese from the Bregenzerwald region.

We dined extremely well and decided that, unless there was a very good reason to go elsewhere, we would eat at the Monaco every night.

We climbed the stairs very slowly and paused in silence outside the rooms. Finally, Zina whispered, "*Spokoynoy nochi*, Harry."

Jeremy, I'm going to nip into the house for a bottle of Coke. If you don't mind, we'll skip lunch. Then, when I get back I'll tell you what happened the next day.

39

*Continuation of the tenth taped session with Harry Posen
Zulla, Virginia June 1st, 2019*

I was up early, so did not see Zina for breakfast. I grabbed a cheese roll and coffee at a street stand and took it to the office. Frau Becker was also in early and accosted me even before I got in the door, flapping about, saying I must call Herr LaCusta in Langley urgently.

As I walked to my office, I was gratified to see that at least half a dozen of our agents were at their desks, including Milton-Jones and Kowalski. Putin was not among them. I imagined that most of his work—whatever that was—would be at the Soviet Embassy on the Erzherzog Karl-Strasse, but that work would have little or nothing to do with Operation Renegade.

"Harry, where the fuck have you been?" Phil was clearly out of sorts.

"Why? What time is it in Langley?"

"Two o'clock."

"It's only eight here, so don't get your drawers in a twist. What's up?"

"We got a tip from Kimberly."

"Kimberly? So he's surfaced?"

"Yeah. I'm not too sure what that means. Maybe some third world country is involved with Sollows and Repnin."

"Who knows? Anyway, what's he got to say?"

"He says you should check out a house in Bermuda."

"Bermuda?"

"Yeah. The house is in the parish of Paget, in the Tankfield area."

"Doesn't mean anything to me."

"He says it's called *Whittingehame*. Apparently, it's named after

Arthur Balfour's house in England."

"Who the hell is Arthur Balfour?"

"Used to be prime minister. He was responsible for the Balfour Declaration—you should know all about that."

"Why, because I'm a yid, you dago?"

"Haha!"

"Yes, I remember the guy now."

"Do you want me to send someone from here?" Phil sad. "They could be there in a couple of hours."

"I think we'd better stick to the terms of reference. I'll send two of my guys right away."

"Okay, by the book it is."

"What about this house? Did Kimberly say anything else?"

"What you see is what you get. Good luck, Harry."

I called Frau Becker over and told her to book flights for Heather Milton-Jones and Maciej Kowalski, then summoned them to my desk and told them what Phil had given me.

"Heather and—I'm sorry, I don't know how to pronounce your name..."

He said something which could have been Marchek, but I didn't quite catch it.

"Take a close look at this place. The chances are very high this is a red herring, but please treat it as if it were both real and dangerous."

"In case there's a difference of opinion, which one of us is the primary?" Heather wisely asked. I was glad she did because I hadn't thought of it.

"It'll be you this time, Heather. Okay: get going."

Zina had instructed them all to have light travel baggage at the office so they could leave at short notice. It might have been my imagination, but it seemed to me that the big, black canvas bag by Putin's desk was more sinister than the others.

Just then Gordon Rattenbury came in, with Zina on his heels. I waved them over and asked how Gordon was doing with his trawl of police forces.

"Not a nibble, Chief."

"Well keep at it."

"There was just one thing—not connected with my trawling."

"Yes?"

"It's this, Chief." He passed me a newspaper, *The Daily Express* of the previous day. "Page three."

It was an article by Chapman Pincher, a British journalist well-connected with the world of espionage, known as the 'lone wolf of Fleet Street'. A few years before he had written a book called *Their Trade is Treachery*—you've probably heard of it—when he unmasked Roger Hollis, the boss of MI5, as a Commie spy. Anyway, I read the article. It was about a Czech called Zatopek who worked for the StB.

"You know anything about this guy, Zatopek?" I asked Zina.

"Does this have anything to do with Renegade? If not, I can't possibly give an opinion or any information concerning a Warsaw Pact agent. You must see that."

"Yes, I'm sorry. Thanks, Gordon. You can go now."

When he had left, I said to Zina, "At least can you tell me if, as far as you know, Zatopek was a loyal Communist?"

"As far as I know, yes."

Then I asked her to leave and called Phil back.

"What is it now?"

"Read yesterday's London *Daily Express*. There's an article there which strongly suggests that Antonin Zatopek, Deputy Czech Ambassador in Britain, was an StB agent—"

"Aren't all those bastards?"

"Yes, but it also says he was a double agent working for the west. Pincher says he is sure he wasn't on MI6's payroll."

"So?"

"Was he working for us?"

"No. I've never heard of the guy in that connection. He's never been on my books, Harry."

"How about Edgar's?"

"I have no idea. Look, why don't the Brits haul him in and grill the bastard?"

"They can't"

"Why not? Diplomatic niceties?"

"No. The bastard was murdered a couple of days ago."

"Christ! Do they know who did it?"

"No, it's a mystery."

"Well, it wasn't us. I don't know what to tell you, buddy. I'll run it past John and the boss, but I doubt they'll have anything."

Reading newspapers was also what most of the others were doing. In the absence of any hard leads from Gordon or our agencies, all they could do at this stage was turn pages and see if anything jumped out at them.

I wandered along to Zina's office. "Did you get any breakfast?"

"Ooh, yes! Lovely pastries and the most delicious preserves. And heavenly coffee."

"I'm sorry I missed it. I left early because I was feeling antsy—"

"What is this antsy?"

"Oh, it means having ants in your pants."

"You are joking? Why would anyone put ants in their pants?"

"It's just an expression."

"You decadent Americans. I will never understand you."

"But you love your decadent pursuits, don't you? Speaking of which, are you free for dinner tonight?"

"Indeed I am. Shall we dine at Oskar's again?"

"Why not?"

At that moment Lousie LeMelutier tapped on the door.

At first glance she looked as if she was no more than about fourteen, but the more you saw of her, the more you noticed that steely gaze, the sinews in her neck and those muscular arms. A dusky woman originally from Algeria, she was clearly not someone to tangle with, and I had heard stories from Paris that before she joined the DGSE, she had been a ruthless police officer dealing with perpetrators of the Rodeo riots. These had involved men of North African descent who stole 250 cars, then burned them in government housing projects of Marseilles, Nancy, Lyon, and Paris. The cars were stolen from more prosperous areas and taken to depressed neighbourhoods to be burned in order to lure police into those areas for street battles. Apparently, Louise had infiltrated the gangs and been instrumental in the arrest of their leaders.

"Bonjour, bosses," she said with a grin. "Probably is nothing but I see this report of two *chirurgiens plasticiens* being killed in Lausanne. You interested?"

"I doubt it," Zina said, "What were their names?"

"Thierry Raymond and Axel Scheel."

"Doesn't mean anything to me. How about you, Harry?"

"Not a thing. How were they killed?"

"One was shot and the other was run down by a car."

"I can't see any connection, but thanks, Louise. Keep looking."

"*Bien sûr.*"

"I guess there are going to be literally hundreds of items like this and about 99.9% of them will be worthless," I said when Louise had left.

"Yes, but we're going to have to sift through them somehow."

"Are you going to sift through some Champagne tonight."

"Just try and stop me."

"You Russians are so decadent. I will never understand you."

"Иди в баню!" Zina said, putting her thumb between her index and middle finger.

40

It was past five o'clock, when Harry stood up and stretched. "If we're going to Middleburg for a steak, I guess we'd better get cleaned up," he said, wearily.

"We don't have to go out, Harry. If you pull out a good bottle of wine, I'll cook some fried potatoes and some omelettes, which we can have with the rest of the ham."

"Yeah, that sounds so much better than schlepping to the tavern. What wine do you want?"

"How about a really top-notch Burgundy?"

"Ah. I've got some *Chambertin* 2002. Will that do?"

"You bet. It should be in perfect condition to drink."

"Okay, I'll go decant the wine. While you're cooking you can let the tape run."

"Right. If you tell me where the spuds are, I'll start it rolling."

"Okay, let's do it."

Continuation of tenth taped session with Harry Posen
Zulla, Virginia, June 1, 2019

I shouldn't really be wasting time and energy on describing that even-ing, but it was special. Very special. I don't think I'd ever been in love before—not really in love, if you know what I mean. Sure, there'd been a few close relationships, but nothing I'd want to make a lifetime deal.

Zina must have been thinking along the same wavelengths as me, because we both made an extra effort to smarten ourselves up. I even abandoned my Hushpuppies for a pair of shiny dress shoes! In my case, I doubt the efforts made much difference—put on my best shirt, dabbed some stuff I found in the bathroom under my arms—but Zina! Oh my God, when she stepped out of the room to walk downstairs, she looked absolutely gorgeous. I've never seen anything like it. I thought my heart was going to stop beating.

Did I tell you she had a very slight double chin and a tiny mole behind her left ear? That really did things to me. Her black, glossy hair was swept back and she had on big, circular, gold earrings. She was wearing a one-piece blue silk dress with a simple brooch matching the earrings. It was hard to believe that this woman was a Communist spy.

Anyway, Oskar was waiting for us at the dining room entrance and ushered us into what he said was the best table in the house, By that point I was in no position to judge because I was so nervous.

I calmed down a bit once we were seated, and noticed a Schrammel quartet playing rather nice music—I think it was Hoffmeyer—and that all the waiters seemed to be ancient, and all wearing knee breeches and white stocks.

"Fraulein Varenko, Herr Posen," said Oskar, "Of course you may have whatever you wish from the menu, but I strongly recommend the tasting experience."

"What is that, Oskar?" Zina inquired.

"There will be a number of courses of small dishes, each with appropriate wines."

"I think I'd like that. Harry?"

"Sure. Let's do it."

Jeremy, you wouldn't believe what we were served! It was certainly a very special meal for what I could tell both of us thought would be a special occasion.

First we had Champagne—a rosé from *Canard Duchene*. Then we had *Dom Perignon* 1975 with beautiful caviar. Coming from Russia, Zina was an expert on that and told me we had been given the best Beluga.

After that we had thin slices of delicious foie gras with a small glass of *Chateau D'Yquem*.

"This is a combination Edgar liked," I said to Zina.

"That man!"

"He had his good points, I guess. I have often wondered why he turned to the 'Dark Side.'"

"It's hard to imagine anyone like him having good points."

"This is clearly none of my business," said Oskar, who had been standing awkwardly, waiting to serve the next course. It was a bowl of clear crayfish broth with delicate shavings of white truffle and a few tiny leaves of coriander.

Following that there was spiny lobster poached in Chablis and served with prawns and freshly-made fettuccine. With that he poured us glasses of *Montrachet* 1978.

Then we had a magnificent cheese board accompanied by one of my favourites, *Château Palmer* 1966.

Finally, we sat gazing into each other's eyes while nursing huge balloon glasses of *Hardy Noces De Diamant Grande Champagne* cognac.

Then we went upstairs and spent the night in Zina's room. That was the beginning of the greatest event of my life.

41

Continuation of tenth taped session with Harry Posen
Zulla, Virginia, June 1, 2019

The following night around midnight, after another splendid dinner, Zina and I were snuggled up in bed when the phone rang. It was on Zina's side of the bed, so she picked it up.

"Yes? Yes, he is. Please hold. Harry, it's for you."

"Hello."

"Chief, it's Heather. I asked to be put through to your room but they said you weren't there. So I tried Zina's."

"Be careful," I said. "There's no scrambler."

"I know. Bad news."

"What? Again, be careful what you say."

"It went tits up."

"Fuck! You okay?"

"Yes. So is Kowalski."

"So, no casualties."

"One."

"Civilian?"

"No one of my crowd. A resident."

"Damn! Don't say any more. Get back here as soon as you can. We'll want a blow-by-blow report."

"Okay. 'Night, Harry."

"What is it?" Zina asked when I handed the phone back.

"Not good. Somebody's dead."

"Дерьмо!"

42

The Royal Gazette

Hamilton,
Bermuda
WEDNESDAY JUNE 12 1985

Explosion rocks Paget. One dead.

A mysterious explosion rocked an area in Paget yesterday, leading to suspicions that the United States Consul General was the target of terrorists.

The place was Tankfield in Paget at an old house equidistant from the residence of UBP Member of Parliament, David Wilkinson, and that of the American Consul General, William S. Jordan.

Bermuda police are being tight-lipped about the cause of the explosion and would only say that a body, that of Francis "Jocker" Johnson, was found nearby. Mr. Johnson is believed to have been employed in an unknown capacity by the British Government.

Contacted for comment, Premier John Swan said: "Let the police do their job. I think it extremely unlikely that this was part of a terrorist attack on the United States. More likely it was an accident."

Mr. Wilkinson, the MP for Paget, said he could think of no reason why anyone would want to get rid of him. "Everyone knows I am a mild mannered sort of chap," he said with a chuckle. "I hardly think I'd be worth the expense of a bomb, although my wife, Ina, might be a different matter."

However, Mr. Wilkinson's colleague, Harry Viera, MP for Southampton West, said the explosion might indicate a resurgence of the Black Beret Brigade, the group which murdered Governor Richard Sharples and Police Commissioner George Duckett in 1973.

Mr. Henry Silva, who has a vegetable plot in Tankfield, told *The Gazette* that he was hoeing his onions about 4.30 yesterday afternoon, when there was a loud blast which knocked him over. "I wasn't hurt," said Mr. Silva. "But I sure was scared."

The office of the present Governor of Bermuda, Lord Dunrossil, said they would comment neither on the explosion itself, nor on Mr. Johnson's possible connection to the government of the United Kingdom.

The investigation is ongoing.

43

I was afraid that having had a really good day yesterday would mean that today Harry would be exhausted and unfit to continue recording. So I was pleasantly surprised when he came downstairs whistling—or making a good effort to approximate whistling.

"Mrs. H, still *hors de combat*?" he asked.

"It looks like it. I haven't been out, but I saw Hernandez down by the cabbage patch."

"I go and check with him."

Through the window I saw Harry cross the lawn and make his way down to where Hernandez was weeding. After a brief conversation with his gardener he came back.

"Yeah. Mrs. H. still out with the flu. Any of that ham left?"

"No, we ate it all last night."

"Did we eat all the eggs?"

"No, there are about half a dozen left."

"Okay. How about whipping up some scrambled eggs? I'll make a bunch of toast."

Eleventh taped session with Harry Posen
Zulla, Virginia, June 2nd, 2019

When we went down to the dining room the next morning there was a vast Viennese breakfast buffet with a wide selection of fresh breads, pastries, butter, jams, honey, cheeses, cold cuts, fresh fruit, yogourts, and hot dishes like eggs. But since we were sick at heart over the loss of an operative and the failure of a mission, we had no appetite so just had coffee.

Until we received an in-depth report from Heather Milton-Jones and Maciej Kowalski, neither Zina nor I would feel like eating. Their flight from Bermuda to Vienna was not expected until mid-afternoon, so some anxious waiting lay ahead of us.

Zina and I thought that it was only a matter of time before our relationship became known in the office, but we saw no reason why we should face that day before we were compelled to. Consequently, we agreed to walk to and from the office separately, and to be careful of our language—both verbal and body—when others were present.

"I guess The KGB has rules about fraternizing with the enemy," I said over our coffee. "Would you face a firing squad for this?"

"It depends on the circumstances," Zina said. "Ordinarily they would have the heavy mob grill you for days on end. In some cases they would call in Dr. Nolkin."

"Who's he?"

"Nikolai Gregorovich Nolkin is a quiet, deadly man of science who knows what substance to inject into a subject in order to get him—or her—to tell all they know."

"Ugh."

"Indeed, he is not a pleasant character, but don't rule him out. We might need him."

"I sure hope not."

"I also."

"Tell me, Zina, are we all right doing...er...what we're doing? I mean, could there be circumstances where the leadership would overlook fraternization? Or am I putting you in danger if they find out about us?"

"No, Harry. They already know."

"What? How the hell did they find out so fast? Who told them?"

"I did."

"*You* did?"

"Yes."

"Why for Christ's sake?"

"For self-protection. Better they should hear it from me rather than from someone like Vladimir Vladimirovich."

"Ah yes. But what did you tell them?"

"I told them that I had you in a honey trap, so I could milk you for information about the CIA."

"Clever you, but it doesn't make me look very good. A poor innocent spilling my guts for a bit of nookie."

"How do you know you're not?" Her laughter rang through the dining room as she grabbed her bag and dashed for the door.

I lingered for a few minutes to allow Zina to arrive at the office first, then slowly strolled around the streets. Pigeons were everywhere, in greater abundance than the tourists. Not for the first time, I wondered why it was that when you were a tourist yourself, other vacationers seemed like nice people, but when you were not they seemed almost contemptible.

When I got in there was a note from Frau Becker on my desk instructing me to call John McMahon. As it was four in the morning in Washington, I couldn't call back until about 2 pm our time.

I asked Gordon Rattenbury to come in and give me another rundown on the various national police forces.

"The problem is, Chief—"

"Gordon, there are two chiefs here. Please don't forget Zina."

"Oh, yes, I am so sorry, Zina. I mean, Chief. The problem is that there is an enormous amount of material, only a tiny fraction of which *looks*, at first glance, like it could be related to Operation Renegade. I try to follow up on those by phone and, so far, none of them have proved relevant."

"It must be very frustrating, Gordon," Zina said.

"Especially when there's always a nagging possibility that some of the ones which didn't seem even remotely connected actually are."

"Have you formed any general impressions?" I asked.

"Yes, I have. I think the enemy's plan has been in place for quite some time, maybe a year or longer, and that they have been able to build up an organization of their own and have been waiting for the right moment to put it into the field."

"What makes this the right time?"

"I don't know, but some events, existing or anticipated, must have dropped into their lap, so to speak, which made it propitious to advance their plan now."

"But we don't know what those events might be."

"Not yet, no."

"And, of course," Zina said, "their agents could be scattered across the world, and Sollows and Repnin could have their hideout—or HQ —in any one of a hundred countries."

"They aren't necessarily in the same place," said Gordon.

"That's a good point, Gordon." I said. "We need to keep open minds on all of this."

I spent the next several hours working with Frau Becker on administrative crap, then, about 2:15, I put in a call to John.

"John, this is a great honour. Usually I hear from Phil, not you."

"The Director has him working on something, so he's tied up."

"I was going to call you anyway. About yesterday."

"Yesterday?"

"Kimberly's tip about Bermuda."

"Oh, yes. How'd that go?"

"It was a shitter."

"How so?"

"It was a trap. A set-up. And it seems our people walked right into it. One was killed."

"Jesus. Who?"

"Guy called Johnson. M16 asset, not one of ours. My team should be getting into Vienna within the hour so I should get a full report then."

"Keep me informed. This is very disturbing. Especially as the source was Kimberly."

"Yeah. Why were you calling?"

"Oh, yes. We got a whisper—and it's only a whisper—that one or both renegades may be holed up on an island off the coast of Ireland."

"Which coast?"

"West coast. The island is normally uninhabited. Has been for years. Called the Great Blasket."

"The great what?"

"Blasket. Monks used to live on it in the olden times. A few families were there until the early 1950s."

"So it might be the kind of place where our traitors might hide."

"Sounds like it. Will you check it out, or shall I ask the Irish GCSIS to take a look?"

"I'll send some guys, but I guess you'd better let the Garda SDU know we might be there."

"Yes, you might need them to rescue your people."

"John, that was unkind."

"Sorry."

"Where did this tip come from? How do we know it's even remotely reliable?"

"It came from Sphinx."

"*Sphinx*? This doesn't sound like his usual kind of tradecraft."

"I know, but to date most of his material has been gold."

"Okay. I'll get right on it. Regards to Margaret,"

Just as I was hanging up Milton-Jones and Kowalski came into the complex, lugging their suitcases. I called them and Zina into my office, where they dragged up the uncomfortable hard-backed chairs.

"Sit down," I said, trying to sound severe. "I wish I could say 'congratulations', but I can't."

"No indeed," Zina added sternly. "I suggest you start at the beginning and go on to the end. "Heather, you were the primary. Proceed."

"All right," said Heather, sitting on the edge of her chair and reading from her notes. "First, on the flight over, they served some contaminated fish and some passengers were very sick."

"Why are you telling us this?" Zina demanded. "Are you suggesting that the food was deliberately poisoned?"

"No, nothing like that. It's just that I had the beef and consequently was fine."

"I'm sensing there is a big 'but' coming."

"There is. It's that Marciej did have the fish and was sick as a dog."

"Yeah," Marciej grunted. "I was out of action the whole time. I couldn't leave the hotel."

"Exactly," Heather continued. "And since protocols prohibited me from continuing alone, I contacted my people in MI6 and asked if we had a resident in Bermuda—"

"Which they did."

"No, they didn't. But they had a part-time asset called Francis Johnson, known to all as 'Jocker'." Heather rearranged herself on the chair. "So I had no choice but to get in touch with him."

"Jocker Johnson," Zina said with a sneer. "Sounds like an upperclass playboy waiting to come into his inheritance."

"You're not far wrong, Comrade," said Heather, also with a sneer. "But I didn't think the KGB had much of a contingent on Bermuda. Maybe I was wrong?" She looked at Zina, waiting for an answer, but none came. "I thought not. Johnson was all I had, so I had to go with him or abandon the mission."

"Knock it off, "I said, "We're on the same side. Go on, Heather."

"Well, we drove down to the Tankfield area of Paget in Johnson's

MG and passed the road, Tankfield Hill, which led to Whittinghame, then pulled over. Johnson asked if we should go on foot, and when I said yes, he turned the car around and we parked on Lovers' Lane."

"Is it really called that?" Zina asked, nudging my foot under the desk.

"Yes. Then we crossed the main road and went up Tankfield Hill. Johnson striding in front. It was very quiet. Nobody about. Blazing sunshine. Lizards on the walls. Palm trees wafting. Manicured lawns and gardens. Beautiful houses painted pink, pale blue, white. Smell of hibiscus and oleander. You get the picture?"

"We do." Zina said. "Your powers of recall make us want to be there."

"It's a nice place, all right. I would say a lot of money lives there. Banking is big business in Bermuda."

"Get on with it," I instructed.

"Okay. Then, when we were about two-thirds along the road—we could see the turquoise coloured sea ahead—we saw the sign. It looked fairly new."

"Whittinghame?"

"Yes. A new sign should have been a warning, but Johnson was all gung-ho and was pressing ahead, saying crap like 'Leave it to me, old girl.'"

"What then?"

"Then, without any warning or confab, Johnson ploughed on right up to the front door and started to turn the handle."

"What did you do?"

"What do you think I did? I screamed 'NO!' and hurled myself behind some eucalyptus trees. Then the world turned extremely red and very loud."

"A simple tripwire," Zina said contemptuously.

"Probably." Heather said, "But we'll never know. Anyway, I made myself scarce by crawling through several gardens, made my way back to Lovers' Lane, hot-wired Jocker's car—he wasn't going to need it any more—and drove back into Hamilton. I parked in Church Street, cleaned myself up as best I could, ditched the car and walked back to the hotel."

"That it?" I asked.

"Yes."

"Good report. Thanks, Heather. Sorry it turned out as it did. What I'd like you to do now is to stay on top of the aftermath from Bermuda. See if you can find out who owned or rented the property in Tankfield and what connections they had. If you get anything, stay with it and hunt it down."

"Got it."

"Maciej."

"Yes, Chief?"

"Next time, stay away from the fish."

When they had left I told Zina about John McMahon's call. I did not, of course, tell her about Sphinx, although I realized that at some point I might have to. I told her I proposed to send Art Smith from the Agency and asked her to name the Warsaw Pact representative.

"I'm tempted to send Putin, but he doesn't seem to have graced us with his presence today, so how about Ivanov?"

"Fine by me. Does he know anything about Ireland?"

"Ah, that's a point. I don't know."

"Does he speak English well?"

"Do the Irish speak English well?" She asked with a laugh.

"You'd better check with him now to make sure."

Zina left and, after conferring with Ivanov, returned, shaking her head. "Not very good. Sergei wasn't even sure where Ireland was, and his English is rudimentary, to say the least. So let's send Gerd Mueller. That okay with you?"

"Sure. You brief them and tell them to be careful. Very careful."

44

My recorded sessions with Harry Posen continued the next day and for days afterwards. But for the sake of chronology of the narrative, and to cover matters in which Harry was not involved, I have inserted the relevant items here even though I did not learn of some of them until much later.

I tracked down Gordon Rattenbury in Upper Slaughter, a sleepy little village in the Cotswolds, a picturesque region of Gloucestershire. He was very old—well into his nineties—and unsteady on his feet, but fortunately his mind was clear and his speech lucid. He lived in a small yellow stone cottage with his daughter, Hilda, who took care of her father and worked as a part time nurse at the hospital, three miles away at Bourton-on-the-Water.

We started our conversation in the garden, a tiny but idyllic plot of green surrounded by climbing roses and gladioli. Seated on a rustic wooden bench, I competed with the loud humming of bees and twittering of birds, as I outlined why I was there and what I had managed to discover to date.

It was clear that Rattenbury was glad to see me and anxious to discuss what he called "the old days." Every now and then he would light an old briar pipe, give it a few puffs and then let it go out. From the lid of his tobacco tin I noticed that he smoked St. Bruno, a blend which had a pleasant aroma. Before filling his pipe he took out a few flakes from the tin and very carefully rubbed them in the palm of his left hand.

"Of course, I'm far too old to be writing a book," he said. "But I could, you know. I've accumulated enough material for several books, but there is no statute of limitations under the Official Secrets Act."

"Does that mean you can't talk to me about those days?"

"No, but it does mean you can't name me as a source until I'm dead.

That shouldn't be too long now."

"I hope not. But I promise I won't reveal your identity."

"Come inside. I've got a lot of notes in my den."

With great difficulty he hobbled away and I followed him, ducking my head so as not to hit the low beam over the door. Hanging roses brushed my shoulders as I entered a quaint and comfortable room, which was quite dark on account of the cottage's very few, small windows.

"Bloody Pitt," Gordon snorted. "We had a window tax for a hundred years, but in 1797 he tripled it to pay for his wars."

"Not a Pitt fan?"

"No, indeed. I imagine the other fellow—Fox—would have been worse, but Pitt bled the country dry. My ancestors, all agricultural labourers, lived in abject poverty because of Pitt. If you want my opinion, he is held in far greater esteem than his record warrants."

"Speaking of records, do you mind if we talk about June, 1985? When the Blasket Island mission came up."

"Ah yes. Are you comfortable? Do you want a cushion?"

"No, thanks, I'm fine."

"Well, what happened was that Posen had asked Verenko to brief Smith and—what was the other fellow's name?"

"Mueller."

"Ah yes. Gerd Mueller. Great big fellow. Anyway, Varenko asked me to do the briefing because she knew sod all about Ireland."

"But you did?"

"Several years undercover in both the Republic and the North. Fighting the IRA. So I got Mueller and Smith in and laid out maps. I also handed them a couple of books about the place. One was *Twenty Years Agrowing* by Muiris O'Sullebhain, and the other was *Island Man* by Tomas Criomhthain. Have you read them?"

"No, I haven't."

"Too bad. They give a wonderful picture of a hard life beyond the boundaries of civilization. The island is off the coast of County Kerry and can only be reached by boat.

"I told them to ask Frau Becker to get flights for them. The choice was fly to Shannon and wait five hours in London or get a flight to Dublin and make a four hour drive to Dingle. I told them if it were me I would choose the latter, and they agreed. I advised them to approach

Dingle by the southern route so they could see Inch Beach, which was, and is, one of the wonders of the world.

"They should get accommodations in Dingle or Ventry, but not any nearer, then slowly, inconspicuously, nose around to Coumeenoole—you can see the Great Blasket from the shore.

"They should pose as tourists, particularly when inquiring about getting a boat ride to the Island. Then they should be seen on the island wandering around with no particular object, but keeping their eyes open for any sign of the criminals."

"Was there any sign of Sollows or Repnin?"

"They called me from the hotel that night to say that they had seen signs of recent habitation, but that there was definitely nobody on the Island at the time of their visit."

"Was that it?"

"No, they found cigarette butts, which Mueller claimed were of a Russian brand. He told me they smelled like an Armenian whore house and said that Varenko had previously told them that Repnin smoked that brand."

"So, mission accomplished?"

"Only in a manner of speaking."

"What?"

"They never came back. The next day their car fell from the top of a mountain and smashed to smithereens."

"Good God!"

"I've got the local newspaper account and the report from the Garda forensics"

He hauled himself up and shuffled over to a chest of drawers, from which he extracted a sheaf of papers. These he handed to me.

45

The Kerryman

KILLARNEY AND SOUTH KERRY
June 14 1985

DRAMATIC CRASH ON MOUNT BRANDON, TWO KILLED

By Eoin Ó Murchú

Whether because of the lack of familiarity with Irish roads or perhaps the over-imbibing of the local stout, two tourists met their doom yesterday when their car left the road at the summit of Mount Brandon.

The highest point in Ireland, at 3,127 feet (Fin McCool's seat is a mere 2,500 feet), was the scene of the fatal accident. Judging by bodies found below it seems that two people occupied the Ford Cortina, hired in Dublin, when it began its descent from the Connor Pass.

What exactly happened is unknown at this point, but something caused the car to swerve and crash through the guardrails and plunge to the depths below. The wreckage was so considerable that the vehicle was beyond any repair. The bodies, both men in their thirties, are believed to have been American tourists. The day before they registered at Benner's Hotel in Dingle as Mathew Smith and Gordon Miller, both of Chicago.

When questioned, local Garda were unforthcoming with information, and quickly incident tapes were erected around the scene. Shortly thereafter plain clothes officers from the GDU appeared but would not comment.

46

GARDA SIOCHANA
REGIONAL HEADQUARTERS, TRALEE
Forensic Laboratory
June 15th 1985

SUMMARY
A thorough examination was conducted on the remains of the two bodies recovered from the crashed 1983 Ford Cortina at the foot of the Connor Pass on June 14th 1985. Insofar as could be determined the occupants' injuries—fractured crania, fractured upper and lower limbs, and severed spinal columns--were consistent with the vehicle having crashed from some height. No signs of any injuries consistent with interpersonal violence were present. In my opinion, both occupants were unharmed until impact.
An examination of the remains of the vehicle revealed the usual injuries consistent with a vehicular accident, but one area did indicate damage not inflicted by the crash, namely that there was clear evidence of the brakes being tampered with and severely damaged. In my opinion this was the cause of the vehicle losing control and leaving the road.

CONCLUSION
Both occupants of this vehicle were victims of a criminal act.

Séamus Callaghan
Senior Forensic Scientist

47

TRANSLATION

Minutes of meeting between General Viktor Mikhailovich Chebrikov and Colonel Olga Andreievna Malashenko

June 15th 1985. Lubyanka Building, Dzerzhinsky Square, Moscow.

Present:
Gen. Shebrikov
Col. Kryuchkov
Col. Malashenko

The meeting was called to order by Comrade Chairman Chebrikov. He indicated that the meeting had been requested by Colonel Malashenko. Also that it be recorded, a request to which he had readily acquiesced.

Col. Malashenko said that her laboratory at Blagoveshchensk had been monitoring various sources in eastern Asia from which it seemed clear that there had been a severe outbreak in Northern China which bore all the signs of Cephalinol. She said that the Manchurian lumbering community of Nin-kiong was completely destroyed and two nearby villages were affected. However, it appears that the regional centre of Aihun has been unaffected.

The Comrade Chairman asked Col. Malashenko if she was certain of her information. She replied that Blagoveshchensk had received notification of the incident before Beijing because the Committee on State Security had agents in place at the Chinese laboratory in Harbin. She said that approximately 90 minutes previously the municipal committee of Aihun phoned the Harbin facility to request medical and scientific assistance. Our agents then informed Col. Malashenko.

The Comrade Chairman asked if Harbin would honour the request for assistance. The Colonel said the question was difficult to answer because[8]

---

8   This page of the minutes is torn at this point, any any other pages ahve been lost.

48

Some weeks after I had returned home after my time with Harry in Virginia, I got a phone call from a man who claimed he had been a senior official in the U.S. State Department. He would give me neither his name nor the position he occupied, but he said had heard (presumably from Pete Roussel, but I am not sure of that) that I was writing this book. He told me he had a copy of the transcript of the phone conversation between President Reagan and Deng Xiaoping, Chairman of the Chinese Communist Party and head of the government of China.

I told him that I had no money, and that if he was looking for remuneration he should try the *New York Times* or the *Washington Post*. He hesitated for a moment, then said that if he took that route his identity would come out and he could be charged under both the Espionage Act of 1917 and the Intelligence Identities Protection Act.

Then he said I could have the document without charge and asked for my mailing address.

"If you do that," I said, "you'd better send it registered mail."

"No, that way I would have to provide a name and address. I'll just put it in the regular mail and hope for the best."

Six days later I received the package.

Minutes of Telephone conversation between President Reagan and Chairman Deng Xiaoping of the People's Republic of China. June 16 1985.

Present (USA): President Reagan, Secretary Schultz, Donald Bouchard, Kenneth Dam, John C. Whitehead. Donald Regan. Arthur Lee (interpreter).

Mr. Lee: You can go ahead now Mr. President, Chairman Deng is on the line.

The President: Good Morning Mr. Chairman. First let me say that we keenly grieve for the tragic and criminal loss of life in your country.

Chairman Deng (per Mr. Lee): Yes. Thank you. I understand that you have discussed this with Mr. Gorbachev?

The President: Yes, about an hour ago. We both understand how the Chinese people feel about such a merciless attack. He assures me that he is willing to put every Soviet facility at your disposal.

Chairman Deng (per Mr. Lee): Yes, I know. I spoke with him early today. He has been most helpful. As I told him that at first we feared that the deaths at Nin-Kiong were caused by a chemical leak from Russian stockpiles at Blagoveshchensk. Comrade Gorbachev assured me such was not the case. Subsequent consultation with our own disease pathologists confirmed his statements. He also told me that two traitors were responsible. You are aware of this?

The President; Yes that is so.

Chairman Deng (per Mr. Lee): I understand that he and you had launched an offensive to find and punish these miscreants.

The President: Yes.

Chairman Deng (per Mr. Lee): Why was the People's Republic not informed and indeed involved at an early stage?

[At this point the President gestured to temporarily halt the feed]

The President: What shall I tell him, George?

Mr. Schultz: What can you tell him? Apologize. Blame me. Say I was supposed to do it, but I slipped up.

The President: Okay, I'll try something along those lines.

[The President indicated to recontinue the feed.]

The President: I apologise. We had a small mix-up with the phones.

Chairman Deng (per Mr. Lee): A mix-up? What is this?

The President: A problem. It has been solved. Let me say, Mr. Chairman, that I am deeply sorry you were not informed or brought in earlier. I gave instructions to that effect, but they…er… were… er…misunderstood by officials.

Chairman Deng (per Mr.Lee): I see. We too sometimes have this problem.

The President: Hah. I guess when you do, the guy responsible doesn't get a second chance. Ha-ha.

Chairman Deng (per Mr. Lee): That is very amusing. (Long silence) Let us now return to the matter at hand. Your operation is established in Vienna.

The President: Yes.

Chairman Deng (Per Mr. Lee): We shall send representatives to this place. They are in the Interior Ministry on the Herrengasse. No expense shall be spared. No effort will be too great until these traitors and Cephalinol had been recovered and destroyed. Our agents will report to Mr. Posen and Ms. Varenko tomorrow.

The President: (whispering to Mr. Schultz) How does he know all this stuff? (aloud) You will be most welcome, sir.

Chairman Deng: 失陪了

Mr. Lee: Chairman Deng says he is sad that he can no longer remain.

Meeting adjourned.

49

For a whole day and part of the next I was on my own, because Harry felt too ill to see me. He did not make an appearance, so I assumed he was keeping to his bed.

Although I was anxious to get back to Nova Scotia relatively soon, I was glad of this development because I knew that rest, and particularly sleep, can help with Primary Progressive Aphasia as it can improve the effectiveness of language and brain health. Rest and sleep would be good because I could tell that when he got tired, Harry's communication issues worsened.

I wandered around the garden about a dozen times, talked to Hernandez, asked about his wife, who was still sick with 'flu, and walked the country lanes. I imagined I was becoming an expert on cattle, grading them and wondering how much they would fetch at market.

On the first day, I walked all the way to Rectortown, a lovely little community with wide-open green fields, beautiful trees, imposing white houses and two neat churches, the Methodist church and Mount Olive Baptist church. The countryside reminded me of parts of England and it was very peaceful, with few vehicles on the roads.

I next saw Harry around noon on June 4th, when he was speaking very slowly and in short, halting sentences. Despite that he insisted we try to do some recording and, since it was a splendid, sunny, hot day, I set up my equipment at the wrought iron garden table.

Twelfth taped session with Harry Posen
Zulla, Virginia, June 4th, 2019

It's all a bit of a haze because there was so much going on, and none of it good. We lost two people, Smith and Mueller, in Ireland. Somehow Sollows's mob got to them and their car fell off a mountain. Then we had the Chinese Cephalinol outbreak. On top of the Bermuda fiasco, this was hard to take because Phil and the Director were giving me hell as if it was all my fault. At the same time, Chebrikov was chastising Zina, which made her difficult to live with.

Then, at the worst possible time, we had the arrival of Deng Xiaoping's additions to our force. More difficult names for me to pronounce, these two were pieces of work—both women—Chun Chen and Hua Zhou.

I say they were women, but they looked like two teenagers of indeterminate age, and were as homely as two bags of rice. They were like machines and absolutely had their own ideas. If Zina or I asked them to do something they didn't like, they would say, "It is not convenient," and walk away.

Zina said she was waiting for an assignment in the South Pole so we could send them there, but I reminded her that only one could go and she had to be accompanied by a NATO rep. We suspected that they were with us, if not exactly as saboteurs, then as spies for Beijing.

Neither Zina nor I, nor any of the other agents, could speak Cantonese or Mandarin, so Chun and Hua could pretend not to understand anything they didn't want to hear. They were a royal pain in the ass.

In addition to all of these difficulties, neither of us was getting any exercise and we were putting on the pounds because of Oskar's wonderful dinners. But we couldn't resist them, and our special table at the Monaco was like an oasis in the desert where we could relax and talk about the intricacies of the operation which we couldn't discuss with others.

This one night—I guess it would have been June 18, 1985—we retreated to our table, but were determined to have something light on the calories. Oskar, as usual, had other ideas.

"Tonight the chef has a magnificent *Gigot d'agneau Jacqueline*. The sauce is out of this world." I can't imitate his High German accent very well, but it was kind of snooty. "It would be breathtaking with a Chateau Canon 1961."

"Stop at once!" Zina said. "This is torture. We must have something light."

"Die Enttäuschung ist groß!" Oskar's face was like a slapped ass. Then, rather like a parent to a naughty child, he said, "In that case, you shall have some *consommé polonaise* followed by a modest portion of chicken with asparagus in a mousseline and green peppercorn sauce."

"What shall we drink?" Zina asked in an apologetic tone.

"Whatever you wish." Oskar said with a sniff.

"In that case, please bring us the Krug 1973," she said.

When Oskar had pranced away, Zina pulled her chair closer to the table, reached out and touched my hand. "Sorry if I have been a bitch lately, but things have been wild."

"I know. It's been a living hell."

"But I have to talk to you."

"Talk away," I said, greatly fearing she was going to say we should stop being intimate.

"On his own initiative, Gordon has been investigating a few interesting lines."

"Oh yes?"

"He calls them 'long shots'. He has been asking how the enemy's operation has been funded."

"The CIA thinks Gorbachev paid them off. That would give them plenty of cash to be going on with."

"You have no proof of that, and I certainly have not been informed that it is the case. May we, for the sake of the discussion, assume that the allegation is untrue?"

"Okay."

"Look at this list." She pushed a piece of paper across the table. "Gordon compiled it. It lists all the major bank robberies, hold-ups, and break-ins in the last few months around the world. That is, the really big jobs."

"Go on."

"The ones underlined are so similar—in methods, execution—that it looks like the same crime repeated in three different locations."

"Assuming they were done by the same people, what was the haul in each case?"

"Over a million marks from the Deutsche Bank in Hamburg. Two and a half million dollars from the Metropolitan Trust in Chicago. And this is—how do you say?—the clincher"-- a quarter of a million in gold bullion from Cairo..."

"Cairo?"

"Yes. It's almost too good to be true. In each case there was a road or street detour to stop the armoured trucks, plastic explosives to blow off the doors, bullets in the leg for each guard. And it all started in Cairo. Gordon is convinced these jobs were done by the same gang."

Oskar and the waiter approached and placed our soup in front of us. It smelled absolutely divine. He opened the Krug and poured each of us a glass.

Zina sipped it, nodded her appreciation, and they went.

"Well," I said when they were safely out of earshot, "at least we don't have to rob banks. We have unlimited funds at our disposal."

"But it again raises the question of how long have Sollows and Repnin been planning this. They must have been *priyateli* for a long time, eh?"

"It would look that way."

"Remind me of the postings Sollows had before his last one."

"Paris, Bonn, Geneva, Vienna, Rome, Cairo, and Moscow."

"Valya was in Paris, Vienna, London, Basle...not a perfect match, but it's certainly possible that they met and formed a business relationship at one or more of the common posts."

"Maybe this isn't the first time they've pulled something rotten. Maybe they've had a lot of practice."

"Possibly. This soup is delicious."

"So is the Krug."

"Harry, I shouldn't tell you this."

"What?"

"It's internal KGB stuff, so you can't share it."

"All right. If you think it's important."

"About fifteen years ago—something like that—there was a plan to destabilize the French currency by flooding the market with millions of francs in brilliantly counterfeited money. Valya was sent to the Riviera to be in charge of the release of the funds."

"Uh-huh."

"But the whole thing failed. The explanation given at the time was that not enough money had been put into circulation at the right speed. But it was hushed up and those of us in the lower ranks never found out what really happened. You see, Valya had powerful friends on the Central Committee and the Politburo."

"Hmm. Edgar made numerous trips to Europe about that time –we assumed they were for cultural reasons—and they could have connected then."

"Here's our chicken."

~

Harry took a deep breath and looked up at the slightly darkening sky.

"Talking about Oskar's food is making me hungry. Mrs H, still out of action?"

"Yes."

"What can we rake up, I wonder? Could you cook us something again?"

"I'll try. It depends on what you have in the fridge."

"Let's go look. If I'm up to it, we can have a short session after we eat."

50

There was a variety of food oddments in Harry's fridge, but not many ingredients which complemented one another: a mouldy loaf of bread; some small chunks of unidentified cheese bearing a suspicious blue growth; two eggs; four strips of very old and smelly bacon; some butter; three withered apples; one onion; jars of mayonnaise, mustard and English marmalade; half a cabbage which had seen better days; two pieces of wilted celery; and one small potato.

"Well, you won't be dining at the Ritz tonight," I said from my examining position on one knee. "This looks like a dog's breakfast."

"Mrs. H. does all the shopping, and with her off sick, I guess supplies have dwindled," Harry said, leaning over to peer inside. "Can you do anything with that lot?"

"I'll try. But it'll need another very good bottle to help wash it down."

"Okay. Burgundy or Bordeaux?"

"We had Burgundy last night, so let's go for Claret. Do you have any Chateau Palmer in your cellar?"

"Palmer was one of Edgar's favourites. Mine too. I have a few bottles of the 1983, 1990, 2005 and 2010. And one of the '66."

"Wow! I don't think we deserve the '66. It needs to be drunk with a beautiful rack of lamb."

"Fuck it!" said Harry, slapping his hand against the fridge. "I'm going to be dead soon. Let's have the damn thing!"

While Harry, with scarily shaking hands, decanted the wine over a candle, I threw the bread and cheese into the bin, then cut up the cabbage, potato, onion, celery and one of the apples. These I put into a pot and boiled it all until it was tender. Then I smashed it into a kind of Colcannon with a huge knob of butter. In a pan I fried the bacon and the eggs and served them with the mash.

It was not my most memorable meal, but the wine turned it into something very special. The bouquet was out of this world—lavender, cedar and some beautiful but unidentifiable fruits. For a 53-year-old wine it was amazingly youthful, and on the palate it was strong yet soft and velvety, with just a hint of tannin to give it backbone. I felt privileged to have experienced it and thanked Harry profusely.

We cleaned our plates and toyed with the rest of the wine, swirling it around in our glasses.

Finally Harry drained his and unsteadily got up. "I think I may be good for another hour."

"Are you sure?"

"Yeah. Let's go for it."

I must again explain how stressful these sessions must have been for Harry, requiring enormous concentration and effort on his part. Frequently I was tempted to jump in and guess what he wanted to say, but he would wave me down and manfully stumble on. The next transcript, much edited for pauses, mistaken words and false constructions, took Harry well over an hour to record.

Here's how the session came about:

"You're from Nova Scotia, aren't you?"

"Yes."

"Where do you live?"

"In Halifax."

"What were you doing in early summer 1985?"

"I was working for Premier Buchanan."

"Premier. That's the same as our state governor isn't it?"

"More or less."

"Where?"

"Where what?"

"Where were you working?"

"In the Howe Building. On the corner of Hollis and Prince streets."

"Is that near Water Street?"

"Very near."

"Okay, cast your mind back. Do you remember an incident on Water Street in June of 1985?"

"Incident?" I racked my brain, and suddenly it came to me. "Yes, by God, I do. There was some kind of explosion and fire only a block away. I recall hearing the bang and watching the smoke rise."

"Treasure Chest Imports."

"Yes! How do you know about that?"

"Switch your machine on."

> *Continuation of the twelfth taped session with Harry Posen*
> *Zulla, Virginia, June 4th, 2019*

I have to back up a bit before I get into that. Right after the Chinese beauty queens arrived, our replacements for Art Smith and Gerd Mueller showed up. Gerd's substitute was Franz Richter, a wiry little Sachsen with an evil glint in his eye. Zina knew nothing about him, and we sure weren't going to ask Putin, so we assigned him research into the criminal enterprises in Eastern Europe which might conceivably have been the work of Sollows and Repnin.

But the real surprise was that, as a replacement for Smith, Phil sent us Herb Chauncey. Don't get me wrong, Herbie was a stand-up guy, but he wasn't a field operative. As far as I was aware, he'd always been a desk man. I didn't know how to interpret this act of Phil's—whether he thought I could use a friendly face or whether he was saying he considered our operation a write-off.

Anyway, a day later Phil called me with another tip he said came from Kimberly.

"Place called Halifax. In Nova Scotia."

"What about it?"

"Kimberly says there is something deeply suspicious about a business called Treasure Chest Imports."

"Why is it suspicious?"

"He didn't say."

"Kimberly's last tip was a trap."

"That wasn't his fault, Harry. He just said there was something worth investigating. And there was. He was right."

"All right, I'll send someone to check it out."

"We can do it. We're much closer."

"We have to stick to the agreement to have someone from the Warsaw Pact on every assignment. Do you have anyone who fits that description working at Langley?"

"Christ, I hope not!"

"Okay, then, it'll have to be done from here. I'll send Tony Aprile.

He's one of yours. Is he any good?"

"He wouldn't be one of mine if he wasn't."

So I consulted with Zina and we decided to send Jan Prochazka from the Czech StB with Tony. It would be a miserable trip for them getting from Vienna to Halifax, but it had to be done.

"Tony, you'll be the primary," Zina said.

"Why him?" Jan demanded.

"Because his English is much better than yours. When we get an assignment to Czechoslovakia, you can be the primary. Understood?"

"*Aano, rozumím,*" Jan grunted.

"That means if there is *any* difference of opinion, Tony's decision goes. Right?"

"*Právo. Dobře.*"

"Tony. Proceed with extreme caution. The bastards have pranged us twice now. We don't need any more casualties."

And off they went.

I'm awful tired. Do you mind if we pick it up after breakfast?

~

I switched off the recorder and said that, unless Mrs. Hernandez showed up with an armful of provisions, there would be no breakfast.

"I'll call H and ask him to pick up some stuff on his way in tomorrow. He usually gets here around 8:30. I guess if he's going shopping for us it will be a little later."

"That's okay. Call him, Harry, then go straight to bed."

51

The ChronicleHerald

June 17 1985

DOWNTOWN EXPLOSION TAKES ONE LIFE

By Don MacDonald, Staff reporter

A mysterious blast rocked downtown Halifax yesterday, causing alarm and confusion and taking one life. What many, at first, thought was the Citadel's noon cannon misfiring, turned out to have been an explosion in a Water Street business premises.

Halifax Fire Chief Donald A. MacDonald said the explosion led to a fire which enveloped 1890 Water Street and spread quickly to adjacent properties. The Chief said the fire took several hours to get under control and that the damage was extensive.

"The building where the explosion took place was completely devastated," said the Chief, "and the nearby buildings are badly affected." He said he supposed most could be restored with extensive work, but that the main premises were beyond repair.

As to the explosion's cause Chief MacDonald was circumspect, saying that a forensic examination, taking days, would have to be conducted. "I would only be speculating at this point," the Chief said, "and I would rather wait until we have hard evidence from the experts."

Dr. David Maxwell, head of Emergency Medicine at the Halifax Infirmary, told the *Chronicle Herald* that at approximately 2 pm a man in an advanced state of injury was delivered by ambulance to the hospital. Dr. Maxwell said emergency surgeons and physicians worked on the patient but he could not be saved and was pronounced dead at 2:45 pm.

Contacted for information about the deceased, Halifax Police Chief Blair Jackson said the man's wallet was miraculously saved from burning, and revealed him to be a Czech national called Jan Prochazka. He said that witnesses in the vicinity think they saw Prochazka with another man some minutes prior to the blast, but that the second man had not been located.

Investigations are ongoing.

52

Harry was up before me the next morning, and I found him in the garden fussing over some flowers.

"'Morning," he called to me as I appeared on the patio. "I think we've got greenfly."

I wandered over and peered at the plant. "It sure looks like that. What can you do about it?"

"I'll get Hernandez to spray them with soapy water."

"I guess Mrs. H hasn't arrived yet with our provisions."

"No. I figure we've more than an hour to wait. Let's go over the fields and see Gordie Holland."

"Who's he?"

"He's a farmer who has horses. You should see them. Beautiful."

"Is it far?"

"About half a mile. You can see the roof of his barn from my fence."

"So long as you won't tire yourself out."

"Don't worry, you'll get your recording."

We set off across muddy fields, and I was glad I had borrowed some rubber boots from Harry. It was rather heavy going, and Harry's progress was slow, but we eventually came to Holland's farm, a spread with well-kept, nicely-painted buildings surrounded by a white niche fence.

Harry told me that Holland kept Spanish Colonial horses, which were descended from the original Iberian horse stock brought from Spain by the Conquistadors. He said they were the main horse of Native American tribes and early settlers, but had become almost extinct some seventy years ago.

Knowing nothing of horses, I had visions of hugely-imposing, majestic beasts, and when we saw them galloping over to see us at the fence, I was surprised to see small, athletic horses, quite low to the ground, with broad foreheads, narrow faces and long tails. But they were handsome and extremely friendly.

As we were admiring the animals a wiry, middle-aged man came out of one of the barns.

"Hi Chester!" Harry called.

""Lo, there, Harry. We don't see you around here too often these days."

"No, I been sick. Is Gordie around?"

"No, he took six head over to Marshall Market to see if he could sell 'em."

"Well, tell him we called. This is my friend Jeremy from Nova Scotia."

Chester looked me over rather as he might a young heifer or a butcher hog, and just nodded silently.

We headed back, this time along the hedges, Harry instructing me on the beauties of redbud, cherry blossom, sweet bay magnolia, flowering dogwood and many more trees, all of which seemed to be in their prime.

We got back just as Hernandez and his wife were pulling into the yard. I was glad to see that both were laden with provisions.

"Mr. Harry," Mrs. H called, "I got your favourite sausages."

"Wonderful. Thank you."

"You eat already? Or you want I cook them for you now?"

"Yes, please, Mrs. H. With a mess of eggs and toast would be good."

"Okay. You go in and sit down and I bring to you."

It took Harry about twice as long as me to demolish the sausages, but they were excellent and we had worked up quite an appetite roaming the fields. We refilled our cups with coffee and went into the study.

Thirteenth taped session with Harry Posen
Zulla, Virginia, June 5th, 2019

Tony called me from an airport—I don't know if it was Halifax, Toronto, or New York—but he was in a terrible state, breaking into Italian the more excited he got. Of course, I told him not to give me any details over the phone, just the bottom line. Speaking in a kind of code language, he said that the mission had failed.

"It was another trap."

"Please tell me there were no losses."

"One."

"Not Jan?"

"Yes."

"I won't ask how—you can tell me that when you get here. But why did it happen?"

"He refused to recognize that I was the primary. He wouldn't take orders from me. I warned him, but he just barged right into the fucking trap like a kid. I was lucky to get clear. I lost all the hair on one side of my head in the blast."

"Thanks, Tony. Get home fast. We'll need a full report."

I called Zina in and told her the news.

'That fucking Czech idiot!" she exploded. "I'm ashamed to admit that I am almost as concerned about Chebrikov laughing at me as I am about Jan's death."

I asked her to get in touch with Alojz Lorenc at the Czech StB, tell him what had occurred and request a replacement for Prochazka.

"Those bastards are one step ahead of us every time," Zina said.

"Looks more like two or three steps ahead of us," I said ruefully.

I was mad. And sick that we had now lost three operatives and, according to forensic reports, all by means of relatively unsophisticated explosives. Sollows and Repnin were making us look like a bunch of amateurs, a sentiment I was sure Phil would echo.

Meanwhile, at any given time, we had eighteen—no, twenty, I forgot Chen and Zhao—combing the world, looking for the proverbial needle in a haystack. I didn't envy them because most of their work must have been boring beyond measure and extremely unrewarding

Zina returned and told me that Lorenc had taken the news calmly and without emotion, and said that the replacement would get a flight from Prague to Vienna and be with us within a few hours.

"Wow. That's efficient," I said.

"And ruthless. We don't like to admit it, but the StB is much more deadly than the KGB."

"Except for Prochazka."

"Except for Jan. Maybe they sent him to us because he was useless."

"Did Lorenc give you a name?"

"Yes. Eliska Svoboda."

"You know her?"

"I might have met her somewhere. But I don't think so."

"Let's hope she's good. Look, Zina, I think we should gather the troops to review our situation, and warn them that more care—much more care—in dealing with leads."

"I agree. Let's do it first thing in the morning."

"Will you do it?"

"If you wish. You can butt in any time, if you feel what I say needs any amplification."

Not much happened during the rest of the day, and that evening Zina and I had another great dinner provided by Oskar at The Monaco. There was some lovely poached wild salmon to start, then roast woodcock with mushrooms for the main course. We followed Oskar's recommendations for wine—a 1978 Chevalier Montrachet and then a spectacular Musigny 1959.

As we sniffed this incredible wine, Zina and I discussed how guilty we should feel enjoying these delights on our governments' dime, and vowed we should come to some agreement with Oskar and/or dine more modestly in future.

When we got in the next morning the gang gathered round except, I noticed, for Putin, who had not graced us with his presence. Eventually, he sauntered in about halfway through Zina's address and sprawled in a chair with his legs—in riding boots—stretched out.

Also late, but for more legitimate reasons, was a young woman—I'd say about 30—who stuck her head around the door and announced that she was Eliska Svoboda. She sat down at the very back of the room. She was a slim, dirty blonde, with a haunting face, looking as if she were on the verge of bursting into tears.

Zina gave a great speech. Shortly after Svoboda's arrival she pitched into the gang like a Master Sergeant addressing a platoon of rookies.

"You are not here on vacation," she thundered. "Just because the circumstances are completely different from normal does not mean you can relax or take fewer precautions than you usually would. We have lost three operatives already because of schoolboy mistakes. The MO was clear. Simple explosive traps, and yet our people got burned. There must not be any more mistakes of this kind!"

"Major, are we allowed to make mistakes of some other kind?" Putin's voice was cold and mocking. For a second I thought Zina might be intimidated, but she lashed into him.

"No, you are not! And if you think losing three men in as many weeks is funny, maybe you'd better go back to Dresden!"

There was laughter and some applause, but Putin's face did not change. He stared insolently back at her.

At the end of the meeting, while people were shuffling back to their stations, I saw Svoboda sidle up to Zina. Then they disappeared into the latter's office.

About half an hour later, Zina appeared at my door with Svoboda in tow.

"What's up?" I asked.

"Tell Mr. Posen what you just told me," Zina said to Svoboda.

"Sit down, Eliska. What is this all about?"

"You understand that I did not know I was to join your project until yesterday?"

"Okay."

"I was not sure at first, but now I know you are serious and that this task force is important."

"Go on."

"Well, three days ago, I was drinking in a bar in Prague—the *Vinor-hady*—you know it?"

"No."

"I do," said Zina.

"Anyway, I was having a plate of cold ham and sour pickles, and a *Becherovka,* when in come this man.?"

"What man?"

"He is Grisha Baltsaiev."

"Member of the StB," said Zina.

"*Ano*. He is being important one time and they say brilliant, but not so much anymore because he is liking too much *pálenka*."

"A kind of vodka."

"Yes. And?"

"Grisha is drunk and he sit down and is trying—how you say— making me, but I not interested in going bed with this smelly man. So he say to me he bet he know something I not know. So I say what is this? And he says the Renegade task force is bullshit."

"Did he, now?"

"*Ano*. He say that is all fake to fool CIA and that Valya Repnin is to come back in—I not know word—*Vítězství*."

"Triumph."

"Yes. That. And he say that Cerny, Prochazka and Varenko will be finished…."

"And the rest, Eliska. Tell Mr. Posen the rest." Zina prompted.

"He say Comrade Chebrikov has arranged whole thing to embarrass Gorbachev and take over USSR."

"Jesus!"

"Thank you, Eliska," Zina said in a kindly tone, "Please go and find yourself a desk. I'm sure this was just the ravings of a drunk. Don't you agree, Harry?"

"Yes, of course, a drunk."

We watched her go back into the main room and unload her belongings onto one of the empty desks.

"What do you think?" I asked.

"It sounds crazy, but…"

"How can you find out?"

"I'll have to find some way to get to Gorbachev."

"That won't be easy."

"No. But I think I know someone who could get a message through."

"Good luck with that. Not a word of this to anyone else. If they got wind of this back in Langley, all hell would break loose."

53

I was deep in a dream about home when I felt I was rolling around. It turned out to be Harry shaking me.

In a daze I reached for the bedside clock and saw it was five-thirty. "What's wrong? What's happened?"

"Wake up."

"Why?"

"We've got to get started. We've got a lot to get through today, and if we don't make a start we may not get it done."

"Okay," I said, swinging my legs over the side of the bed. Can I have a wash and shave?"

"You're not going to be seeing anybody important today. Come on!"

"Do we get any breakfast?"

"That can wait. Maybe we can grab some when Mrs. H. arrives at 8.30."

Still half asleep, I stumbled downstairs, followed Harry into the kitchen and saw that he already set up my recorder.

"Are you ready?"

Fourteenth taped sessioin with Harry Posen
Zulla, Virginia, June 6ᵗʰ, 2019

At breakfast the next day, Zina and I had an emergency confab. Speaking almost in whispers over eggs, coffee and pastries, we tried to figure out where we were going wrong, and how to use our best assets more productively.

"I feel like an allied general in the First World War, just hurling cannon fodder at the enemy guns."

"I know. It is not a nice feeling."

"One thing I think I have decided on."

"What's that, Harry?"

"I'm not going to accept any more tips from one of my sources."

"Who is it?"

"Nice try, Comrade."

Zina grinned. Of course I was talking about Kimberly, but I couldn't give a KGB major any details.

I don't want to leave you with the impression that the only missions we ran ended in death and disaster, because there were dozens of leads the team tracked down when nothing was found and nothing bad happened. But the unsuccessful missions worried me, and the loss of team members weighed heavily on Zina and me.

All aspects of our investigations bothered me. As I had intimated to Zina, I was worried about our sources. I didn't know what, if anything, had happened to Kimberly, but his so-called "intelligence" had led to four deaths. I was determined there wouldn't be a fifth. I knew it would lead to an argument with Phil, who swore by Kimberly, but I couldn't help that. Either Kimberly had become corrupted by someone—I feared by Edgar—or he was being fed intelligence from an unreliable source, namely Sollows through an intermediary.

'We don't have a lot of choice except to go chasing after these tips wherever they may lead us," said Zina. "We can't just sit in Vienna and wait."

"No. I'm certain something very big is coming. I'm convinced that what we've witnessed so far from the enemy are only rehearsals."

"Rehearsals for what?"

"If we knew that, we might be able to take preventive measures. I've been racking my brains but I can't settle on any one thing which would be big and dramatic."

"Are they really in this for the money? They must be quite rich from their bank robberies."

"And especially if Gorbachev paid them off not to attack Ukraine."

"I have told you there is no truth to that!"

"How would you know? It's not like Gorbachev would tell you. Besides which, the Ukraine attack did not happen. Why was that?"

"I don't know," she said sullenly. I noticed the beginning of a tear in her eye. "Harry, I don't want us to fight. If we are not united this mission has no chance of success."

"Yes, you're right. I'm sorry. Did you manage to get a message through to the big man?"

"I think so."

"How?"

"Just between us?"

"I swear."

"My favourite uncle, *Dyadya Vanya,* is a great friend of Boris Yeltsin, and as you know he has been a big supporter of Gorbachev's reforms. He will go to see the Chairman."

"Really? You amaze me."

"I am not just a pretty face."

"Indeed you are not, but your face is very pretty."

"Yes, I think so. Anyway, my uncle will go to Mikhail Sergeyevich and together they will confront Viktor Mikhailovich and find out if there is any substance to the rumour."

"Wow! Well done. What do you think will come of it?

"It is hard to know, but you know that Chebrikov has also been a supporter of the Chairman."

"Hmm. When does Tony get back?"

"Dorothea said it would be late tonight or tomorrow morning."

"Zina, I think we'd be deceiving ourselves if we didn't expect the enemy to lay more traps for us. Don't you agree?"

"I do. I have an idea they won't use explosives again. They will think that by now we are prepared for that approach."

"What do you think they will use next?"

"Harry, I have no idea. But let's face it, we know that all the agencies represented here in Vienna have used hundreds of tricks, dirty and deadly, and Sollows and Repnin will be well versed in all of them."

"On that cheerful note, we'd better get into the office. You go first. I'll follow in a few minutes."

~

About ten o'clock that morning, I got a call from Phil. As expected, he gave me hell for sustaining another loss of life.

"If you want to recall me and replace me with someone else, go ahead," I said. "Maybe you would be a better fit yourself."

"Me?"

"Yeah, you've got all the answers. Why don't you take over?"

"Tread carefully, Harry. That's insubordination."

"You know I can't help what happens in the field. I can only tell my people to be careful. They're all fully trained operatives in their own jurisdictions. If they act foolishly, it's not my fault."

"All right, calm down."

"I'll calm down when I've caught these bastards."

"Okay, okay."

"Did you just call to give me a hard time?"

"No, I have another lead for you."

"If it's from Kimberly, I'm not interested. I don't trust anything coming from him anymore."

"It's not Kimberly, it's Sphinx."

"Sphinx?"

"Yeah, he says there's something suspicious about an abandoned church."

"Where?"

"Let me see. Yeah, here it is, a place called Monmouth in the UK."

"Here we go again."

"No, I think this could be gold. Sphinx has never let us down. You know that."

"All right. Give me the details. I've got just the person to look into this."

"Who?"

"Heather Milton-Jones from MI6."

"Sounds like somebody out of a Carry On movie."

"I've got work to do. I guess you do, too."

"Yeah. See you, Harry."

I called Zina in and told her what Phil had relayed to me. She could tell I was not entirely comfortable with the assignment.

"I know you can't reveal anything about this source, but is it reliable? Is that what is bothering you?"

"Yes."

At that moment there was a tap on the door and in walked Putin. He even clicked his heels!

"Майор, я только что получил известие от товарища Эриха Мильке из Берлина." He said, addressing Zina.

"Colonel, you must speak English, please. Мистер Posen does not speak Russian well."

"And I not English speak so well."

"Do you want me to translate?"

"No, is okay. I try."

"Harry," she said, "Vladimir Vladimirovich says he has received a tip from Erich Mielke of the MfS."

"The head of the Stasi. That Mielke?"

"Apparently so. Go head, Colonel."

"He say for to investigate place in England."

"What place?"

"Is called Monmouze."

"Monmouth?"

"Da. I have wrote details in Russian on paper," he said, handing Zina a page from his notebook.

"Спасибо, Colonel. We will take it from here."

"Is it the same place?" I asked her when Putin had gone.

"Yes, it is. What an extraordinary coincidence."

"Maybe, maybe not. But I guess we have to go see."

"Could we send more people? Three or even four?"

"It would be awkward. Too much like a gang. Too obtrusive."

"You're right. Then who should we send?"

"Heather is the obvious choice to be primary on this"

"Agreed. I think she can look after herself. Who would go with her?"

"Do either of your guys speak English?"

"Ivanov does. Very well."

"Then Sergei Ivanov it shall be. Is he level-headed?"

"I think so. He is in great physical shape and is a gold medallist in martial arts."

"What are his weaknesses?"

"He fancies himself as a great ladies' man, but then what man doesn't?"

"Me. I don't."

"No. But you are special."

54

Harry abruptly got up from the table and went to the window. "Switch off the recorder. Mrs. H. has arrived, so we can have some breakfast. What do you fancy?"

"I don't mind what it is so long as it's food," I said, doing as he instructed. "I'm absolutely starving."

"You know what would be good?"

"What?"

"Steak and eggs."

"Oh, yes."

"I'll get Mrs. H. on the case right away. I like rare steaks at night, but with eggs it can't be pink. You agree?"

"I do. Yes."

"Good. Shall I ask her to fry up some potatoes to go with that?"

"Why not?"

"And mushrooms?"

"Sure."

He left to go and talk with Mrs. Hernandez, and helped speed her along by getting all the ingredients and laying them out on the kitchen table. I watched him through a crack in the doorway, and despite his illness, which slowed him down dreadfully, and his age, 76, I could see that physically Harry was still in better shape than many other men as old as he was.

I thought it tragic that the buildup of unwanted proteins and mysterious changes in brain tissue could render such an otherwise fit and interesting man into someone constantly groping his way through life. The difficulty in finding words or the names of objects and people, problems with grammar and sentence structure, occasional inability to repeat phrases or sentences, and the painful hesitancy and pauses during speech must have been a constant torment to him.

The doctors had said that in time—they could not predict how fast the disease would progress—he would not be able to understand spoken or written language, and eventually have a total loss of the ability to communicate. Selfishly, I hoped I would never see him in that condition; even now it was heart-breaking to watch him.

Mrs. H. produced a magnificent breakfast. I tucked in with gusto, but I was distressed to see that Harry could only finish about half of what was on his plate due to difficulty swallowing, occasional drooling and once almost choking.

He pushed his plate away, gurgled on a cup of coffee, and then put it down. "Let's get on with it," He said slowly, his voice filled with despair and resignation.

Continiuation of the fourteenth taped interview with Harry Posen
Zulla, Virginia, June 6th, 2019

About half an hour after we had given Milton-Jones and Ivanov their marching orders, Tony Aprile got in from the airport. We were glad to see him, but couldn't help laughing at his appearance. It was true. The blast in Halifax had neatly removed all his hair on one side of his head and had turned the skin red. He looked rather like some strange jester at the court of Francis I.

"*Bon Giorno*, Tony," Zina said. "It is good to see you alive, if not exactly in one piece."

"You think it's funny? You shoulda been there. If I didn't know he had a mother someplace, I'd be glad that asshole bought it."

"Was it that bad?" I asked.

"Boss, you got no idea. From the minute we left this building he was giving me grief. Even on the plane going over he refused to abide by protocols that we should keep apart, and kept coming to my seat to tell me jokes. And piss poor ones, too!"

"Sit down, Tony," I said, "and give us your report."

"Can I smoke?"

"If Zina doesn't mind."

"Just this once. If you must."

Tony pulled out a pack of Camels and smoked one after the other as he poured out his account.

"After the aggravation on the plane—during which he was swigging beer like there was no tomorrow—he argued about the connecting flights even though he knew fuck all about them, then, when he finally got to this God-forsaken place, he argued about which cab we should take."

"Go on."

"Then, at the hotel, after we checked in he decided he wanted my room, so I had to lug all my stuff out. During dinner he was loud and letting out stuff about the job, for God's sake, and I could have killed him right there."

"Skip to the day, Tony," I said.

"*Va bene*. We went to this street near the waterfront. The sidewalks were made of brick, if you can believe it, and in the rain—it was tipping down—it was shit slippery. So the idiot decides to go sliding, drawing all kinds of attention to himself."

"Was that the same street where the suspicious property was?" Zina asked.

"Yeah. So we saw this place, Treasure Chest Imports, and the place is in darkness—in the tourist season. That's fishy right there. So I said to the Polack—"

"He's Czech, not Polish."

"Right. So I said to him that it smelled even higher than the fish on the wharf. He called me a *Kočička* and even though I don't speak his lingo I knew it was an insult."

"You were right," Zina said. "It was an insult. It means 'Pussy'."

"Anyway, I told him that I was the principal and we should not force the street door, but carefully look at the building from every angle."

"Quite right."

"He didn't think so. He said I was a *Kočička* again and went ahead."

"What did you do?"

"I let him go. I didn't follow until he called out that it was clear. Even then I crept in on little cat feet, examining everything to see if there were trip wires or anything like that."

"There weren't?"

"Not on the floor or walls. Not that I could see. Then the idiot went to a big desk and said, 'Let's have a look in here.' I shouted, 'No!' and got the hell out of there as fast as I could. I think I dived out of the door."

"And then?"

"That's all she wrote." Tony stroked the naked side of his head. "The place went up like a match thrown into a box of fireworks."

"I take it you didn't hang around?"

"*Assolutamente no, cazzo*! I got myself away to a nearby hotel—I didn't go back to check out of mine—got a cab to the airport and took the first flight out of there. To some place called Fredericton, for God's sake. From there I had to go to Boston, then back here."

"Thank you, Tony," Zina said, "Are you sure you haven't left anything out?"

"I don't believe so. If I think of anything I'll let you know."

"Okay."

"But do me a favour, okay?"

"What's that?"

"Don't send me any place with more Czechs. I had a bellyful of them."

55

𝕸onmouthshire 𝕭eacon

June 21 1985

American style shoot-out and high speed car chase ends in death and mystery

By S. H. Clarke

The peaceful, sleepy back streets of Mediaeval Monmouth and the leafy country lanes around Cross Ash were transformed two days ago into something resembling a real-life action Hollywood movie. These dramatic events occurred on Wednesday between twelve noon and two o'clock, when they came to a sad and mysterious end.

The main actors in this incredible drama were the deceased, a woman who went by the name of Claudia Morgan (her real name is unknown), a Russian named Ivanov, also deceased, and another woman whose identity has yet to be discovered.

These scraps of information I discovered by overhearing conversations between the local Heddlu and the mystery woman at the scene of the crash. When the officers realized I was listening in they quickly shooed me away.

As far as can be ascertained this is what happened.

At about noon the Russian, Ivanov, and the mystery woman went to ancient Glendower Street, for unknown purposes, and were seen breaking into the old, unused, abandoned Congregationalist Church. Then it seems they were disturbed by a woman calling herself Claudia Morgan. Morgan opened fire on the other two, and persons in the vicinity said they heard as many as twenty shots fired.

It was shortly before the shooting that I was in my office in St. James' Square when I was alerted by Mr. Harry Williams of Glendower Street, and urged to rush to the scene. I did so at once and was able to observe the action from the safety of my Mini.

Apparently, the couple were firing back at Morgan who was using a parked car—not her own white Jaguar—as cover. During this Wild West shoot-out, Morgan shot and killed Ivanov, then escaped in her car.

The mystery woman got into her own car (since found to have been a rental vehicle) and followed Morgan in hot pursuit. I followed in my Mini. The white Jaguar sped through the town and up the Rockfield Road, apparently heading for Skenfrith and Grosmont where, presumably, she thought she could lose her pursuer. However, just past Newcastle she took a sharp left on the B4347, then left again on the B4521 making for Cross Ash.

By this time the cars were going at breakneck speed, and at the notorious Cross Ash U-bend in the road near the Dawn of Day turn-off, the Morgan woman lost control of her Jaguar and it madly careened from side to side, eventually crashing into a farm manure wagon opposite The Three Salmons public house and going off the road at high speed into a large tree.

Fortunately, Police Sergeant Tabby Evans and Constable Perce Thomas, were taking lunch in the Three Salmons and emerged on hearing the crash and hurried to the Jaguar. After conducting an examination of the vehicle, Sergeant Evans announced his belief that the driver was dead—something which was later confirmed by an ambulance crew from Nevill Hall Hospital in Abergavenny.

At this point the woman pursuer attempted to unobtrusively turn her car around and return to Monmouth, but Constable Thomas prevented it by stepping in front of the vehicle. No doubt the constable required her to give evidence as a key witness to the crash. The woman got out of her car, took Constable Thomas aside and handed him what looked like an identification document, whereupon Thomas summoned Sergeant Evans, who also examined the document. The two men saluted her and allowed her to leave the scene.

When I asked the Heddlu officers who the mystery woman was and why she had been allowed to depart, they asked me if I had "had one too many pints for lunch" and suggested I "was seeing things." Inquiries to Gwent Police Headquarters in Cwmbran have gone unacknowledged.

Many other questions remain unanswered: Who was the mystery woman? Is she a person of wealth and influence? Is she police? Why did she and the Russian, Ivanov, go to the abandoned church on Glendower Street? What was the shootout all about? What was the real identity of the crash victim, "Claudia Morgan"?

One thing is certain, however, and that is that this ancient town, the birthplace of Henry V in 1386, is unlikely to see another day filled with such excitement and death any time soon.

56

While we were taking a short break, Harry said, "Say, I have something which might interest you."

"Oh. What is it?"

"A souvenir I kept from the Renegade operation."

"Was that legal? I thought all records and documents had to be handed in."

"If it had originally been the property of the United States, then I could have gone to jail for keeping it. But I guess this belonged to Russia. Zina gave it to me."

He went over to his bookcase, pulled down a copy of *War and Peace*, and took out a piece of paper.

"I imagine I can still smell her," he said very sadly, sniffing the paper, "but, of course, it's all in my head. God, how I miss her even after all these years!"

With tears in his eyes he handed it to me.

Всем товарищам и соратникам операции "Ренегат": Это еще раз подтверждает нашу приверженность жизненной важности этого проекта и его успешному завершению. Все руководство Союза Советских Социалистических Республик едино в стремлении к быстрому решению проблемы, поставленной подлыми предателями.

Подпись:
Генеральный секретарь ЦК КПСС Михаил Сергеевич Горбачев.
Виктор Михайлович Чебриков, председатель Комитета государственной безопасности.

"Nice isn't it?"

"I guess," I said, "but what the hell does it mean?"

"Switch your recorder on and I'll tell you."

Continuation of the fourteenth taped session with Harry Posen
Zulla, Virginia, June 6th, 2019

The next couple of days saw a plethora of individual investigations with similar results. Lead in Warsaw: False alarm. Lead in Tangier: False alarm. Lead in Sao Paulo: Nothing. Lead in Rotterdam: *Zilch*. Silkeborg: *Nada*. Marseilles: *Rien*. Tel Aviv: *Bupkus*. It was all very frustrating and depressing. We had taken hits from the enemy but we had not made any scores against them.

Then I saw Zina coming towards my office with a big grin on her face. I hoped the grin meant good news at last.

"Here," she said, handing that very document to me.

"What is it?" I knew a little Russian, but, just like you, I couldn't figure it out.

"My Uncle Vanya came through with the goods."

"Really? Then he's a greater success than Chekhov's Vanya was."

"Indeed. A very depressing character."

"Well, what does it say?"

"Roughly, that Chebrikov and Gorbachev are definitely on the same page, that they are united in wanting 'Renegade' to be brought to a successful conclusion."

"That's a relief. You should show it to Eliska Svoboda."

"I'll do more than that. I'm going to call the Warsaw Pact agents together and read it to them."

"Better to tell everybody. The NATO people need to know, too. Oh yes, and Chun and Hua. We don't want anyone to feel excluded."

"You're right."

We went out into the large room and Zina called for their attention. They were all present except for Milton-Jones, Ivanov, and Putin.

"I have received a communication from the highest level in the Soviet Union and I thought you would want to hear it."

> To all comrades and associates of Operation Renegade: This is to reaffirm our commitment to the vital importance of this project and its successful completion. The entire leadership of the Union of Soviet Socialist Republics is united in its desire for a quick solution to the problem posed by the vile traitors.

> Signed:
> Mikhail Sergeyvich Gorbachev, General Secretary of the CPSU Central Committee
> Viktor Mikhailovich Chebrikov, Chairman of the Committee for State Security

"This makes it clear that the leadership is united on this matter. That's all. Please go back to your work." She gave a pointed glance to Svoboda, who smiled and appeared relieved.

When I returned to my office I saw my phone light was flashing. It was Frau Becker.

"Herr Posen, I have a Sir Christopher Curwen on the line from London."

"Okay, Dorothea, put him through."

"Mr. Posen, do please forgive me for disturbing you, but I felt I had to under the circumstances."

"Hello, Sir Christopher." I could tell by his exaggeratedly courteous manner this would be bad news. "What can I do for you?"

"I have to convey a message to you from Heather Milton-Jones."

"Oh?"

"Yes, she called me yesterday to report an incident attendant upon her investigation in Monmouth."

"Please just tell me what she said, Sir Christopher."

"Certainly. She is now on her way back to Vienna, so will give you a full report, but she asked me to let you know that the mission was a failure and that Sergei Ivanov was killed. Shot."

"Jesus! How did it happen?"

"I know no more than you do, Mr. Posen. I'm sorry to be the bearer of sad tidings."

Zina almost cried when I told her. She and Sergei hadn't been particularly close, but she liked him much more than the other Russian agent on the team, Nikita Bakunin. Mostly, she was downcast because we had sustained another loss with nothing to show for it. Particularly annoying was the fact that, instead of running and hiding, the enemy was arrogantly and repeatedly taunting us with apparent impunity.

I think Oskar must have seen it on our faces when we got back to the Monaco, because as soon as we had washed, changed and seated, he produced a bottle of *Canard-Duchene rosé* Champagne which we devoured, much more quickly than we should have.

It had been a hell of a week, not made any easier to bear by the constant pressure from Moscow Centre and Langley, who tinged their condemnation of our efforts with ridicule. We knew it was only a matter of time before they decided the project needed new leadership.

"Oh, my dear Harry, I don't think I could stand it if they recalled me to Moscow."

"You could defect."

"Could it be done, I wonder."

"If push comes to shove, I could arrange it. It would be much more difficult if we were on the other side of the Iron Curtain."

"I will think about it."

"In the meantime, we can't go on like this."

Her face fell.

"No, I don't mean us. I mean the project. If we go on like this, pretty soon you and I will be the only ones left."

"It is not our fault that our agents are dying like flies. We are dealing with true experts who have built their own organization over time, and with skill. Langley, Moscow Centre, Prague, Warsaw, London and all the others seriously underestimate what we are facing and—you must have noticed it—have not been sending us their best talent."

"No, we sure aren't getting the cream of the crop."

"Sir Christopher told you that Sergei was shot, didn't he?"

"Yes."

"That would suggest a departure from their usual explosive traps."

"We predicted they'd change their MO. We'll find out tomorrow, when Heather reports."

"She's good."

"Yes, but unfortunately she and Gordon—and Lemultier—are exceptions."

We finished the champagne, and ordered a half bottle of Meursault to go with the *Potage St. Germain* we had ordered. We sipped the white Burgundy and quietly toasted our love affair.

"Harry, has it occurred to you that Repnin and Sollows might have someone on the inside?"

"Inside? A spy inside 'Renegade'?"

"Yes."

"Hmm. If they have, I can't think what value they would be, at least at this stage."

"But that person would be of great value if our operation were to go on the offensive at any time in the future."

"Sure would. Do you suspect anyone in particular?"

"I wondered about Kowalski. His being sick in Bermuda could have been an act. It made sure he was miles away when the explosion went off."

"True. I've had my eye on Marcel Labelle. I don't know why, but he looks shifty."

"Yes, he does. But I think if he were corrupt, Louise would be on to him."

"She's dynamite. I wouldn't want to get on the wrong side of her. What do you make of Putin?"

"He's not really a member of the team, is he? He comes and goes as he pleases, and half the time he's missing when we need him. We can't upbraid—is that a word?—upbraid him because he outranks me, and I am sure he thinks he also outranks you."

"I wonder what he does when he's not at headquarters. Do you think we should put a tail on him to see where he goes?"

"It would have to be a good one. Someone who could fade into the crowd."

"I might have a word with Gordon about that."

"Good."

The soup came, beautifully bright green with a swirl of cream. It was delicious. Then we had an *entrecôte de beouf* with tiny potatoes, green beans and morels.

With the main course, we had a half bottle of Volnay 1972. When we were halfway through, Oskar came along to inquire if we approved of the meal.

"Lovely," I said, joking. "Coming here is just like going home to *Muter*."

"Praise indeed. *Danke*." Oskar bowed.

"This is nothing like my home!' Zina said emphatically. "The food here is light years away from the dreadful *ersatz* stuff my mother used to feed me!"

"Fraulein Zina, we will attempt to compensate for those years of deprivation." He bowed again and drifted away.

"If we do succeed with 'Renegade,'" Zina said plaintively, "Do you think you could get President Reagan to talk to Gorbachev to get me released?"

"I talk to the president twice a day, so I'll put in a good word for you." Then I said, "Let's get the job done. Then we can see what is possible."

We sat silently for several minutes, drinking the last of the Volnay. We wanted neither dessert nor coffee today, just each other.

57

Harry did not appear at all the next day, and I assumed his lengthy ex-
ertions of yesterday were responsible. I was getting worried—not only
for Harry's well-being, but also because I had now been in Zulla far
longer than I expected, and was anxious to get home. From the outset I
had not been prepared for the slow and tortuous way our recordings
proceeded, nor for the enormous amount of editing they subsequently
required to deal with the many long pauses and mistakes in choice of
words and phrases.

Harry judged that he was about two-thirds of the way through his
narrative, meaning that I would be here for many days to come. I had
pressing matters to deal with at home, but if I went to attend to them I
did not know when I would be able to return to Zulla. More to the point,
I did not know how much Harry's condition would have deteriorated
in the meantime.

I could not publish a book which told only part of the story, so I
resigned myself to a long stay and hoped for the best.

When it became clear to me that I would not be seeing Harry that
day, I wandered over the field to Gordon Holland's farm to look at the
horses. They were wonderfully friendly creatures, thrusting their
heads over the fence to be scratched and stroked. Surreptitiously, I
slipped them sugar cubes I had stolen from Mrs. Hernandez's kitchen
cupboard, and imagined what their names might be. Given their ancient connection with the Spaniards and Cortes who brought them to
America in 1519, maybe they were called Maria, Pedro, Santiago,
Miguel or Catalina. Alternatively, because they later became favourites
of the Choctaw, perhaps their names were Nahsoba, Talako or Halli.

I chatted for a while with Chester, who spat tobacco juice between
sentences, and told me—at greater length than I needed—that these
horses were different from the wild mustangs found in Nevada. Gordon

had returned from Marshall, Chester said, but had since gone on to Blackstone to "look over some stock."

I ambled back through the country roads admiring the greenness of the fields and the fine cattle, went back and, at random, read snatches of books in Harry's library. I was surprised at the range of his tastes.

I had a little cold supper and, bored, went to bed early.

The next day I was relieved to see Harry looking, and sounding, fairly well, and soon he was again relating his experiences.

Fifteenth taped session with Harry Posen
Zulla, Virginian, June 8th, 2019

At breakfast the next morning, I could tell Zina was agitated about something and was itching to tell me. After the waiter had fussed around the table delivering coffee, toast, eggs and pastries, she leaned across to me.

"Harry,"

"Yes?"

"I think I know."

"Know what?"

"I figured it out in bed last night before I went to sleep."

"Thanks for the compliment!"

"These disasters we've been having," she said, pretending not to understand my joke. "They're not traps."

"Not traps? They sure seemed like it. So what are they?"

"Last night, we discussed the possibility of there being a spy in 'Renegade.'"

"Yes."

"Well, instead of these events being traps, supposing they are genuine leads—genuine in the sense of being sincere, though unfruitful..."

"I think I understand," I said, struggling with her strange use of English. "Go on."

"Okay. The reason our agents have been waylaid has not been because the enemy set traps, but because the enemy was told in advance where they were going to be."

"And a mole would do that!"

"Precisely.

"Well done, my love. You are not only ravishingly beautiful but also extremely brilliant!"

"This I know," she replied with a smug grin. "So you will talk to Gordon today?"

"Yes, I'll ask him to tail everyone."

"Everyone? Even Heather and Louise?"

"Everyone."

"That will require Gordon to set up an entirely different operation."

"Yes. I'll speak to our friend, The Minister of the Interior, Franz Löschnak, and see if he will lend us some bodies."

"Good. Some day you will become a decent officer," she said with a smirk, before munching a jam-covered croissant.

When I got to the headquarters, I called Herr Löschnak and explained my dilemma. He could not have been more helpful and offered full co-operation, saying he would provide, on a short-term basis, ten of his Criminal Intelligence Service (BK) officers, and two rooms on a floor below ours so Gordon could move between locations without difficulty.

Then, when Heather Milton-Jones arrived, I called her and Zina into my office.

"Alright, Heather, please let's have your report."

"The expurgated version or the blow-by-blow version?"

"Give us the expurgated version, then if we need further details we can ask you."

"Right. Bare bones. As soon as we got to Heathrow, Sergei started brushing up against me, and after we got our car and were out on the M4 he suggested we needed to obtain only one hotel room in Monmouth."

"Сволочь!" Zina said.

"Yes, bastard. I told him to forget any notions like that. He let it go for a few miles, then started to stroke my neck saying how much I would enjoy his attentions."

"What did you do?"

"I told him I was a lesbian."

"Are you?"

"No, not that it's any of your business, Zina."

"Извини."

"That's okay. No need to apologize. Anyway he wanted to see

Stonehenge and, as we had plenty of time, I indulged him."

"Then what?"

"After Stonehenge we went to Monmouth—lovely little town—and checked into The Punch House. That evening, when we went down to dinner there was a woman—a real looker—sitting at a corner table. Needless to say, he was eyeing her up all through the meal and, towards the end, he left me high and dry and walked over to her table, sat down and started a conversation with her."

"Just like that?"

"Just like that. I finished my dessert and waited a bit, but noticing they were now drinking Cognac and getting along like a house on fire, I left and went to my room."

"Go on."

"Next morning, on my way to breakfast, I knocked on his door but got no answer. Worried, I snagged a maid—I think she was Filipina—and asked her to unlock the door, and after a lot of sign language, she eventually did."

"And?"

"Empty. Bed not slept in. So I went down to the dining room and there he was—hung over and grinning from ear to ear. He told me he had got off with the woman the previous night, that her name was Claudia Morgan, and that she was a sales rep. for a fashion house.

"Of course I grilled him to find out what he had said to the woman, but he said he couldn't remember because he'd had a lot to drink. So, I ordered him up to his room and gave him seventeen kinds of shit.

"Finally he admitted that he had boasted about who he was and what he was doing in Monmouth, but said he couldn't see what harm it could do."

"What happened then?"

"We went to the site, had a peep inside, found nothing of consequence and prepared to leave. Lover boy was ahead of me, and as soon as he put his nose outside, shots started thudding into the walls. As I whipped out my Glock 17, I caught a glimpse of the Morgan woman crouched down behind a parked car across the street.

"Her fourth shot caught Sergei between the eyes and he went down like a sack of spuds. I got off a few shots but she managed to get to her car—a white Jag—parked a few feet away. She took off like a bat out of hell, whereupon I sprinted to our car and went after her."

"Were you able to catch her?" Zina asked.

"If I had, I would have made sure she stayed alive so we could sweat her for information about who she was working for."

"Quite right."

"We raced through the town, but when she got out into the countryside I lost her, and the next I knew was coming round a bend and seeing her car off the road and smashed against a tree."

"Were the cops there?"

"Very quickly, because they'd been sneaking a few pints in the pub across the road. I hung around until they told me she was dead, then buggered off out of there. I called Sir Christopher and put him in the picture—you know he's my boss—and he said he would call you."

"Thank you, Heather. A good report. Please would you send Gordon in?"

"Now we know!" I said when Heather had left.

"Know what?"

"What their next tactic would be—the Honey Trap!"

"Ah yes. Always works with men like Sergei. Here's Gordon. I'll talk to you later."

~

Gordon was an old-fashioned copper's copper, having been seasoned in war, and familiar with all manner of detection and police work. If he was lacking in looks and youth, he more than compensated for that in knowledge and wisdom.

"What's up, Chief?"

"A delicate matter for your ears only."

"That include my oppo?"

"Your oppo?"

"My opposite number, Heather."

"Yes, I'm afraid it does—for the time being. Are you okay with that?"

"Not comfortable, but orders are orders."

I explained to him what I had arranged with the Interior Minister, stressed that he would be heading an entirely secret and separate operation from 'Renegade', and that he would share his findings only with me.

"Alright, Chief. So what is it?"

"We have a mole."

"Ah-hah!" He exclaimed, tapping his briar on his lower lip. "Any ideas who?"

"Yes, but I'd prefer not to influence your thinking. You start fresh with no preconceptions."

"Fair enough."

"Gordon, be very, very careful. Some of our crew, like Putin, LeMelutier, Heather—and, for all I know, Chun and Hua—are very experienced agents and will have their eyes peeled as a matter of course."

"I understand."

"I'm glad you do. All your people must look and act like they are Austrian police—which they are—doing grunt work, so if they are rumbled it will look as if they are engaged in local crime work."

"Got it."

"And include Becker, Lena, Annika and Johanna in your investigations."

"Will do."

"Surreptitiously find out where all our people are staying, give me the addresses—including room numbers if in hotels—and let me have the list."

"Certainly. Why?"

"When I have the list, I'll arrange with the Minister to have all their phones bugged."

"Good thinking."

"Any questions?"

"Er...where is my...er...other office?"

"Two floors down. Room 17. But you must not be seen going in or coming out. There are backstairs and a side entrance in Haarhof Street."

"Gotcha."

"Good luck, Gordon. Do not fail. We can't afford to lose any more people."

He touched his forelock in mock salute. "Leave it with me, Guvner."

58

Mrs. Hernandez cooked a splendid meal for us that evening. It was roast chicken, roast potatoes, mashed turnip, Brussels sprouts and lovely gravy. She had also made an intriguing stuffing from ground chestnuts, mushrooms and sausage meat. It was quite delicious.

Harry told her not to bother making dessert because, having polished off the chicken and vegetables, we would not have room for it.

To go with dinner, Harry said we needed something special, and disappeared into his cellar. I could hear him stumbling around for about five minutes, and just as I was about to go down to see if he was all right, he emerged holding a bottle encrusted with years of dust.

"I thought it was down there somewhere," he said. "I've looked for it many times but only just now did I discover it behind a case of old Barolo."

"It looks like it's been down there a long time."

"It has. Guess what it is."

"I have no idea."

"Heitz Martha's Vineyard 1964."

"Wow! Is it still drinkable?"

"We'll find out as soon as I decant it."

"Would you like me to do that?" I asked, remembering how he had shaken when he last performed the function.

"No, I'm fine." he said and inserted the corkscrew into the bottle. When he tried to light the candle, his hands trembled so much, he gave up. "You'd better do it. We don't want any accidents with something so precious."

The wine turned out to be wonderful. I remembered having tried it around 1980, when it was still a brutal blockbuster, black as ink and so ferociously tannic that it was impossible to drink. The years had softened it and given it many exquisite dimensions of odour and flavour.

After dinner, Harry said he might be good for another two hours recording, so I cleared the table and set up my machine.

Continuation of the fifteenth taped session with Harry Posen
Zulla, Virginia, June 8th, 2019

I did not bother Gordon for some days and let him get on with the task.

After he left my office, Zina came in carrying a file. "Have you read this?" she asked.

"What is it?"

"Gordon's file."

"I skimmed it when we were first established."

"It's very interesting. Gordon has had quite a history."

"Yes, I got that impression, too."

"He was born in a slum tenement in Nottingham, struggled through grammar school, went into the army and then into the police force. Apparently, he could have become a Chief Constable in one of the county forces, but instead he applied for, and was accepted by, the Special Branch, and from there he went to MI6 because he believed Britain was in danger of an extremist takeover through the Labour Party and the unions. He saw how money was being filtered to various leftists groups in the UK from Moscow and Beijing."

"That is interesting."

"Now here's a note which will interest you. It says here he vigorously opposed being sent to 'Renegade' because he loathed the idea of working alongside communists!" Zina said with a laugh. "But Sir Christopher overruled him and told him to pack his bags and get out here!"

"Has he shown any animosity towards you?"

"Not so far. Maybe he has seen that Communists are not so bad after all."

"It must be because you are so sweet and so kind."

"Quite so." Zina pulled up a chair and sat down. "Harry, why are they doing it?"

"Why are who doing what?"

"Repnin and Sollows. What are they getting out of all this? It can't just be for the money."

"I think they're dangerous lunatics."

"There must be more to it than that. In Valya's case, it could be the thought of having and wielding power. With their resources they could subvert several little third-world countries, if they wanted to."

"With Edgar, it might be the ability to accumulate valuable works of art. I think he would really get his rocks off having all kinds of priceless objects and knowing that nobody could see them except him. Rather like Goering did. The stuff he looted from all over Europe was worth $3.6 billion in today's money."

"That's a lot of art!"

"Tell me, Zina," I said suddenly. "Do you miss him?"

"What on earth do you mean, Harry?" Her eyes flashed.

"You know what I mean."

"How did you know about us?"

"Chebrikov shared Repnin's file with Casey. It was all in there about your affair with him."

"Yes, of course it would be. I should have known."

"How long were you...together?"

"Several years."

"But now it's over?"

"Of course it's over!"

I shouldn't have upset Zina like that, but I needed to know—from her reactions—that she was completely cured of her attachment to Repnin. Of course, you can never be completely sure of things like that, but I had to be reasonably certain that I wasn't sharing her affections with a ghost.

Not much happened during the next few days except for more false alarms, some from as far away as Vladivostok, some as close as Graz.

Nikita Bakunin, the KGB resident from the outset of 'Renegade', was as silent and inscrutable as always, not showing an atom of emotion, even when his buddy Ivanov was killed. Ivanov's replacement, Tatiana Nikolaevna Kuznetsov, arrived and settled in well, although I sensed some tension between her and Zina. Apparently they had known each other at Moscow Centre and although Kuznetsov was a captain and Zina a major, I gathered they had been quite friendly.

Since Zina was not forthcoming with additional information, I could only guess at the problem. They were both very attractive women, so maybe jealousy was involved. Maybe they had even vied for Repnin's attention prior to Zina's winning out.

The Bobbsey Twins, Chun and Hua, had developed into excellent investigators. Louise LeMelutier was a human dynamo, but her fellow DGSE officer, Marcel LaBelle, continued to skulk around the place, avoiding work whenever he could. The GDR replacement for Gerd Mueller, a very young Saxon called Franz Richter, seemed rather over-whelmed by 'Renegade' and completely intimidated by his fellow teammate, Vladimir Putin.

The FRG contingent from Bonn, Karl Mauser and Henrich Bach, was industrious and inconspicuous, and eager to undertake any task assigned to them. Also lively and conscientious were the Czechs from the StB, Eliska Svoboda and Maytyas Cerny. However, the Poles, Jacob Wencell and Maciej Kowalski, were hopeless. When they did agree to undertake a job they usually screwed it up. More than once I toyed with the idea of having Zina call Władysław Ciastoń, the head of the *Służba Bezpieczeństwa in* Warsaw, and ask him to recall Wencel and Kowlaski and send us fresh talent, but Zina advised against it.

It had been almost three days since I gave Gordon Rattenbury his special assignment. I was engrossed in some background files when my phone buzzed.

"Chief, it's me."

"Gordon?"

"Yes. Meet me in the alley behind the building in five minutes."

I walked out of the complex, along the corridor and down the back stairs, and out into the street. Gordon was leaning against a wall, furi-ously puffing on his pipe.

"I thought it better if I wasn't see going into your den."

"What have you got, Gordon?"

"First, Putin."

"Yes?" I was expectant.

"Forget him. When he leaves the office he goes to the movies, swills vodka in a trendy bar, visits massage parlours, sometimes he goes to a gym."

"Nothing suspicious at all?"

"Not a sausage."

"Okay, then who *is* suspicious?"

"Well, all of them are suspicious in their own way. Some visit pros-

titutes, some have lesbian relationships, some have homosexual liais-
ons and so on. One has dubious contacts."

"Who?"

"Annika."

"The secretary who works with Frau Becker?"

"Yes. Her behaviour is not always consistent with those of your run-
of-the-mill Carinthian secretary in the big city."

"How so?"

"She does not mix—socially—with her own kind. She goes to places
where the *Piefke* hang out."

"Germans. What's wrong with that?"

"These are *Ossis Piefke*. East Germans."

"Hm. Even so, it's not necessarily suspicious."

"But she has also occasionally contacted the mole."

"The mole? You know who it is?"

"Certainly I do."

"Then for fuck's sake tell me who it is."

"Mauser."

"Mauser? But he's *West* German."

"I can't help that, Chief, I'm just telling you what I know."

"You're sure?"

"Absolutely 100%. Several times before our team members have
been going out into the field, he has called a number and has been
heard relaying the information."

"What's the number?"

"It's different each time. Herr Loschnak's people say the calls are
made to bars, restaurants, barber shops, that sort of thing."

"Does your set-up downstairs have something soundproof which
can serve as a cell?"

"Give me twenty-four hours and it will have."

"Okay. As soon as you have it ready, get a plain-looking van, grab
Mauser off the street, take him to the cell and sweat the bastard."

"Understood, Chief."

"We must get him to tell us where Sollows and Repnin are hiding
out."

"By whatever means?"

"By whatever means."

59

Sixteenth taped session with Harry Posen
Zulla, Virginia, June 9th, 2019

Mauser was coming out of a pastry shop on the Kohlmarkt when we snatched him.

Gordon had disguised the van as a VWA vehicle—the Vienna Water (Municipal Department 31)—so was able to get away with driving the only vehicle in a narrow street thronged with pedestrians. It was a simple operation, made easier by Mauser having both hands occupied with stuffing a huge *Kouign-amann* into his face. Two guys in Municipal overalls hopped from the back doors and just tipped him in, then bound and gagged him.

Once they got back to headquarters they bundled him up the back stairs and into Room 17. Immediately, they dragged him to the improvised sound-proofed cell, and tied him to a chair. It was here that Gordon intended to conduct the interrogation.

Gordon, and a particularly unpleasant, giant Austrian from the Ministry, questioned him for a day and a half. I was present for the initial session and dropped by from time to time.

Mauser sat on one side of a wooden table with Gordon, the giant—whose name was Elias—and I on the other.

"Do you know why you have been brought here, Karl?" I asked quietly.

"I guess it's some kind of exercise. That or a test."

"No, it's not an exercise, but it may turn out to be a test of your endurance."

"I don't understand."

"You will. And quickly, too. We have caught you having communication with outside persons, passing on information about Renegade's plans. Is there anything you want to tell me about that before we get to the important stuff?"

"I was reporting to my boss."

"I am your boss. What other boss do you have?"

"Hellenbroich, of course."

"Hellenbroich?"

"Yes, he's head of the BDN in Bonn."

"I know who he is. Why were you reporting to him?"

"He wanted to be kept in the loop."

"Well, that'll be easy to clear up. I have to call Heribert shortly to get a replacement for you."

"Why am I being replaced?"

"You went missing. Didn't you know?"

"Missing?"

"Listen, you piece of shit!" Elias jumped in. His voice was extremely loud and threatening. "Tell us where they are!"

"Who?"

"Sollows and Repnin, you bastard!"

"I don't know. I thought that's what all of us were doing. Looking for them."

"Karl," Gordon intervened almost sweetly, "We can do this the easy way or we can do this the hard way. You know very well how it works. I'm going to ask you a great many questions for the rest of the day and tomorrow, and if you don't tell me what I want to know, I shall leave you with Elias. He is not particularly friendly."

"I can see that."

"You will save everyone a lot of time if you start by telling us where Mr. Sollows and *Gospodin* Repnin are."

"I don't know. I swear it."

"Right," I said, getting up. "I'll leave you to it. Let me know if he wises up. I may be back after I've spoken with Heribert Hellenbroich."

"Okay, Chief."

"Gordon, Elais, you have carte blanche with one proviso."

"What's that?"

"Don't kill him."

When I called the BND in Bonn, Hellenbroich was out of the office. They said he was in conference with the Chancellor, Helmut Kohl and the Minister for Special Affairs, Wolfgang Schäuble. I left a message with his secretary to call me when he got back to his office.

It was almost time to go home to The Monaco when the call came through.

"Herr Hellenbroich, you know who I am and something about the project of which I am joint head?"

"Yes, Herr Posen. I have been briefed. And I sent you two of my best men. How are they performing?"

"Henrick Bach seems to be excellent."

"And Mauser?"

"I need a replacement for him."

"Really? What's happened? Is he dead?"

"No, but currently he is being questioned for making unauthorized calls to persons outside the 'Renegade' operation."

"*Scheiße*. That is not good."

"He says he made those calls to you."

"To me?"

"Yes. Did he call you?"

"No, why would he be calling me?"

"That's what I thought. So, he's lying."

"Clearly, although I can't see why he would tell a lie which would so easily be disproved."

"Me neither. I'll let you know if we discover what is behind this lie. In the meantime, may we have the replacement?"

"Certainly. Do you have any glamour on the team, Herr Posen?"

"Er...glamour...er...Major Varenko is very beautiful and the women from England and Czechoslovakia are not bad looking. Why do you ask?"

"I will send you Gisela Munsinger. She used to be a film actor before she joined the service."

"What kind of film actor?"

"Haha! Form your own conclusions. She will be with you tomorrow."

"Um...thanks."

"*Gern geschehen. Auf Wiedersehen*, Herr Posen."

When the team seemed to be engrossed in their work, I slipped out again and went down the back stairs. They were becoming familiar to me. Whereas the rest of the building was spotless and well maintained, these stairs were seldom used and were quite dirty. The brass on the balusters and handrail was tarnished, the paint on the walls peeling, and some of the cove mouldings were badly scuffed and coming away from the steps.

Also, the lighting was poor and very weak, giving a pale yellowish green complexion to everything. I thought this would be an ideal setting for scenes in movies about gangsters or spies. Or, maybe, movies starring Fraulein Gisela Munsinger.

After telling Gordon what had transpired in my phone call with Hellenbroich, we went into the cell to confront Mauser. He looked like hell and it was obvious that Elias had been knocking him about. I frowned at Elias to warn him to ease up and then gave Mauser the news.

"Herr Hellenbroich tells me he has received no calls from you. What do you say to that?"

Mauser looked as if he had been slapped around the face with a twisted towel. He just stared incredulously, wide-eyed, with his mouth hanging open. Either he thought he *had* been talking to Hellenbroich, or he was the best actor in the world.

"I must have been duped. The man told me he was my boss, Hellen-broich."

"Oh yes? Didn't you recognize the difference in the voices?'

"No, the telephone line is not the best and before this I'd only spoken to him once or twice."

"I think you spoke to Edgar Sollow," Gordons said, "and when we confronted you, you gave us the first name you could think of. You panicked and gave us Hellenbroich. It wasn't even a nice try—*ein Schöner Versuch*—was it? A pathetic attempt to play for time. Pathetic."

"Which brings us back to the main question," I said. "Where are Sollows and Repnin?"

"I don't know. *Denn Gott ist mein Zeuge*, I do not know!"

"All right, if that's the way you want to play it, I think it may be time for you to meet another friend of ours."

"Who?"

"You'll find out soon enough."

When I got back upstairs, I went to Zina's office. It was so much nicer and cleaner than mine, with flowers and wall hangings.

"Two pieces of news."

"Oh?"

"One: A former film star—I suspect porno movies—is joining us. Name of Gisela Munsinger."

"You're joking?"

"No, she's Mauser's replacement."

"What's the second piece of news?"

"Mauser says he thought his calls were to Hellenbroich, his boss in Bonn, but I called him and found out it was a lie. He's keeping *schtum* on anything else."

"Impasse?"

"Yes."

There was a long silence, during which I wrestled with my conscience about our next step. I didn't want to do it, but I didn't think I had much choice.

"Zina..."

"Yes?"

"How soon could you get Dr. Nolkin here?"

"It's come to that?"

"Yes. I think so."

"I'll call Moscow now. If he's not out of town on assignment, he could get here in five or six hours."

"Please do it."

"Alright, if you're sure."

"There's no other way."

60

I interrupted Harry because I needed to be reminded who Dr. Nolkin was, and I wanted the information clearly on the record. He said he would tell me later, but that this seemed a good point at which to take a break.

He got up and stumbled down the passage and out onto the lawn. I decided not to go with him, as he seemed to want to be alone. I watched him make a circular tour of the flower beds, then he tottered down to the back fence and clung on to it for support as he looked out at the field.

It must have been about twenty minutes before he came back and sat down heavily.

"Okay." He motioned towards the recorder.

Continuation of the sixteenth taped session with Harry Posen
Zulla, Virginia, June 9th, 2019

Dr. Nolkin was not someone I knew. I'd never heard of him until Zina mentioned him one day. She told me he was a legendary figure in the KGB who had the rank of major but who normally only took orders from the very top. He was a scientist—a doctor of chemistry and pharmacology—who was also a medical doctor. Zina told me he'd been a leading researcher into SP-117, a successor to other drugs used by the KGB which were effective in making a subject lose control of himself but would have no recollection of what had occurred.

Apparently others had tried administering the drug in various drinks, but Nolkin believed that injecting the subject was quicker and more effective. Zina told me that, judging by the screams reported by guards stationed outside his injection locations, he didn't inject the concoction into the usual places on the body.

Nolkin didn't reveal the precise contents of his injections, but said

they were thought to be some combination of ethanol, scopolam-
ine, quinuclidinylbenzilate, midazolam, nirazepam, sodium thiopental
and amobarbital. I'm not sure I'm pronouncing those right, or that
you'll ever have heard of them—I sure hadn't—but you get the idea.

I'm not sure what I expected—some kind of huge Frankenstein figure, I guess—but when he arrived later that day he was a tiny, very
quiet, extremely polite individual, dressed in a smart black suit, well
shined black shoes, a black homburg, spotless white shirt and a polka
dot bow tie.

Zina had arranged for us to meet him in a café on Herrengasse so the
others would not see him, and then we took him round to the alley, and
up the back stairs to Room 17.

As soon as we'd introduced him to Gordon, we got the hell out of
there. Call us cowards, but neither of us wanted to hang around to see
or hear the effects of Dr. Nolkin's ministrations upon Karl Mauser.

The next morning I tapped on the door at Number 17 and Gordon
let me in. It was very quiet and deserted.

"Where's Dr. Nolkin?"

"He's long gone, Chief."

"Where to?"

"Moscow."

"When did he go?"

"3:26 this morning. Washed his hands, put his coat on, called a taxi
and went straight to the airport."

"Well, what was his report?"

"He says Mauser does not know where Sollows and Repnin are."

"Is he sure?"

"He says there is absolutely no room for doubt."

"Shit."

"He also says that Mauser really did believe he was talking to
Heribert Hellenbroich and taking instructions from the West German
BND."

"Oh, my God! The poor bastard."

"Don't worry, Chief. Apart from some severe tenderness in the gen-
ital region, Mauser won't think anything happened after we questioned
him. We gave him a sedative before Nolkin arrived. He has no idea the
good doctor was even here."

"Good job, Gordon. Tell him our information was wrong, that we're sorry we doubted him, and that he should take some well-earned leave and go home to Bonn."

"Will do, Chief. When should I say he might be coming back?"

"Let's leave that open. His replacement has already arrived. Tell him we'll be in touch."

~

When I told Zina about the developments on the lower floor, she frowned and shook her head.

"What's wrong?"

"It's too easy."

"How do you mean?"

"If you were Valya and Edgar, what would you think we would think?"

"You're not making any sense."

"My English is not always perfect."

"Try again."

"If you were them, wouldn't you think we would be suspicious?"

"In what way?"

"That we would suspect we had a mole and would try to find out who it was."

"Ah."

"So, why not provide one?"

"On a plate?"

"What is this plate? Harry, we are not talking about food."

"'On a plate' means presented nicely."

"Yes, nicely presented. That is what I am saying. We were meant to find this mole."

"But—"

"They would not know that we would bring in Dr. Nolkin."

"And if we continued to think Mauser was a real mole we wouldn't look any further."

"Yes. And that means—"

"The real mole is still in place."

"Yes."

"Could it be Anikka?"

"Maybe, but I don't think so. She is around the office, but is she privy to our field operations?"

"No."

"So, who is it? Are we back to Labelle or Kowlaski?"

"Maybe. How did we first get on to this mole business?"

"I don't know. I think you came up with it over dinner."

"It didn't start with one of your sources?"

"No, I don't think so. In any case I'd stopped accepting information from Kimberly—"

"Aha! So his name is Kimberly!" She gave a triumphant laugh.

"Damn! One point to you."

"What about the other source?"

"No, I'm sure I never got any intelligence from him on the possibility of a mole."

"Should you ask him what he knows?"

"I might..."

At that moment, Frau Becker tapped on the door.

"Herr Posen, a call from Herr LaCusta in Langley. Line four."

"Thank you, Dorothea. Phil, what's shaking?"

"Not a helluva lot, Harry. I heard about your latest screw-up. Gunfights in the street and all."

"Thank you for your concern, Phil. How can I be of service to you?"

"It's what I can do for you. Got a little tip for you."

"Not Kimberly? You know I won't act on anything we get from him unless it's corroborated by other sources."

"No, Not Kimberly."

"Who?"

"Sphinx. He says you might have a little, furry creature embedded in your outfit."

"That's old news. It's been dealt with."

"Really? Good for you Harry."

"When did this come to you, Phil?"

"I was away for a couple of days with John and the Chief. We had to go to Camp Peary, to The Farm. It was on my desk when I got in today. Sorry about that, but there was nobody with clearance to decode it."

"That fits."

"What fits?"

"Oh, nothing. Thanks, Phil."

"What's going on, Harry?" Zina asked after I had hung up.

"Right on cue, my boss called with a tip about the mole from the very source we were just talking about."

"No!"

"You might as well know that the other source is called Sphinx. We're a team, so let's not play these games anymore."

"I agree."

"Remarkable, isn't it? That information came to Langley three days ago."

"Three days? We know now that Mauser's being a mole was false, a plant—a distraction—but we did not know that three days ago."

"No. We didn't."

"So this intelligence should have reached us about the time we first thought that Mauser was –how do you say—fishy?"

"Yes. And if it had reached us then we would have seen it as corroboration, and therefore we would have been much more inclined to believe he was a genuine mole."

"And without Dr. Nolkin's findings, we would not even have questioned it."

"That must mean that there is a link between Sphinx and the enemy. Could it be that somehow Sollows and Repnin are tapping into Sphinx's messages before they get to Langley? Would that even be possible?"

"Or maybe they, too, are clients or customers of Sphinx and that he is getting paid twice for the same intel?"

"Holy cow! That would take some nerve! If either customer found out, retribution could be terminal."

"Who is Sphinx, Harry?"

"I don't know."

"What?"

"I've never known. He's very big stuff."

"Somebody must know. If we could reach him, maybe he could lead us to the enemy."

"John MacMahon might know. If not him it would have to be Casey."

"Call LaCusta back, Harry."

I checked my watch and figured it was about four in the afternoon in Washington, so Phil would not have gone home yet.

"Phil."

"You must be psychic."

"Why?"

"I was just about to call you again."

"What about?"

'Sphinx."

"That's why I was calling you."

"Harry, the files have gone walkabout."

"*What*?"

"They've disappeared. I was starting to smell a little rodent and went to Central to do some digging and, pouf, they were gone!"

"Computer?"

"Wiped."

"Holy shit! What were you looking for?"

"I wanted to find out who the son of a bitch was."

"Who?"

"Sphinx."

"You didn't know."

"No."

"Why didn't you ask the Chief?"

"Casey? How the fuck would he know?"

"Didn't he bring Sphinx in?"

"Christ, no. It was before Casey joined the Agency."

"And you don't know who originally brought him in?"

"No."

"Who ran him?"

"I did."

"And you didn't know who he was?"

"No. It was strictly 'need to know'. You know how uptight these people can be. Apparently there was a rule established—I don't know when—that only the finder should know the identity. To cover their asses. That's why I was digging. I wanted to find out."

"Dear God. I think I'm going insane."

"*You* are? The Director's blood pressure is through the roof. Not a fucking word in the place on his two top informants."

"Hold it, Phil. Did you say *two* top informants? Who's the other one?"

"Kimberly."

"His stuff is gone too?"

"Yes."

"Shit! Who ran Kimberly?"

"Sollows until he disappeared, then me."

"Did he find him and bring him in?"

"Yeah."

"What the fuck is going on, Phil?"

"Fucked if I know. But I'm going to find out!"

"How?"

"I'm going to see Dick Helms."

"Is he still alive?"

"And kicking. He's only 72. He was Director here from '66 until '73. He was boss when Kimberly was brought in. I'm going to see him to-morrow."

"Where does he live?"

"He retired to Maine. He's driving down tomorrow."

"Phil…"

"What?"

"For Christ's sake, get Helms protection immediately. These bas-tards are capable of anything."

61

Time was marching on and my bills, rent payments and correspondence were piling up at home. It was giving me a nasty, almost sick feeling when I thought about it.

The more Harry taxed his brain and body, the pricklier he got, so I dared not ask him when he thought he might be finished. I debated with myself whether it would be best if I just threw in the towel and headed out.

But I sensed that there was more of Harry's story behind him than there was ahead. In Churchill's words, it was not the end, nor was it the beginning of the end, but it was the end of the beginning. So I knew I would have to hang on until the end, which I hoped would not be bitter for either of us.

When he came down the next morning I could tell he was in no mood for small talk, so I kept my mouth shut and ate my eggs in silence. Harry only managed a piece of buttered toast, on which he choked and involuntarily drooled over. He turned away, his face contorted with rage and embarrassment.

At length, he turned back to me. "Let's do it."

Seventeenth taped session with Harry Posen
Zulla, Virginia, June 10th, 2019

The day after Phil told me he would be meeting with Dick Helms, we all had a nasty shock. Hua Zhou and Franz Richter came into my office, where Zina and I were having a cup of tea. They were in high spirits because they said that they had just calculated that we had circulated 50,000 copies of Sollows and Repnin's photographs around the world.

"Fifty thousand? That doesn't seem possible," Zina said.

"Is true!" Little Hua said, uncharacteristically bouncing up and down with what looked like joy.

"It will be just a matter of time before some policeman somewhere recognizes one of them and we will have them!" said Franz.

"Good work, gang," I said.

As everyone knows, pride cometh before a fall, and ours couldn't have cometh any quicker, because Rattenbury soon appeared in the doorway with a face like a bulldog chewing a wasp.

"What is it, Gordon?"

"The news is not good, I'm afraid,"

"I knew it. You're always the bearer of bad tidings."

"Sorry to rain on your parade, but you'd better have a look at this."

He handed me a copy of a Swiss newspaper dated some weeks before. It was in French and, since my command of the language is only fair, I asked him to give me a translation.

"It's a report of the murder—actually it looks like a double murder —in Pully. That's near Lausanne in Switzerland."

"What's that got to do with us?" Zina asked.

"The first body was that of a Dr. Reynaud and the second was his assistant, a Dr. Scheel, both killed within an hour or so of each other."

"So?"

"Dr. Reynaud is—or rather, was—one of the top plastic surgeons in the world."

"I'm starting to feel sick," I said. "Go on, if you must."

"According to clerical staff at Reynaud's clinic, immediately before their deaths they had been working on two men, neither of whom had been seen by anyone other than the surgeons."

"Do we have any idea of the extent of the changes made to their appearances?"

"One of his secretaries said the operations were conducted over the best part of a week, but that they had some work done a few months previously."

"*Oy gottenyu!* What about records?"

"Conveniently destroyed in an explosion."

"Shit!" Zina said, drawing surprised glances from the others.

"They paid in Swiss francs by way of a series of cashiers' drafts on a Geneva bank. Naturally, we can't find out the name on the account."

"Even if we could, it wouldn't tell us where they are."

"Take away the confidentiality of the banking system, and the Swiss have very little left to bolster their economy," said Gordon philosophically.

"So," Zina said with a long, troubled sigh, "we have no idea what the enemy looks like today."

When they left the office, I looked up at the calendar. It was June 29th. Only one day to go to the end of the month. The enemy had never been precise with the timing of their ultimate threat nor what their optimum target might be, but for some time I'd had this feeling that once we were into July, the time for procrastination would be over. The only thing that could save us, I thought, was a great big lucky break.

Maybe it wasn't as big a break as I wanted, but progress was made when I heard back from Phil. I had been working late and was just about to put my jacket on and go back to The Monaco when my private line light flashed. Zina was still in the office, so I signalled to her to pick up and listen in.

"Just had lunch with Helms," Phil said, getting straight to the point.

"Where'd you take him—The Oval Room?"

"No, Mr. K's."

"On K Street?"

"Exactly."

"Didn't know you liked Chinese."

"I don't, but I'd heard that Helms did."

"Just the two of you?"

"No, I had to take Casey along. Without him, Helms might not think I had enough authority."

"Smart move on your part."

"Fortunately, the Director let me do all the talking."

"Smart move on *his* part."

"Glad you think so. Anyway, stay with me and I'll try to give it to you as it unfolded."

"Okay."

"So I said to Helms that I was gonna bounce a few things off him and get his reaction. He said okay, go ahead. So the conversation went like this:

"Kimberly."
"Good product, but expensive."
"Who brought him in?"
"Edgar Sollows."

"Who ran him?"

"Sollows did, naturally."

"Did it automatically follow that the finder would do the running?"

"Not always, but often it seemed logical."

"How did Sollows find Kimberly?"

"Let me think. Yes, we got a tip from the cousins—"

"The British?"

"Yes. They said there was a big fish on the market, but that they didn't have the budget for it. They figured if they gave him to us, they could share in the product—at least that part of it which affected them."

"Do you know who he is?"

"Sure, I do."

"Who is he?"

"Bill, is it okay if I tell him?"

"Casey said it would be fine and to go ahead and tell me."

"Antonin Zatopek."

"Zatopkek? Is that the Czech?"

"Yes, Deputy Ambassador in London, but really Alojz Lorenc's man in the UK."

"No wonder we got good stuff from him"

"Yes. Still getting quality goods?"

"We're not so sure."

"Too bad."

"Let me try another one on you."

"Okay, fire away."

"Sphinx."

"That was at the tail end of my term at the Agency, but as I recall, he was also good and not as expensive as Kimberly."

"What was his specialty?"

"I wasn't directly involved, but my recollection is that he was your basic corroborator. He was used to double check our material from other sources."

"Was he Russian?"

"I never knew. Apparently, he was well-placed somewhere

within the Warsaw pact. His input helped us to determine the worth of any intel which seemed either kooky or dynamite."

"Okay. Who is Sphinx?"

"I don't know."

"What?"

"I was on the way out, Phil, I didn't need to know, so I didn't. You could ask whoever ran him after I left."

"That was me."

"And *you* didn't know?"

"That's really interesting," said Helms, grinning.

"Why?"

"The finder being the only one to know."

"Who was the finder?"

"Do you believe in the theory of circularity, Phil? Things, events, people moving in circles and everything comes back to where it started."

"Sounds like a deeply flawed theory to me. But what's the point?"

"It's just that I was present when Sollows announced the discovery of Sphinx."

"*Sollows* found Sphinx?"

"No."

"I'm confused. Then who did?"

"Kimberly. Kimberly brought him to us."

"Fuck me!"

'Exactly!"

"But you told me some time ago that Zatopek wasn't one of our assets."

"I didn't know then that he was. I was only vaguely aware of the guy's existence. When you asked me about some report in a British newspaper by—what's his name?"

"Pincher. Chapman Pincher."

"Yeah, if Pincher was right that he was a NATO spy and he wasn't a Brit asset, he had to be working for the French or West Germans."

"Where the hell does that leave us, Phil?"

"Let me know when you find out."

Zina and I looked at each other in amazement. We couldn't get our heads around what we had heard.

After the call ended, she frowned deeply. "When was Zatopek murdered?"

"I'll have to look it up…er…yes, the report was on June 11, so he would have been killed on the 10th," I said.

"That's eighteen days ago."

"That's right."

"Are any bells in your head, Harry?"

"What kind of b…oh, shit!"

"Yes, my darling. We have been getting intel from Kimberly—"

"After he was dead!" I said.

"Indeed. So if he could not be giving us info because he was no longer in the land of the living, who the fuck was sending it to us?"

"*Farshiltn! Farshiltn!*" I was mad as hell.

"The conclusion is inescapable. Messages from Kimberly have been coming from Valya and Edgar."

"Which means that the tips *were* traps after all—"

"Yes, and that they guessed—or knew—that we would bring in Dr. Nolkin and find out that Mauser was innocent—"

"So we would think there was another mole and throw the whole operation into a paranoiac chaos," I said.

"They are diabolically clever. More clever than either of us thought."

"The dirty bastards!"

"Let's go home, Harry, I need a drink."

"I need more than one."

62

"Speaking of drinks," said Harry, motioning for me to turn off the recorder, "I could do with one right now. To perk me up."

"Physically or mentally?"

"Both, but heart sickness, too."

"I guess talking about Zina always makes you sad."

"You have no idea. Even thirty-five years later it hurts. It hurts more than this goddamn disease."

"I think you'd better have that drink. I'll fetch it for you. What will you have?"

"Scotch, single malt. The Dalmore 12 year old Sherry Cask. Will you join me?"

"Oh no, it's much too early in the day for me."

"It's past four."

"Good God. I had no idea. In that case I might try a small drop. Will you have yours neat or take it with something?"

"An ice cube and a little soda, please. I don't agree with the so-called 'experts' who say it has be drunk with water. I think the bubbles bring out the flavour of the whisky better."

"I agree with you. Dalmore sounds good. I'll have the same."

I went into the room where Harry kept his liquor on top of a fine, polished cabinet. He had just about everything any guest could want, although I would rather imbibe battery acid than some of them, like Ouzo, Chartreuse (green and yellow) and Drambuie. The thought of these concoctions made me shudder, so I took the Dalmore, soda and glasses to the table and poured them out there.

I poked my head around the kitchen door to ask Mrs. Hernandez for some ice and found her preparing a magnificent rank of lamb for our dinner.

"How you and Mr. Harry like it? Good or bleeding?"

"I think we both prefer it pink—not quite bleeding."

"*Mierda*! Do you want your potato no cook too?"

"Now, Mrs. H. You know very well we like them *asado*."

"*Si*." She sighed. "I got coliflor to go with. Is alright?"

"Yes, that will be fine, thank you Mrs. H. Please may I have some ice, *hielo*."

"Sure." She pulled a tray out of the freezer and passed it to me. "Mr. Heremy, you like Mr. Harry, no?"

"Yes, I do like Mr. Harry."

"Is so *triste* that he is going to die, no?"

"It is very sad, Mrs. H., but he will not die today."

"No, señor, not today."

"Maybe not for many months. Maybe another year. Possible two?"

"You think?" She brightened up, giving me a big smile. "Me and Hernandez, we worry about our jobs."

"I'm sure you do," I said. I picked up the ice and took it into the next room.

At first, I was annoyed that Mrs. H's sadness was more about herself and her husband than about Harry, but then I thought I was not much better than them, worrying if he would last long enough to allow me to finish the book.

I mixed the drinks and, reflecting that in labour law a decision could simultaneously be motivated by both legitimate and unlawful reasons, took them to Harry.

"Mrs. H. is cooking rack of lamb."

"Oh, goody!" Harry cried. "That means we will have to have another great wine. What do you suggest?"

"Do you have any *Château Pichon Lalande*?"

"Yes, I have some 1982. Will that do?"

"Wonderful. Why don't you take a break while I go and decant it? Mrs. H. says dinner will be ready about seven."

"Sounds good. Better still, why don't you just keep the recorder running? That way you can take all the time you need. And I won't feel embarrassed about speaking so slowly."

I switched on the machine and went to take care of the wine.

I had not actually been down in Harry's cellar before and was surprised it was so small. Although shelf space was limited, it was loaded with quality bottles from all over the world, especially France, California and Italy. A few bottles of *Vega Sicilia* were all he had from Spain, and two bottles of 1977 Graham's port from Portugal.

I took my time decanting the *Château Pichon LaLande* as there was a lot of sediment in the bottom of the bottle, which I knew would make the drinking unpleasant unless I excluded it, and because I sensed Harry wanted me to stay away longer.

It was almost seven when he tottered in, saying he was "done in" and didn't know how to switch off the recorder.

I went in and saw that the tape had run off the reel, so I put it back on, rewound it, then rejoined Harry, who was sniffing the decanted wine appreciatively.

Continuation of the seventeenth taped session with Harry Posen
Zulla, Virginia, June 10th, 2019

Zina was fretting even more than usual the next day and decided to call the troops together to see what, if any, ideas they might have. Clearly, she thought, the top-down management model was not working well for us, and she was right. After all, it was the agents who were putting their lives on the line, not Zina and I, and it was quite possible some of them had thought of something we had not.

"We've lost four of our own people, in addition to a local agent who was assigned to us." She addressed a full house—even Putin was present. "We have travelled thousands of miles, spent enormous amounts of money and we have little to show for it except evidence which shows how naïve we have been and how many times we have been fooled. We now know that several previously-credible sources have been corrupted and can no longer be relied upon. We are also fairly certain that both Valentin Repnin and Edgar Sollows have had extensive plastic surgery and no longer resemble their photographs— all of which must be withdrawn."

There was a loud groan throughout the room.

"Yes, withdrawn immediately. We have seriously underestimated the enemy's preparedness, the extent and efficiency of their organiza- tion, and the deviousness of their thinking. Mr Posen and I would like to receive your ideas. If you are able, please keep your comments pos- itive—not because we can't handle criticism, but because time is of the essence."

"Why is time of the essence?" asked little Chun Chen.

"We can't say for sure, but Mr. Posen thinks—and I agree with him —that the enemy is planning something big and that it will happen soon—unless we can stop it."

"How soon?" asked Jacob Wencel.

"We don't know. Mr. Posen's instincts—"

"Instincts!" Putin snorted.

"I know, I know, Vladimir Vladimirovich, you cannot take instincts to the bank, but he has a strong feeling something will happen in July."

"But that's tomorrow!" Louise LeMelutier cried.

"Exactly. So if any of you have any ideas, let us have them."

"Please to excuse." Gisela Munsinger stood up at the back, causing a gasp from some of the men who turned around to look at her. In her early thirties, she looked like someone who had just walked off the ramp at Yves St. Laurent. "I am new to be here, so is perhaps not right I should speak."

"No, no, Gisela, go ahead."

"Do I understand it to be right that, before today, we have been— how do you say—*reagieren*?"

"Reacting."

"*Ja*, reacting."

"That is so," said Mattayas Cerny, springing to his feet. "We vait here until something comes in, then we go investigate and then we get val- loped!"

"I think that is something of an exaggeration," Zina said, "We will still have to check out leads which come in, taking more care to protect ourselves. But if we did less of that kind of work, what would we be doing instead? What is the alternative?"

"We go to them," said Gordon very quietly.

"Take the battle to the enemy," Tatiana said.

"Take the initiate, the offensive," piped up the usually silent and sullen Marcel LaBelle.

"And how do we do that?"

"Please tell us more about the personal habits of these men, their tastes, their pursuits, and particularly their weaknesses," said Heather Milton-Jones.

"*Da*, weaknesses. Идите за слабостями! That is the way!" Putin's intervention was uncharacteristically enthusiastic.

"Alright," Zina said. "Repnin is vain. He loves fines clothes, expensive cars, superb food—"

"A capitalist!" Putin sneered.

"But above all, Repnin is an opera freak—something like myself—who absolutely, fanatically, adores opera."

Tony Aprile broke out in a surprisingly good tenor voice.

La Donna e mobile. Qual piuma al vento
Muta d'accento, E di pensiero

"Very good Tony." Zina said. "*Grazie tanto.*"

"*Prego.*" Tony took a little bow.

"When did you last go to the opera, Zina?" asked Franz Richter.

"Good point. I will go as soon as I can."

"Both opera houses stop performances for summer recess next week," said Henrick Bach. "You better go soon."

"Thank you Henrick. I shall do as you suggest."

"Can I come with you?" asked Nikita Bakunin.

"Maybe some other time, Nikita Andreiovich. Now, back to business. Harry, can you tell us about Sollows?"

"He is also extremely vain," I said, "and he is a snob who loves fine art, an expert on food and wine. He is used to very expensive things."

"So what are we waiting for?" Louise shouted. "Let's contact the best restaurants, galleries, showrooms, suit makers, and wine merchants in the world and see if they had any mysterious new, very rich, clients in—when was this plastic surgery done?"

"Nineteen days ago"

"In the last two weeks. No, allowing for recovery time maybe only one week."

"Yes, that makes sense. I could not have said it better myself," said Zina. "Louise, you and Nikita decide which places to contact and designate agents accordingly."

"*D'accord. C'est ci bon, Madame!*"

"Thank you, everyone. Get your marching orders from Lousie and Nikita. Let's hope the new approach brings results."

"Very soon," I added.

63

"That was a lovely drop of *Pichon Lalonde* last night," said Harry the next morning. "I hope it didn't embarrass you when I was drinking it."

"No, not at all," I said, although, in truth, it had.

"Not even with the lamb? I have to admit that I committed something of a social solecism there. This disease has turned me into a very sloppy eater."

"The lamb was superb. It's too bad you weren't able to enjoy more of it."

"Increasingly, I'm losing control of the throat muscles. I've tried eating softer foods and taking smaller bites, but I've only had limited success."

"I wish there was something I could do to help."

"So do I. I sometimes think the people around me suffer almost as much as I do because they feel so helpless."

"Do you feel up to recording a little more today?"

"No. But let's do it anyway."

Eighteenth taped session with Harry Posen
Zulla, Virginia, June 11ᵗʰ, 2019

It was a joy to watch and hear Louise and Nikita handing out the assignments the next day. Usually the office was fairly quiet, but now it was buzzing. The mood of the place had changed as we finally felt more like the pursuers than the pursued.

Louise told each agent to contact his or her national domestic security service (the equivalents of the FBI and MI5) and have them check out specially-targeted exclusive retail outlets for unusual activity during the past week. They were not to ask for, but to demand on pain of prosecution, information on any particularly abnormal or expensive purchases or, in the case of restaurants, bookings. If the results were affirmative then our people would be dispatched to the scene to investigate. We had assurance from the top that there would be no intra-agency rivalry or troublesome lines of jurisdictional demarcation.

Names I had only read about were humming through the air as Louise called them out, and the agents immediately got on their phones. I heard Gagosian Galleries mentioned, along with Hauser and Wirth and David Swirner of New York, Perrotin of Paris, and Victoria Miro in London.

Nkita, pronouncing them atrociously, shouted the names of bespoke tailors such as Gieves and Hawkes and Henry Poole of Saville Row, along with Dege and Skinner and Anderson and Sheppard in London. Even shirt makers Turnbull & Asser and shoemakers Loeb were called out and acted upon.

The wine merchants Berry Brothers & Rudd and Corney and Barrow were on Louise's list, as were Lavinia, known for its massive selection, and historic retailers like LeGrand Filles and La Cave des Papilles and Le Garde Robe.

Famous two- and three-star Michelin restaurants to be contacted included Alian Ducasse at the Plaza Athenee, Arpège, Le Pre Catalan and Amador in Paris; Le Gavroche in London; The Waterside Inn at Bray; and Steirereck im Stadtpark in Vienna.

Nor was tobacco left out of the mission, given Repnin's strange tastes, and La Civette and Tabac du Palais in Paris and Pfeifen Fischer in Vienna were flagged for early investigation.

"And have you done your part yet?" I asked Zina, who was sitting on a desk, listening to the hubbub and smiling at the welcome activity.

"What do you mean, Harry?"

"Have you got your ticket for the opera? You've only got today and tomorrow."

"Damn! I forgot!" she cried. "They'll be all sold out for the final gala show on Tuesday. There may be some left for tonight's performance. I must go immediately!"

She rushed out, her heels click-clacking like a typewriter as she went. A laugh went up from the crew and cat calls in a variety of languages followed her out.

It was about an hour later that I looked up and saw Zina, white as a sheet, trembling and clutching the door frame for support. Heather, who was nearby rushed to her and led her to a chair.

I went over, worried that she was seriously ill. "What is it, Zina?" I said. "Tell me darling, what's happened?"

Heather gave me a surprised look, and tactfully moved away.

"I have seen him," she said, her voice hoarse and wavering.

"Seen who?"

"Valya."

"No! Where?"

"We've sent people all over the world looking for him and he is here in Vienna!"

"Where did you see him?"

"At the *Staatsoper*. He was no more than fifteen feet away from me."

"Take your time. Tell me everything."

"There were huge, long lines of people waiting to buy tickets and I was stuck in a slow-moving one. Two blasted Italian tourists who could speak no German were holding everything up.

"I was thinking I would be stuck there until midnight when I heard a voice saying, 'No, no, no, I do not want a seat in the centre of the *parterre*. I want a chair in the lowest possible loge.' I froze, because instantly I knew the voice. Then it went on, 'I don't care about the singers and the sets. I want to see the conductor!' Then I knew for sure it was Valya."

"Did you see where the voice was coming from?"

"Yes, it was a much younger, darker Valya with a finer nose and wider mouth. I would not have recognized him from sight alone, Harry, but the voice was unmistakable."

"What did you do?"

"When the tourists had finally got their tickets, I paid for mine and turned around slowly, holding my hand over my mouth to hide my face. There he was, standing in the foyer. I could even see the red stripe on his ticket—the stripe tells you the seat does not have a full view of the stage—and I watched him put it in his pocket."

"Did you follow him?"

"Yes, at first. I tailed him to the street, but then I thought I might blow it, because he is a highly trained operative and knows when he is being followed. If he intended to use his ticket, I figured, we would know where to find him and would be prepared."

"Smart thinking," I said and called Rattenbury over to tell him what had happened.

"Zina, are you absolutely sure?" Gordon asked. "The man is a thorough-going professional. What are the chances he would show himself in public and draw attention to himself by arguing with a ticket clerk?"

"Opera is his great love. He's a fanatic," she said, "And I never met anyone else who insists on the worst seat in the house just so he can see the conductor. He had another face, but it was his voice."

"Dorothea," I called out to Frau Becker, who came across and joined us.

"What's going on?"

"Dorothea, could you please get us a floor plan of the Staatsoper and a list of how many red stripe seats have been sold?"

"Give me twenty minutes," she said.

No sooner had Frau Becker left, than Zina and I were both called to our offices to take incoming calls. To my considerable surprise, my call was from the Director.

"Posen, Casey here."

"Yes, sir."

"You don't need me to tell you to get your ass in gear and get this job done."

"No, sir."

"So I'm gonna tell you to get your goddamn ass in gear and get the fucking job done!"

"Yes, sir—"

"Posen, the President just got another threat from those bastards. Message can't be traced, obviously. Says their patience is running out and that we should ante up the money very soon."

"Sir, we have just had our best lead to date."

"Oh yeah? How many agents' lives will this cost?"

"I hope none, sir. We had a positive sighting of Repnin today—"

"Where?"

"Right here in Vienna."

"Did you, by Christ? So?"

"We're pretty sure we know where he will be tonight at a certain time—"

"Where's that?"

"Sorry, sir, that info is on a need to know basis."

"Enjoyed saying that, didn't you?"

"Kind of. We will be there ahead of time. The big problem is that it is a public place and there'll be lots of people around."

"Argh! For Christ's sake, don't be killing civilians, Posen."

"I'll try not to, sir."

"What time will that be?"

"About five hours from now. Shall I call you direct when we get a result?"

"Hell no, my wife is dragging me off to some dinner party. Call John McMahon or LaCusta."

As I heard the line go dead, I looked up and saw Zina. She still looked a little shaky but the colour had come back to her cheeks.

"I just got a call from Chebrikov."

"Me, too. I mean, I got a call from Casey."

"I'm guessing it was the same message."

"Yeah. Get the job done or else."

"In your case, the 'or else' would only mean demotion. In my case it could mean Siberia, or a shot in the back of the head in the cellar of the Lubyanka."

"Don't even joke about such things. Besides, we're going to nail the bastard tonight."

We went out into the main office and saw Gordon, Nikita, Gisela, Eliska and Louise poring over a large plan which Frau Becker had laid out on the table.

"If what you say is true, Zina," Gordon said, "then we figure he will have to be sitting in one of four seats—two on each side. These are the only red striped seats that have completely unobstructed view of the conductor."

"But apart from having sharpshooters from the Austrians stationed in these balconies," Eliska pointed, "we dare not have anyone close to him. Even if he didn't see them, a trained professional would sense their presence."

"Harry, we think you and Zina should place yourselves up here where you can duck behind the curtain if you need to." Gisela said.

"Okay."

"We can put our people—two each—here, here, here and here to try to grab him when he leaves," Louise said.

"But once he get past of us and into crowd in foyer, it will be difficult to nail him," Nikita said. "We for certain cannot use weapons because of fear for killing other peoples. One or maybe two of us would have to get at him and physically pull him down on ground."

"A good old fashioned rugger tackle might do it," Gordon said.

"What is this rugger tackle?" Zina and Nikita asked as one.

"It's from a game they play in England, but in France we are better players," Louise said. "We beat them in 1983. And last year."

"Okay," I said. "Has the Austrian ministry been contacted?"

"Not yet," said Gisela.

"Then do it! Now! Tell them this is the very highest priority but do not tell them what or where. If they send the snipers to us an hour before we leave, they'll get their instructions then."

"Everybody, synchronize watches," said Zina. "The curtain goes up at seven o'clock. So we should be in our places well before six. And everyone should approach the opera house from the back streets, and should go in a few at a time. Gordon, will you coordinate that, please?"

"Yes, Chief."

"We will have a dozen people there—including the snipers—and excluding several squads of the regular *Bundespolizei*, who will be told to be in the general vicinity, but no closer than four blocks away," I told them. "The danger is that if we have too few people, he could slip through the net, and if we have too many, he will see one or more of them and smell a rat."

"What is this rat you are smelling, Harry?" Gisela asked.

"*Den Braten riechen*," said Zina.

"Haha!" Gisela broke into laughter.

"What's up with her?" I asked.

"In German, it means to smell the roast."

64

On the next day, I did not see Harry until after noon. Clearly, having recorded for such a relatively long time the day before, he was worn out and needed rest.

I was lounging in the garden, watching Hernandez weeding the flower beds, when he finally appeared. I could tell he was keeping his reserves of strength and concentration for the task ahead, and was not interested in small talk.

He motioned me to fetch my recorder from the house and bring it to the wrought-iron table underneath the willow tree.

Nineteenth taped session with Harry Posen
Zulla, Virginia, June 12th, 2019

I'd like to tell you we got our troops to the *Staatsoper* like a military operation or a well-oiled machine, but it was a shambles—the only time in the entire operation that Gordon let us down. I think he had decided in his own mind who should go with whom, but if he told the people concerned, they didn't understand. If our approach and entry had taken place even half an hour later it would have attracted so much attention that Repnin would certainly have been tipped off. The only ones who were calm and quietly organized were the three Austrian snipers, who received their instructions only at the last minute.

Anyway, we were all in place well before the doors opened to the public and hunkered down for a long wait, because the opera that night was Mozart's *Don Giovanni* which, in case you don't know, the performance lasts about three hours and twenty-five minutes, including an intermission. Since we were installed an hour before curtain, it meant a four and a half hour stretch, which is okay if you like opera, but absolute murder if you don't.

Fortunately, while a lot of opera is not my cup of coffee, I do like Mozart, and 'The Don' in particular.

After what seemed like an eternity, the red velvet curtains parted to reveal Donna Anna's house which, if you know the opera, is set at sunup so we couldn't see the audience in that light. Zina had her opera glasses and was constantly scanning the two front rows of *sessels* to the left of the stage, but she could not yet see Repnin.

When Scene Two opened, it was early morning in the square at Seville, so it was much lighter.

As Leporello was scolding Don Giovanni for his scandalous behaviour and his many conquests, Zina grabbed my arm so tightly I nearly cried out loud.

"There he is!" she said, handing me the glasses. "Over there in the lowest tier."

I looked and, for the first time, saw the enemy's other half in the flesh. He certainly didn't look like his photograph, so the plastic surgery had worked wonders for him. He was leaning forward in his seat, seemingly doing his own conducting with one hand. He looked every inch the fanatic Zina had described, and I wondered what it was about this man that had induced her to become his lover.

We agreed we couldn't attempt anything during intermission, and our team had been told they could go to relieve themselves, provided they went to the toilets quietly and unobtrusively.

The audience trooped back in and, as the house lights were going down, Zina hissed in my ear, "He's not there! The bastard must have caught on."

At that moment, Gordon thrust his head between us.

"Chiefs, he went to the balcony bar, got a drink, but when people started moving back to their seats he wasn't there. He must have bolted."

"Where did he go?"

"Don't know. We lost him in the crush."

"Take me to the bar. Now!"

It was only yards away, and within minutes we were in the long room, empty save for a solitary bartender. Instinctively, all of us immediately held up our police identification. I was about to go up to him to question him when he put his finger to his lips and pointed to some open doors leading to the outside balcony.

I motioned Gordon to go along the bar and approach the doors from the other side, while I advanced to the near side. Carefully, we edged forward and squinted through the gap.

The Viennese night was starry and the sound of traffic drifted up from below. I could see nothing, but Gordon made a sign to me, scribbled on a cardboard drinks mat and slid it across the floor to me. It said:

> I can see the toes of his shoes.
> He's hiding in a niche eight feet
> to the north of the windows

I gave Gordon the thumbs up, and whispered to Zina to go out and tell the Austrians to approach from outside the building.

I drew my Glock and stepped out onto the balcony. As quietly as I could, I edged along until I was only two feet from the niche. I was betting on his not carrying a weapon, otherwise he would have had trouble getting through security at the front doors.

"Okay, Valya," I said. "Come out with your hands in the air."

I heard him gasp and saw him leap away from me, but his shiny shoes slipped on the flagstones and fell forward. He balanced for a second on the parapet, then over he went.

I rushed to the balustrade and looked down. Far below, Repnin was stretched out on the sidewalk, showing no sign of life.

An ambulance arrived, pronounced him to be *kaum noch am Leben* and rushed him to the nearest hospital, where the *Bundespolizei* mounted a guard outside the operating theatre.

The attending physician told us that Repnin had fractures of the tibia, femur, ilium, seven broken ribs, and a severely punctured lung. When pressed, he said that even if he came through the surgery, the patient's chances of survival were no better than twenty percent.

"If he dies before we can talk to him," said Zina, "we won't know where Sollows is."

"I'm acutely aware of that," I said. "Send for Dr. Nolkin. Tell him to come immediately—if not sooner!"

"I'll call right away."

I lost track of the time. Every hour spent waiting in a hospital corridor is like three days anywhere more pleasant. They told me Repnin was in theatre for nineteen hours before being transferred to the ICU.

I called the Minister of the Interior and asked him to intervene to make sure Repnin had his own unit, to which only we would have access. He said the medical personnel would loudly protest but he would make sure that his colleague Dr. Franz Loderbauer, the Minister of Health, would give appropriate instructions.

When Loderbauer's orders had been carried out, Zina and I took it in turns to sit with Repnin.

It must have been at least twelve hours after his surgery before he regained a kind of consciousness. We plied him with questions, but could get nothing out of him, whether due to his condition or because he was faking it.

Eventually we gave up, went out and waited for Boris Nolkin.

He arrived much quicker than we anticipated, travelling from Moscow, he told us, on one of the Soviet Union's brand new twin-seater Su-25UBs. He seemed delighted to inform us that the flight had taken only one hour and twenty-five minutes and had flown at 590 mph.

As usual, he was dressed all in black, save for his white dress shirt and polka dot bow tie, except that now I noticed he had a red ribbon on his lapel, indicating he had received the Hero of the Soviet Union award since we last saw him.

When we took Dr. Nolkin into the room, Repnin appeared to be in agony as Nolkin had told us, by phone, to stop administering morphine and all other narcotic analgesics. Repnin's skin was a ghostly white, he was dripping with perspiration and was moaning loudly.

After conducting an examination of the patient, Dr. Nolkin turned to Zina. "You leave now."

When she had gone, he said to me, "Under the circumstances I cannot recommend conventional methods."

"To hell with that," I said, "We can't afford to lose more time."

"You misunderstand me," he said, bowing his head stiffly. "My country's safety is at stake. Comrade Gorbachev told me so himself. So of course we cannot wait, but as a medical man I must advise that there are serious risks."

"Understood. Proceed."

He carefully put on his white lab coat and opened his case of instruments. "This patient will be unable to respond to my previous serum, nor will he be able to do so to pentathol or amytal given singly. I have no choice in this matter."

He gave an injection directly into Repnin's groin, with the result that the latter kicked and screamed horribly.

Nolkin looked at his watch. "In three minutes we shall know." He lightly tapped his perfectly manicured fingers on the edge of the bed. "Tell me the most important piece of information you want from him. We might not have time for anything else."

"We need to know where to find Edgar Sollows. And, if you do have time, we need to know what they plan next."

Nolkin nodded silently, then took another glance at his watch.

"Valya," he said in an almost dreamy, toneless voice, "where is Edgar Sollows?"

"Monte Carlo," Repnin said in a hoarse whisper.

"Where in Monte Carlo? Where?"

Repnin coughed, blood spraying from his mouth, then, his body contorting violently, he fell back.

"Mr. Posen, We'll get no more from this man," said Dr. Nolkin quietly. "The traitor Repnin is dead."

"Spasibo, Doctor."

"Не упоминай об этом."

As Nolkin was taking his lab coat off, I began to search the corpse. It was not a pleasant task but you never knew what might be hidden about the body.

It was just inside the rectum, covered in blood and feces. I wiped it off as best I could and held it under the light.

It was a tiny, black book with rounded corners and what looked like numbers on its pages. I didn't dare run it under the tap in case the ink ran, so I took some surgical cotton wool from Dr. Nolkin, and continued to carefully clean it.

"What is it?" Nolkin asked.

"I don't know. It looks like numbers. There is an eight digit number at the bottom of the left hand page here."

"It means nothing to me."

"It could be anything, I guess," I said. "The combination to a briefcase, a lottery ticket. Anything, really."

"I must go now," said Dr. Nolkin. "I am sorry I was not of more use."

65

The New York Times

Tuesday
July 2 1985

PRESIDENT REAGAN—
"I'VE NEVER HAD SO MUCH FUN IN MY LIFE"
White House joins the nation in preparing for huge Independence Day celebrations

By Mitch Barrett

As Ronald Reagan swings into his second term with style and gusto, the 74-year-old president is belying his age. The president, who says he has never felt better, demonstrated how he felt to reporters by doing a series of six push-ups on the Oval Office carpet yesterday. "I don't have time now to do more," said the president with a coy grin as, slightly out of breath, he retreated behind his desk.

Mr. Reagan stated that it was 209 years ago that the United States declared its independence from Great Britain, and that all Americans of whatever race, colour or creed should be proud of the country's achievements, especially in the fields of technology and human rights.

The president said there would be celebrations right across the country, involving fireworks, artistic performances, the flight of a massive, specially-decorated hot air balloon, marches by the Young Americans for Peace movement, and a coordinated display by the United States Armed Forces. Mr. Reagan said he would be spending the day travelling across the nation, visiting various cities on the East Coast and in the Midwest. He said he was fully involved in the preparations and was thoroughly enjoying it. "I've never had so much fun in my life," he said.

On the international front, the president said he felt that relations with the Soviet Union were thawing and showed promise for the future. Mr. Reagan said that Mikhail Gorbachev was very new in his role as leader of the U.S.S.R. (he became General Secretary of the Russian Communist Party in March of this year) so not too much could be expected of him this early in his tenure. "However," said the president, "I am cautiously optimistic. I don't think I'll be telling him to tear down the Berlin Wall just yet," he said with a laugh, "but, who knows, maybe in a year or two?"

Mrs. Reagan will be accompanying her husband to all Independence Day celebrations despite being scheduled for surgery later this month. Her staff said a polyp had been discovered on her colon, but she was maintaining "business-as-usual" and was not in immediate danger.

66

Twentieth taped session with Harry Posen
Zulla, Virginia, June 13th, 2019

While I was anxiously waiting for the lab report to come back on the tiny notebook I had discovered in Repnin's rear end, I acted immediately on what his dying words had told us: *Monte Carlo.*

I ordered three teams to that city to hunt for Sollows. It seemed natural that Marcel LaBelle and Louise LeMelutier should be the principals in two of the teams and Heather Milton-Jones in third because she was fluent in both French and Italian; and I assigned Gisela Munsinger, Jacob Wencell and Matyas Cerny to work with them. I was tempted to send more teams, but since the place is only two square kilometres and is the second-smallest independent country in the world, after Vatican City, with a population of 38,000, I figured they would be getting under each other's feet.

"I will call the *Chef de la Sûreté Publique*, Monsieur Marangoni, and let him know you are coming and why," I told them sternly. "Literally, leave no stone unturned. Search high and low until you have found the bastard."

"Will we be subordinate to the Monte Carlo police or will we have a free hand to act as we see fit?" Heather asked.

"I'm not sure, to be honest. But I will try to get as much autonomy as possible. Prince Ranier is very sensitive where his country's honour is concerned. Now, all of you, go! Let Zina or me know the second you find anything."

"Leave M. Marangoni to me," said Louise. "I will befriend him and tell him he is the handsomest policeman I ever saw."

"As it happens, he is very handsome, though starting to lose his hair," said Zina, "but what would you have done had he been short and fat?"

"Ooh, la la! I have my ways," Louise said slinkily.

"Enough of this chitchat," I said. "Go! Get out of here!"

As they were noisily leaving the headquarters, Frau Becker indicated that both Zina and I had incoming calls. Mine was from the crime lab on Wagramer Strasse.

"Guten Morgen Herr Posen, Ich bin Doktor Heinz Lube, der Leiter des Kriminallabors."

"Good morning. I'm sorry, but could you speak in English, please?"

"Please excuse me," said Dr. Lube. "Of course. As you probably know I am calling you about your little black book—although not so black as it once was."

"Yes. What did you find?"

"Mr. Repnin's is the only DNA we can find on the booklet. We can confirm that the numbers you noticed were 29434561."

"Was there anything else written in it?"

"Not written in it, but stuck to one of the few pages was a small card."

"A card?"

"Ja, a business card."

"Is it legible?"

"It was difficult, but after a series of processes had been applied, we were able to perceive what was on the card."

"What did it say?"

"I have it here. I'll say it slowly so you can write it down:"

Septimus Johnson
98, Beech Road,
Stourbridge,
West Midlands UK

"Nothing else at all in the book?"

"Nothing, except traces of excrement, but I assume you are not interested in that."

"No indeed. Thank you so much, Doctor. I am much obliged to you."

"Auf Wiedersehen und viel Glück."

I called out to Gorden to come to my office, and as he entered, Zina was rushing over from her own office. She looked extremely upset and obviously wanted to talk.

"Harry, something dreadful has happened."

"One moment, please, Zina. I have to deal with Gordon first. Both of you sit down."

I explained what the lab had discovered and asked them if it meant anything to either of them.

"It means nothing to me," Zina said.

"I know where Stourbridge is," said Gordon. "It's roughly in the middle of England, in what we call 'The Black Country', with a population of about 65,000."

"Who is this Septimus Johnson character?"

"Sorry, Harry, no clue at all. I've never heard the name before."

"Okay, Gordon, get over there and find out. Take Eliska with you."

As soon as Gordon was gone, I told Zina to shut the door and tell me what was troubling her.

"Kryuchkov just called me."

"Remind me who he is."

"He's is Chebrikov's Number Two."

"Of course. What did he have to say?"

"He said that now that Repnin has been neutralized, there is no remaining threat to the Soviet Union. He says that Nikita, Tatyana, and I must return to Moscow in three days' time."

"The dirty, rotten bastards! Does that apply to the Czechs, Poles and East Germans, too?"

"He wasn't clear on that point. But, Harry, don't you see we have to make a decision in the next two days."

"About your defection? Yes. I will have to talk to John MacMahon and see if it can be done cleanly. And if not, then clandestinely. You do know that there is no earthly chance that Reagan will talk to Gorbachev about it?"

"Yes," she said sadly, "I know."

"I know it's your motherland and all, but I think the USSR pulling out now is absolutely disgusting."

"I cannot disagree," Zina said quietly.

"I'll call John now and see what I can do."

First I told John that Kryuchkov had called and told us that the Ruskies were pulling out.

"The swine!" It was not often John cursed. "I'll get the Director to call Reagan and see if we can get this reversed."

"Thanks. That sure would help. But there's something else."

"What?"

It took some time to explain to McMahon what had developed between Zina and me and that we had to act soon because we were on a deadline imposed by Moscow.

For a few seconds he was silent. "Harry, you know you've been a horse's ass to get involved with this woman? It's against all the rules and protocols."

"I know."

"How do we know she's not a sleeper—excuse the expression— who was sent by the KGB precisely to seduce you and come back to the states as a plant?"

"She's not. Trust me."

"Famous last words."

"Please, John."

"Okay. Secretly book a flight to the US for her and advise me of its arrival time and date. I'll make sure she's not held up at Dulles, then I'll have her brought here for a debriefing. Be warned she will get the full treatment. We will question her as if she was any other foreign agent. No special consideration. You understand?"

"Yes."

"She'll be held here until you come back. Tell absolutely no one else."

"Right."

"None of the Warsaw Pact agents there must have any idea of this. And when she goes, she must just disappear as close to departure time as possible. No goodbyes."

~

By this point in his narrative, Harry was weeping copiously, and I begged him to stop and take a break.

After I had fetched some 7-Up from the house and he'd taken a drink, we slowly toured the garden. Then I advised him to sit and have a nap under the willow tree.

He agreed and slept there for over two hours.

67

Continuation of the nineteenth taped session with Harry Posen
Zulla, Virginia, June 13th, 2019

It was around noon the next day when Louise gave her report to us. I put her on speaker phone so Zina could hear it. The three teams had been fast and, with the help of the *Sûreté Publique*, which had put officers in the field expressly for that purpose, they had been thorough. Every hotel, every *pension*, every doss house had been visited and searched from top to bottom, which was quite an achievement considering that the city had about a hundred of them.

Louise said that Monsieur Marangoni had, quite seriously, indicated that his record showed there were 370 men aged around fifty in the principality and he had sent 270 of his 515 "flics" or officers to visit every one of them. None of them was of the right age, height or weight for Sollows. While 70 officers stayed doing their regular jobs, 100 were checking the hotels and pensions, 20 had been charged with calling property companies to see if any new arrivals had tried to buy or rent premises, and the remaining 55 had been dispatched to keep a 24-hour watch at the Casino.

I told her that it was Repnin, not Sollows, who had been a big gambler, but she said she thought the casino might be somewhere a visitor might blend in with his surroundings. Only five men who could conceivably have been Sollows were stopped and interviewed, but all had perfectly reasonable alibis.

"Patron," said Louise with finality, "that man is not here. I think you have to consider the possibility that Repnin was lying."

"Dr. Nolkin didn't think so."

"Then I can't explain it. Anyway, there's no point in the six of us hanging around here. I have ordered taxis to take us to Nice airport and we should be back in about five hours."

"I've come to a startling, but not particularly brilliant conclusion," I told Zina when Louise had hung up, "but first, I have to call Dr. Schober at the *Bundespolizei* for a brigade of cops. While I'm doing that, could you assemble the entire gang, please?"

There were only ten of the crew at headquarters, the others being in Monte Carlo or England, so I asked Frau Becker if we could also use Lena, Annika and Johanna as foot soldiers, in addition to officers from the *Bundespolizei*. The looks on their faces as they gathered around suggested they were expecting good news of some kind, so I felt bad about not providing it.

"Sorry, guys," I said, "Louise and the gang have drawn a complete blank in Monte Carlo. I'm satisfied they have been more than thorough and that Sollows is not there."

"Then where the hell is he?" Herb Chauncey called.

"I think we have to operate—at least for the time being—on the assumption that he and Repnin were here in Vienna together. So we now have to beat the bushes here. How is your German, Vladimir?"

"*Gut, natürlich. Ich bin seit einiger Zeit in Dresden stationiert,*" said Putin with a smug smile.

"Alright then, Vladmir, you are in charge. Tony will be your second in command. Liaise with the Austrian police. Make sure all hotels are covered. Check for recent rentals or purchases of property. We have to do here what Louise and company did in Monte Carlo."

"Christus! This is a little bigger," Franz Richter said.

"A lot bigger. One and half million people as opposed to fewer than thirty thousand. So this will be a lot harder. Fortunately, Dr. Schober has set aside 500 officers to work with you. Vladimir, why don't you assign 50 cops to each of our people? Lena, Annika and Johanna will be on standby here in case you need errands run."

"Da, boss," he said with a huge grin. "Would I be right in thinking that we should start in the centre and work out?"

"Good thinking. It is not certain, but it's more likely that Sollows would be closer to galleries and restaurants than in the suburbs."

"Off you go," Zina said, "and good luck!"

Noisily they trooped out, leaving a cavernous, empty space now occupied only by ourselves, Frau Becker, and her girls.

"What was it you wanted to tell me, Harry?"

"First, you should know that I have booked you on three different flights to Washington over the next few days. The tickets are locked in my desk. I don't think you should be carrying them around. Here's my spare key. Remember, you must be ready to leave at a second's notice."

"What will be the sign?"

"How about if you see me stretching like this." I put my arms above my head. "I choose that because it's something I never do normally. After I've pretended to stretch I'll saunter out and circulate around the desks. That's when you come in, get the ticket, call a cab to the *Bruno Kreisky Gasse* and sneak out via the side stairs. Put the ticket in an inside pocket and don't take anything else with you. No briefcase, no files, certainly not that clunky Toshiba, only the handbag you would usually take with you to the washroom."

"Okay. What is the other thing?"

"It's really so simple as to be ridiculous. We've been so busy and so preoccupied with...er...other matters that I guess I didn't have time to think it through."

"You're talking in riddles, Harry."

"You know how we were so royally messed about by Kimberly and Sphinx?"

"Yes, but we now know that Kimberly was Zatopek."

"Yes, and we know that Sollows found him and was running him, but we never really knew who Sphinx was, and we weren't sure which western government, if any, had him on their payroll. We knew it wasn't the CIA or MI6."

"Yes, we thought it might be the French or the West Germans."

"Well, I thought I should make double sure, so I got LaBelle and Bach to make inquiries with their agencies, and both came up blank. Which means that Sphinx *was* Sollows, just using the alias to milk gobs of money out of the agency in return for fake intel. And, of course, to reinforce—to corroborate—whatever intel Kimberly fed us."

"Sounds right. He's a diabolical genius, when you come to think of it."

"I'd rather not think about the way he's had us running round in circles."

"You know, Harry, there's something else which has been bothering me."

"What's that?"

"I have been wondering how much Cephalinol they stole, how much they have used to date, and how much they have left."

"That is a very good question. It might give us an idea of their future capability. How can we find out?"

"There is a woman, a brilliant scientist who works at one of our Siberian stations, Olga Maleshenko. I will try to contact her to find out."

"Excellent! It could be crucial. What time is it at whatever God-forsaken place she is?"

"Blagovoschensk."

"Where the hell is that?"

"In the Amur oblast, about two miles from the Chinese border—to the east of China."

"My god, talk about the back of beyond! Was she sent there as a punishment?"

"No, don't be ridiculous, Harry. This woman is a colonel in the KGB and is highly respected. Let me see, Blagovoschensk is seven hours ahead of us. What time is it now? I left my watch on my desk."

"Two thirty—give or take."

"Only nine-thirty there. She is sure to be up. Now I have to figure out how the hell I can get a call to Siberia."

Zina hurried back to her office to make the call. After about half an hour of arguing with various operators, she finally got through and was soon yammering away in Russian like they were old pals. At length, she came back to me with a long face.

"What?"

"Malashenko told me that Sollows and Repnin used most of the Cephalinol they stole in their previous attacks. She figures there is only enough left for one last strike of any size."

"So, our hunch that they—only Sollows now—have one big bang to come. We thought it would come soon, and with Repnin out of the picture, I am sure Sollows would want to move quickly."

"Whatever it is, wherever it is, we have got to get wind of it ahead of time."

"And how do we do that?"

"I don't have a clue. Let's hope our gang finds the bastard here in Vienna before he can instigate his plan."

68

The twentieth was the final recorded session by Harry Posen. It took him all day to do it, finishing long after dark. It was dreadful to watch his painful struggle and, sensing he wanted to be left to suffer without a witness, I wandered off into the fields. Twice, I swung by the house, and if I saw him through the trees, still trying to record, I would creep away and recommence my long walk.

It was getting late when I returned for the last time, and I noticed that Harry was gone from the garden table and that the recorder's reel was spinning, the click-click cutting through the quiet of the night. I stopped the machine, picked it up and went into the house.

Hearing a strange noise in the kitchen, I peered around the door to find Mrs. Hernandez sobbing.

"Oh Mr. Heremy," she cried, "Mr. Harry has gone to hospital. They take him to Warrenton."

"When was this? What happened?"

"About an hour ago. He come in very tired and gasping and he collapse on floor."

"Oh, no! What is the name of the hospital in Warrenton?"

"I think is called the Fauquier."

"Do you know the phone number, Mrs. H?"

"Is on fridge. Mr. Harry write number on paper on fridge long time ago."

I called the hospital and inquired about Harry, and when they asked me if I was a relative, I lied and said I was his nephew. After a long wait, I was connected with a nurse who told me that Mr. Posen could not see visitors and was in considerable discomfort. He had lost consciousness for some time, but had since regained it. His breathing was heavy and he was unable to communicate.

When I asked when he would be able to come home, she put me on hold so she could consult the attending physician. She came back on the line and said Harry would be in hospital for at least a week, but that, while his condition was ultimately fatal, he was in no immediate mortal danger.

There have been few times in my life that I felt as wretched as I did then. I was desperately concerned about Harry, but I knew I could not possibly hang around for a whole week. I had been there far too long. My normal life was falling apart and it was only the belief that one or two more days might complete the task that kept me there.

I would have to go home and, after having transcribed his final tape, would have to finish the story by resorting to such other sources as I might be able to find.

Reluctantly, I packed my bags, called a taxi to take me to Dulles, said adiós to Mrs. H. and left, racked by guilt but knowing I had no other option.

After I got back to Nova Scotia, I occasionally called Zulla to see how Harry was, but he could not talk to me (or anyone else) and the best I could get from Mrs. Hernandez was "he not good, Mr. Heremy."

It strikes me as amazingly cruel that it was almost two years before Harry died, two years which must have been agony for him and horrible for those around him. Virginia still does not have a law permitting medical aid in dying, but it was only 80 miles from Zulla to the District of Columbia where it was permitted, and I often wondered why Harry did not avail himself of the service. Maybe his Judaism was more Orthodox than I suspected.

I stuck by my pledge that I would wait until his death before proceeding with this book. It was the least I could do for one of the most interesting and courageous people I have ever met.

Twentieth and final taped session with Harry Posen
Zulla, Virginia, June 14th, 2019

It didn't take many hours for reports to start coming in on the sweep of Vienna. The *Bundespolizei* had done a remarkable job of combing the city's lodging houses and apartment buildings. The hotels had been mostly handled by our team, where Putin had been extremely efficient. They had proceeded on the assumption that Sollows must have either purchased, rented or leased accommodation, and if all of those angles were pursued the enemy's presence would be revealed.

I was not as sanguine as the others. To me it seemed like the pro-verbial needle in a haystack. I thought it nigh on impossible to properly check every single place of interest in the time available, and that it might even be that Sollows had bribed some police to bypass him. So I figured we would need an enormous break.

When it came, it was a combination of the search and luck and, in-cidentally, again showed how block-headed Zina and I had been. As reports came in, Frau Becker and her girls coloured the streets, or blocks, as cleared so that the once-white map was now almost seventy-five percent pale green. Within another hour, all but one block was filled in.

Tony Aprile was the last to report. He came in and slammed a file on my desk.

"That's the lot!" he exclaimed, "I never imagined there were so many hotels in one city. I even found one underneath the train station, for God's sake!"

"But you got nothing?"

"I wouldn't say that, Boss," he said with a grin. "I got two good leads. The receptionist at the Prince Leopold and Jennie, a lovely bit of gear on vacation from New Jersey. I'm seeing one of them tonight."

"In your dreams, Tony. It'll be all hands to the pump around the clock until we find this bastard. So behave yourself."

"Yeth, luvy," Tony said, extending his wrist.

"What the hell was that for?"

"Joking. You're staying at a faggy hotel."

"What the hell are you talking about, man?" Zina demanded.

"Your hotel."

"What about it?"

"It's a gay hotel."

"Don't be ridiculous!"

"Are you mad?"

"No, I was there checking it out and I met the old queen."

"Who the waiter?"

"No, the guy who owns the place."

"What, Oskar?"

"He's not gay," said Zina, "at least not to my knowledge,"

"What are you babbling about Tony? When were you there?"

"Very early this morning. I was let in by some hundred-year-old guy who showed me up to Herr Oskar's apartment."

"And...?"

"Well, he came to the door in only his pants. When he leaned on the door jamb I noticed it."

"What?"

"He shaves his armpits."

It took several seconds for Tony's words to sink in, then Zina and I turned and gaped at each other. It was like being hit over the head with a sledge hammer.

"Oh, fuck! What a pair of fucking fools we have been."

"Ебать!" Zina screamed.

"What's up, Boss?"

"It's just that you see before you, Tony, two of the biggest idiots in Vienna."

"How come?"

"You see, Tony," Zina said quietly, "Edgar Sollows is alopecic."

"Say what?"

"It means he has no hair. Anywhere."

"You mean...?"

"Yes, that was Sollows you spoke to."

"And you know, Harry," Zina said, almost in tears, "Repnin didn't lie to us. When he said Monte Carlo he meant Monaco."

"That's the name of the hotel."

"Quite so, Tony. Go round up six bodies from the squad room and let's get over there right now!"

Of course, we were too late. Sollows was a sufficiently experienced agent to know when the jig was up. No doubt, as soon as Tony left the hotel, Sollows/Oskar had fled into the streets, who knew where to.

And, as we had guessed, we found microphones under our bed and under our regular dining table. Upstairs in "Oskar"'s apartment, we found the equipment to which they were connected. Sollows had been privy to all of our conversations, intimate and otherwise. I can't re-member ever feeling so utterly embarrassed and such a complete fool.

We searched the place from top to bottom and questioned the staff. None had seen him depart. They all assumed he would be back in time to preside over dinner, and seemed heart-broken when we told them the place had to close immediately.

Just before we turned the scene over to the forensics from the Interior Ministry, I riffled through some books by his bedside and chanced to see a copy of *Hugh Johnson's Pocket Wine Book*. Suddenly it came to me.

"Zina!"

"What?"

"I know what the numbers mean."

"What numbers?"

"The numbers in Repnin's little book. 29434561."

"What do they mean?"

"They are the last two digits of each of the four best Bordeaux vintages this century."

"Really? So what do we do now?"

"Head for the cellar."

When we descended the steps we saw shelf after shelf after shelf of twinkling bottles, and several shelves with bottles which were dull with dust and age. I wondered how much of this collection had been here already when Edgar had acquired the hotel, and how much he had been able to buy since then. God knows he had enough money to enable him to assemble one of the finest cellars in Europe.

"What are we looking for, Harry?" Zina asked.

"Unless there is vital information written on the labels, then I very much fear what we are looking for is inside the bottles."

"But how many bottles would that be?"

"I don't know, but I pray there won't be many."

"Why?"

"Because we're going to have to break the bottles to get at the contents."

"NO!" she cried. "Can't you take the corks out?"

"It would take too long. Most of those corks have been almost cemented in by the passage of time. But let's see how many bottles there are which have been re-corked and how many vintages are involved. If we're lucky there won't be many."

"Have you drunk those vintages?"

"I've had a few 1961s, One 1945. But no 1929s or 1943s. They're supposed to be the greatest wines ever made."

It was cool and dark in that cellar and the lighting was by a single, unshaded bulb hanging from the ceiling, so it was difficult to read the labels. Fortunately, the cellar had a kind of system in that the shelves were arranged by decade, so the ones we were concerned with were at the back.

We had to brush—in some cases scrape—the dust off the labels until finally we had exposed all the ones in our decades.

There were only four 1929s, a *Cost D'Estournel*, a *Lynch Bages*, a *Château Latour*, and a *Château D'Issan*. The 1945 vintage was represented by a *Vieux Château Certan*, a *Cheval Blanc*, a *Mouton Rothschild* and two *Petrus*.

There were only three from 1943: *Haut Brion, La Mission Haut Brion* and *Château Margaux*. But there were almost thirty bottles of the 1961, mostly from *Châteaux Palmer, Canon, Lafite,* and *Domaine de Chevalier.*

Even if we only took the bottles which looked as if they had been re-corked recently, it would still take hours to open these and then even more hours to see and then extract whatever they might conceal. I was almost in tears when I called in several of the *Bundespolizei* and told them what had to be done.

The captain told me he had never known the real meaning of being "heart-broken" until that moment.

The cops got to work and a sublime aroma arose in a cloud around us as bottles were smashed and checked for secret contents. They had to destroy twenty-eight bottles which appeared to have been opened and re-corked since the wine was made.

About fifteen minutes later we stood amid a pool of wine and a litter of broken glass, and in our red-stained hands were miniature metal tubes containing twenty-eight tiny strips of celluloid. In one way I was relieved, because if I had been wrong and the exercise had been for nothing, I think I would have crawled away and died.

"It's like going to a funeral," said Zina sadly.

"Let's go, my love. We'll get these to forensics and see what they have to tell us."

"All that lovely wine gone, Harry."

"Not quite. I stole two. Put them in your handbag. We'll have them later."

The lab did not take long to process the microfilm and advise us of the contents. They contained all the details of the Sollows and Repnin organization, which was infinitely more extensive than we had imagined and had been in place for far longer than we had thought possible. The names of the employees—or agents—were listed, with their addresses and terms of remuneration. Among this information were some nasty shocks for both the CIA and KGB, namely the identities of traitors to each side. There were banking records, flow charts and other material.

But there was no indication of where Sollows might go to hide or to what final use they intended to put their remaining Cephalinol.

Zina and I wandered back to[9]

---

9   Recording ends here.

69

Continuation of taped interview with Gordon Rattenbury
Upper Slaughter, United Kingdom, August 2019[10]

AKERMAN
Please tell me about your mission to Stourbridge.

RATTENBURY
Ah, I thought you would ask about that. I have my notebook here to jog my memory.

As soon as Mr. Posen gave me the order, I cast my mind back to the brief time I had spent in and around Stourbridge, a medium-sized town in what used to be the industrial heartland of the UK. In 1985 there were many remnants of coal mining, iron and steel production, glass manufacturing, and engineering still in evidence, although it was greatly reduced from what it had previously been. This area was the cradle of the Industrial Revolution, and the filth produced by the hundreds of mines and factories gave it the name "The Black Country".

The Black Country covers the three metropolitan boroughs of Dudley, Sandwell and Walsall as well as the City of Wolverhampton. A geological definition follows the South Staffordshire coal seam. Stourbridge is on the southwestern edge of this region and there has been heated debate as to whether it is really part of the Black Country. The people of Stourbridge say, "Yes", the people of the other areas say, "No."

But this terminological altercation has nothing to do with the mission with which Eliska Svoboda and I were entrusted. Our job was to go to Beech Road in Stourbridge and ascertain who Septimus Johnson was and what his connection with Sollows and Repnin was.

Flying by Austrian Airlines Flight OS 331, we touched down at

____

10   The first part is in chapter 44.

Heathrow early in the morning of July 3rd, where we were met by Julian Clarkson from MI5, in whose car we proceeded to the town via the M4, M25, M40, M42 and then the A491 to our destination.

Please forgive my provision of detail, Mr. Akerman. It is not my intention to be pedantic, but to be precise.

A: I quite understand. Please go on.

R: We arrived in Stourbridge at 12.38 and took an initial run to Beech Road, just driving past slowly to observe. The house had nothing unusual about it, being very much like all the others in the street—you know, red brick, semi-detached, what you call duplexes—built between the wars, I should guess in the late 1930s.

This district was known as Norton, and as we drove around it we noticed several pubs and a social club quite near Beech Road. Seeing two elderly gents on a bench outside the club, I pulled up, stuck my head out of the car window, said we were lost, very hungry and could we get a sandwich and a pint there?

"'Ow bist?" asked one of the men, whose names were Fred Bradley and Enoch Guest. They told me the facility was for members only, but if I gave them the money and told them what we wanted they would bring it out to us.

So Eliska, Julian and I sat down on another bench and started talking to Enoch while Fred went inside to get our provender. Of course, Julian and I did all the talking because Eliska's accent might attract too much attention.

After beating about the bush for a while and sinking a pint of Banks's bitter, I delicately broached the subject of the occupant of Number 98.

"Ah," said Fred, "Yo know Septimus?"

"Only by reputation," I said. "We called at the house, but nobody was home."

"E'll be out doin' his shopping. Gittin' the babbie a new bonnet. 'E should be back by the time yo've 'ad anuther point."

"So, are yo in the aero-engineering business, our kid?" Enoch asked.

"Er...yes." I was not sure what he meant, but I decided to go along with it.

"Brilliant mon, they says," said Fred. "Bostin."

"Really?"

"Yeah, he used to be professor in Brum. Got all them PDhs and everything. 'E still does work for folk wi' money."

"Roit intrestin' it is," said Enoch. "I think so, any road, 'though Fred here cor be bovvered."

"No, I cor be wettirin about thot. I got me pigeons to keep me busy. I got six Janessens, four Trentons and a Bandit. Yo loike pigeons, our kid?"

"Sorry, no," I said, not having a clue what he was talking about. "Well, we best be going. Thanks for helping us out and for your excellent company."

"Tarra a bit," said Enoch.

"Tra tra," said Fred.

We parked the car near a kind of park or playing field and walked up the street to Number 98.

A: This was on the other side of the street from the park?

R: Yes. Eliska stayed in the car—with emergency instructions for what to do if we weren't out in an hour—while Julian and I knocked on the door. It was answered by a small, balding man of about 65, wearing gold rimmed spectacles and a tatty old cardigan of indeterminate colour.

"Good morning sir, I'm Chief Inspector Rattenbury of the Special Branch and this Sergeant Clarkson," I lied only because no member of MI5 ever admits they are with the agency.

"Oh good heavens!" he exclaimed. "You'd better come in."

He led us through a narrow hallway into a small but comfortable living room, where we sat down.

"Tea, Chief Inspector?"

"No, thank you, sir. We've just had lunch," I said, brushing away the cat which had just climbed on my lap.

"Let me take Tiddles away," said Johnson, who removed the animal and put him outside.

"What is your line of work, if I may ask, sir?" I asked when he returned.

"I used to work in the aircraft industry," he said, taking off his glasses and polishing them with the end of his tie. "I was with Lockheed during the war—at Leamington—and for a while I was with Handley Page. Then I taught at Brimingham University for a while. After that I was partner in a small business which manufactured flight instruments."

"And are you retired now, sir?"

"Semi-retired. Look, what is this all about?"

"Just routine inquiries, sir. I'll be more specific when I know more about what you do here and now."

"Ooh, that sounds ominous." Johnson seemed to be enjoying his interrogation. "Now, I make pieces of equipment to order—machinery which needs to be adapted to particular needs. You could say I'm a bit of an inventor, in my own small way."

"I see."

"Would you like to see my workshop?"

"Very much, sir."

He led us out of the back door, through a small garden planted neatly with flowers on one side and vegetables on the other. We picked our way along the tiny dividing path until we reached a structure of several sheds joined together.

Inside, we were amazed to see a clutter of thousands of bits and pieces hanging from the roof; dozens of boxes filled with pieces of metal, screws, nails, pipes, and wire; and rack after rack of hand tools and power appliances. On one side were several sophisticated metal lathes and a series of tanks labelled argon, carbon dioxide, helium, nitrogen, acetylene and oxygen; and welding equipment. Along one wall were dozens of dials and meters and a variety of electrical equipment.

"Have I been getting into trouble, Chief Inspector?" Johnson said with a smile.

"That rather depends, sir."

"Depends on what?"

"Have you seen this before," I said, producing a photograph of the card found in Repnin's little book.

"Yes, it's my name and address."

"I'm aware of that, sir. Do you recognize the typewriter which typed it?"

"Of course I do. It's my typewriter."

"Could you explain how this card came to be in Vienna recently?"

"Vienna! Good heavens!"

"Who might you have given it to, sir?"

"One of my customers. I have so few these days I don't want to incur unnecessary expense by getting printed cards so I type them out when needed."

"Do you keep a record of the jobs you have done?"

"Of course I do."

"In that case may I see the description of work performed during the past six months?"

"Certainly, here it is." He passed me a ledger the size of a school exercise book.

I looked carefully. A lawnmower fixed with a grass collector on the side of the machine, a hot house sprinkler automatically activated when moisture levels dropped, a bicycle fitted with a radio under the saddle. Then something different.

"What this?"

"A directional detector."

"What's that?"

"Er...it's what some call a 'fuzz buster'."

"Radar cheater?"

"Yes."

"Huh. What about this job here?" I pointed to another entry.

"Ah, that's a bit technical. Do you know anything about altitude and air pressure?"

"Why don't you tell me, sir."

"I'll try to explain in layman's language. This is an altimeter which, at a certain height, activates a releasing mechanism."

"What's that?"

"I'm not entirely sure. Somebody else would have made that part of the equipment."

"Why didn't you do it?"

"The customer didn't ask for it."

"Okay. At what altitude does this release take place?"

"I set it at 1,000 feet but it was made so it could be adjusted."

"Let me see if I understand. If an aircraft going up or coming down reached a certain altitude something—we don't know what—would be released."'

"Not down," said Johnson, "only up. The design was specific to ascent. That's where the subtleties of air pressure come into play. Activation would occur when ascending but be closed during descent."

"How big would this releasing mechanism be? What would it look like?"

"I couldn't possibly say. It could be as big as a tank or as small as a matchbox. It would depend upon the requirements of the client and the skill of the engineer."

"Alright," I said. "Tell me about the client who ordered this."

"Well, he was well dressed, well-spoken, but I could tell he was foreign."

"American?"

"Oh, no. And not German or French. I became familiar with both during the war."

"Is that him?" I showed him a photograph.

"Yes! That's him. He paid cash in advance, plus a bonus."

Septimus Johnson had identified Antonin Zatopek, alias Kimberly.

I found the nearest telephone box and, with some difficulty, put in a call to Mr. Posen.

~

Gordon Rattenbury died 17 months after I saw him. Later, his daughter told me his funeral was well-attended, but she said she did not know most of the people who were present. She said they did not introduce themselves and did not go to the repast following the service. When I told her that her father was a hero who had worked for MI5, she accused me of mocking her and hung up on me.

70

I finally caught up with Heather Milton-Jones in Wales in early October. At first she refused to see me, but after I pestered her with repeated telephone calls she relented and told me to come to her house in a tiny, remote village called Abergwesyn.

It took me a long time to find the place because my car broke down and I had to wait while a tow truck came and took it to the garage. By the time the car was fixed it was late, so I found a place to stay in the little town of Llanwrtyd Wells and called Heather to ask her if I could come the next day. She was annoyed but reluctantly agreed.

The next day was beautiful and sunny, one of the few entrancing days in Wales when it is not raining, or about to rain. The leaves were starting to turn gold and brown at the edges as I wound my way up the narrow road north to Abergwesyn.

I was fifteen minutes early, so I turned up the Irfon Valley on the road which eventually leads over the mountains to Tregaron. That stretch of road with mountains on both sides, and the river winding alongside, is one of the most magical places I know. I would have lingered there, but did not want to upset Ms. Milton-Jones further by being late.

She lived in a tiny cottage nestling into the hillside, within a few miles of the wild and desolate upland Desert of Wales. An old MG convertible stood in a narrow driveway. Contrary to my expectations, the garden was untended and untidy and the house itself was none too clean either.

Heather would then have been about eighty and was thin and rangy, but still with smooth skin and bright eyes. "So, you're here." She said grimly.

"Apparently. Thank you for seeing me."

"We'd better get down to business. I have to be in Builth Wells at noon."

"Most of the information for my book came from Harry Posen, but unfortunately he was unable to complete the story."

"What are you missing?"

"I especially want to know what happened when your colleague, Gordon Rattenbury, reported on his mission to Stourbridge. And then I would like a description of how Zina Varenko came to leave."

"All right. I can help you with both. Would you like coffee?"

"Yes, please. Black with sugar."

When she left for the kitchen I took a look around the walls and saw that she had a number of rather lovely post-Impressionist reproductions. Four were by Cézanne, two by Gauguin, and one by Georges Seurat.

She came back with the coffee, put the tray on a small table, sat down and lit a cigarette.

> I was conferring with Harry and Zina when Gordon's call came in. It was about four in the afternoon on July 3rd. The look on Harry's face was priceless as he listened. After grilling Gordon for a few minutes, he put the phone down.
>
> "Son of a bitch!" he said. "Gordon's nailed it. He found out that Zatopek had a contraption made which could release the remaining Cephalinol when an aircraft attains a certain altitude."
>
> "An aircraft?" Zina said. "Does that mean Air Force One?"
>
> "No," Harry said, "I don't think so. Unless I'm mistaken, I think it means a balloon."
>
> "A balloon! Of course!" Zina jumped up. "President Reagan is scheduled to tour eastern America in an army balloon tomorrow."
>
> "And if Cephalinol is on board that balloon, it would wipe out not only the president but half the Eastern Seaboard."
>
> "You must call Casey right away," Zina said.
>
> Harry put on the speaker phone, got on the line and eventually managed to make contact with the CIA director. I thought Casey would have a heart attack, but he said he would call Donald Regan, the president's Chief of Staff, right away.
>
> We hung around the office, talking about nothing in particular, until about an hour later Phillip LaCusta called to say that

the army had searched the balloon, found the Cephalinol and destroyed it. He was obviously in a good mood and was showering us with congratulations.

He told us he had been in the office when President Reagan had called Casey and expressed his delight. Apparently, Reagan himself said the only remaining problem was, "Where the hell is that fellow Sollows?"

When we told the gang in the squad room, they cheered loudly and broke out some liquor and passed it around in paper cups. Word must have gone around the world quickly, because Frau Becker announced that the Austrian Minister of the Interior had asked that Harry go to his office to accept his personal compliments.

As he left, we all cheered him wildly.

71

From pages 212-213 of the unpublished diaries of Viktor Vasilyevich Grishin, Member of the Politburo of the Central Committee of the Communist Party of the Soviet Union, from 1971 to 1986. State Library of Russia, Moscow.

July 3rd, 1985

Today we were informed that Operation Renegade had been successfully concluded. The Politburo met this evening, quite late because most members had departmental duties to attend to during the day.

I was early for the meeting, but when I arrived at the chamber Gorbachev and a few others were already there, just lounging around drinking tea from the huge samovar.

When Chebrikov came in, there was an amusing exchange which I later dubbed "the meeting of steel and flesh."

Mikhail Sergeyevich said, "Hail, the conquering hero! Well done, Viktor Mikhailovich. My hearty congratulations."

"I was glad to have been of service," Chebrikov said with his usual false modesty.

"So, your protégée Varenko has done us proud?"

"She is not exactly my protégée, Mikhail Sergeyevich."

"But she has done good work for the country. I have not yet decided what medal she should be awarded."

"I have heard she has formed an attachment with the Jew Posen," Chebrikov said sourly.

"Posen is a Jew? I didn't know that. An attachment? What sort of attachment? Do you have evidence?"

"A romantic attachment, Mikhail Sergeyevich. Yes, I have been reliably informed."

"I am sorry to hear this. She was probably seduced by the Jew. Who is in Vienna with her?"

"Captain Bakunin and Private Kusnetskov, and Putin."

"Vladimir Putin? What is he doing there? I thought he was in Dresden."

"He was, but Mielke sent him to Vienna as a member of the GDR delegation."

"How strange! I wonder why Comrade Mielke wanted him out of the way. Some corruption, no doubt. Look into it, Viktor Mikhailovich."

"I shall, Comrade Secretary. Is that all?"

"No. Contact Putin immediately and instruct him to escort Varenko and the others to Moscow."

"When?"

"Today. Now."

"I will. Are you still going to give her a medal when she arrives?"

"I think so. Will you promote her?"

"If I might make a suggestion..."

"Certainly."

"Why don't we reward her for her good work, but at the same time punish her for this unfortunate liaison with the Jew?"

"And you would do this...how?"

"Promote her and send her to Saskylakh."

"Where the hell is that?"

"It is the administrative centre of the Anabarsky District in the Sakha Republic."

"How far is that from here?"

"It would depend on how she travelled there. By air, maybe 2,500 miles "

"And by road?"

"If she could get through, maybe 3,800 miles."

"Here come the others," said Gorbachev. "It's time we got this meeting under way."

72

Heather Milton-Jones lit a cigarette. I noticed her cigarettes were called Senior Service, had no filters and were very strong.

The room was quite small and, despite the weather being mild, she had closed the cottage door. The smoke was seriously bothering me, hurting my throat and making my eyes water, but I had to hang on in order to complete my story.

"What happened after that?" I asked.

"First, I should tell you what happened just before Harry left to see the Minister."

"Okay."

"On his way out he stopped and beckoned me to one side. He told me he thought Annika might have been working for the opposition, but he didn't know how innocent or malignant her intent had been. His instructions were that Zina and I should 'sweat her', as he put it."

"And did you?"

"Yes. We asked Frau Becker to bring her to Zina's office, and when they came we told them both to sit. We questioned them thoroughly about the recommendation of the Monaco Hotel and why she had told Dorothea about it. She said she had never been to The Monaco but had heard it was good from someone she met in the bar she regularly visited. Further questioning suggested that the 'someone' was Repnin, which made perfect sense, because she said he was handsome and charming. She said he had mentioned the place to her on 'maybe three or four different occasions.' We let her go because neither of us could detect a trace of malice in the girl."

"That's it?"

"Yes, but as she was leaving we saw and heard a courier arriving from the Soviet Embassy with an urgent message for Putin."

"Did you see it?"

"Later, I'll show you." She lit another cigarette and puffed on it. "I watched Putin go first to Bakunin, mutter something to him, then both of them went to Kuznetsov and muttered to her. Then the three of them came directly over to us.

"'Comrade Varenko,' said Putin sharply, 'we have been urgently called back to the USSR. We must go immediately.'

"I thought Zina was going to collapse. Her face went white and a look of sheer terror crossed her face.

"'Now, please, Major!' Putin's voice got harsher. 'Comrade Kuznetsov will assist you.'

"Tatyana went around and roughly grabbed Zina's arm and Nikita took the other. They almost frog-marched her out of the office. There was nothing I could do. I knew that if I tried there would have been a Wild West shootout between the NATO folk and the Warsaw Pact people right there in the office. In two minutes it was all over. They were gone."

"The message," I remind her.

"Oh, yes, I have it here. I've kept it all this time. A memento of one of my most unsettling moments, and one which confirmed my hatred for Communism."

She handed me a yellowing, somewhat tattered piece of paper.

Генеральный секретарь поручил мне приказать вам немедленно сопроводить майора Варенко обратно в Москву. Немедленно отправляйтесь во Флугафен Вена вместе с Бакуниным и Кузнецозом, где Туполев ТУ-134 будет ждать. На табличках написано, что он направляется в Ригу, но капитану было приказано перенаправить рейс на Москву. Подпись В.М. Чебриков, председатель Комитета государственной безопасности.

"What does it mean?"

"What you'd expect. That he was ordered to take Zina straight to *Flughafen Wien* and board a TU-134 which was supposed to fly to Riga, but had been ordered to divert to Moscow."

"Jesus! When did Harry get back from seeing the minister?"

"About twenty minutes later. He asked where Zina was and I said she had gone. He started to say that he didn't understand why she hadn't waited for his sign, then stopped, looked around and saw all the long faces at the desks. Then he realized what had happened."

"How did he take it?"

"How do you think? He let out a blood curdling howl like an animal caught in a leg trap. I've never heard such anguish, such pain as was in that cry, not even from people being tortured. He fell to his knees, helplessly sobbing. Gisela came in and together we tried to comfort him, but it was no good. When we went home for the night, we left him there, crying his heart out."

"That is inexpressibly sad," I said.

"By this time almost everyone in the office knew about their affair, even if not all of them knew that they were in love."

"I gather you kept in touch with Harry after Renegade."

"Yes, both professionally and personally. I liked him."

"Tell me, when did the Soviet Union open up to foreigners?"

"The Berlin Wall came down in November of 1989, but it wasn't until 1991 that the U.S.S.R. was officially dissolved."

"When that happened, Harry must have gone to try to find Zina."

"Yes, of course, but not for a while because, while travel restrictions gradually eased, official regulations continued to apply and it was not easy to get beyond Moscow. And especially not for someone who was known to be an American spy."

"When did he get the necessary clearance to go to Siberia?"

"Not until 1993. He had no difficulty getting to Moscow, and not much getting to Tomsk. But he told me it was a nightmare getting north to the Sakylah region."

"But he finally made it?"

"Yes, but Zina was not there."

"Where had she gone?"

"Apparently, before the Soviet Union dissolved, she had been transferred to Chuktokta."

"Where on earth is that?"

"North of Kamchatka. It's over 10,000 miles from Moscow by road."

"Bastards! They really mean to bury her. Was Harry able to get out there?"

"No, It was impossible. But he later learned that Snezhoyne—the place she had been moved to—was badly flooded when the River Anadyr broke its banks."

"She drowned?"

"Her death was recorded as 'presumed drowned.' But nobody really knows."

"So, she could be out there somewhere."

"I suppose so, theoretically. I have to go to Builth Wells now. I doubt we shall meet again, Jeremy."

We never did.

73

By 2020 I had gathered most of the material I needed for this book, but it took a long time to sort through, decide what to keep and what to set aside, and put it in chronological order. So it was not until 2024 that it was ready to be printed.

But just before I had done my final proofing, I noticed an article in *Decanter* magazine.

The headline was "Newcomer Makes a Splash in Sainte-Croix-Du-Mont". The article, by someone called Sebastian Smyth, described how a wealthy person, Roger Dawson, had rescued *Château les Deux Oboles*, a run-down but formerly great winery, had refurbished it and was now producing excellent sweet wines.

Since I am not partial to sweet wines, I only skimmed the article, but my reading was slowed down by the opinion of Mr. Dawson that sweet wine was the perfect accompaniment to every kind of food.

That opinion is one which is shared by quite a few people (though I am not one of them) so it was not particularly remarkable, but it niggled at the back of my mind throughout the day. Finally, I fished through the waste basket and re-read the article.

What I had not seen on perusing it for the first time, was a number of photographs of the winery. One of them made my blood run cold.

There, staring from the paper, was a middle-aged man holding a bunch of grapes. Even from a poor reproduction, the eyes bored into me and I had no doubt I was looking at Edgar Sollows.

END

Jeremy Akerman

About the author

Jeremy Akerman is an adoptive Nova Scotian who has lived in the province since 1964. In that time he has been an archaeologist, a radio announcer, a politician, a senior civil servant, a newspaper editor and a film actor.

He is a painter of landscapes and portraits, a singer of Irish folk songs, a lover of wine, and a devotee of history, especially of the British Labour Party.

Jeremy's first novel, *Black Around the Eyes,* was published in 1981. Other projects required his attention until recently, when he was able to take up fiction again. From the start of 2023 to the end of 2025, he wrote and published twelve novels.

See: moosehousepress.com/authors/jeremy-akerman